David Willox

Poems and sketches

David Willox

Poems and sketches

ISBN/EAN: 9783744722124

Printed in Europe, USA, Canada, Australia, Japan

Cover: Foto ©Andreas Hilbeck / pixelio.de

More available books at **www.hansebooks.com**

Yours Fraternally

POEMS

AND

SKETCHES

BY

DAVID WILLOX.

GLASGOW:
ALEX. MALCOLM & CO., 34 ANN STREET, CITY.
1898.

DEDICATED

(BY PERMISSION)

TO THE

RIGHT WORTHY BRO. WILLIAM JAS. HUGHAN,

PAST SENIOR GRAND DEACON OF ENGLAND,

PAST SENIOR GRAND WARDER OF EGYPT, IOWA, &c.,

IN APPRECIATION OF HIS

WELL-DIRECTED RESEARCHES AND VALUABLE PUBLICATIONS

RELATING TO

FREEMASONRY,

AND ESPECIALLY RESPECTING

THE "OLD CHARGES" OF THE FRATERNITY.

BY

DAVID WILLOX.

PREFACE.

At the last moment I have, quite unexpectedly, been called upon to write a Preface to the present volume. At the first glance this may appear a superfluous undertaking in presence of the fact that a biographical sketch is already in type, but my talented compiler, Mr. A. G. Thomson, Editor of *Scottish Nights*, assures me that I should say a word or two as a personal introduction to the work. What can I say? To fully three-fourths of those whose names appear in the list of subscribers, at the end of this book, I am personally known—to many of them for the better part of a lifetime, and to others, more recently; hence I can hardly expect to say much that will be fresh or new to them.

If authorship has its rewards, it certainly has also its penalties, and one of these is that an author, however humble he may be, is too often expected to be original. I will make no attempt to be so in this instance, but confine myself to a few plain facts.

For the present volume the general reader is indebted to the frequent solicitations of the "Brethren of the Mystic Tie," at whose hands I have received many marks of kindness and consideration. In this instance, whether their kindness for me has outrun their discretion or not, time will tell. Originally, I had no intention of publishing in book form the musings of my leisure hours, but having been frequently urged to do so by some of the most eminent members of the " Craft," I resolved "either to make a spoon or spoil a horn."

In the arrangement of the matter I have been greatly assisted by my friend Mr. Thomson, already referred to : indeed I have left that part of the work almost entirely in his hands, and I take this opportunity of acknowledging his kindness.

Whatever merit there may be in the work now offered to the public, I claim that as my own, and am prepared to bear whatever blame my venture may entail.

It is perhaps an unusual thing for an author to criticise his own work, but I am so sensible of the defects in the present volume that I cannot refrain from saying that could I have brought my mind to the task of revision, many of the pieces might have been improved : but revision has always been distasteful to me, hence you have them as they are—in many cases printed from the first pencilled impression of a passing thought, caught, perhaps, amidst the din and toil of the forge and rolling mill, or in the silence and solitude of some sequestered nook, far from the bustle and hurry of commercial life.

Should the reader enjoy but half the pleasure in the perusal of the book that I have had in its composition, my time will have been well spent.

Yours truly,

D. WILLOX.

INDEX.

Biographical Sketch of the Author.

Poetry and Song have been and are characteristic of the Scottish race. From the days of Thomas the Rhymer down to the present time the " land of brown heath and shaggy wood " can lay claim to more poets than any other country, ancient or modern. The poetic element has been a living power in Scotland, which has gained increased vigour and strength with age, adorning and brightening the everyday life of the race with the light of cultured thought and beauty.

Men gifted with the divine fire have sprung from, and are still to be found amongst, every class of the community. Many of them in humble stations have borne the brunt of the battle of industrial or commercial life, and have left behind them memorials in their poems and songs that go far to adorn the literature of Scotland. This they have done while discharging their duties as citizens, and fighting the battle of life, and that often with the odds against them. Amongst such men Mr. D. Willox, better known as " Tam M‘Phail," deserves a place.

Born on the 3rd June, 1845, in what was then the rural village of Parkhead, but now included within the boundaries of Glasgow, Mr. Willox has spent the greater part of his life in his native place.

His father was a handloom weaver, a class from which many who have made a name in the world have sprung. He was a first-class workman, of a free and careless disposition, fond of company, but did not always pay that attention to his home which duty demanded. Conse-

quently, his children were dependent upon their mother
for that love and care which the father too often neglected,
preferring the company of his fellow-workmen to the society
of his family.

To his mother, therefore, Mr. Willox owes much. She
appears to have been a woman of a gentle, loving disposition, fond of her husband, and of her home and her children, doing her duty faithfully and unflinchingly, in the
face of hardships and trials, many of which a husband's
forethought might have averted. Bravely she struggled
on, teaching her children, in her own simple way, their
duty towards God and Man, and impressing upon them
that truth and honesty are the cardinal virtues of life—a
task which the modern matron is too apt to forget.

Born, as has been said, in Parkhead, in a street, or
" land," known by the unique name of " Nae Place," which
name it still bears, Mr. Willox's childhood was spent in the
quaint village, where the rattle of the weaver's shuttle was
heard all day long, and, doubtless, on his young ears fell many
a curious and now-forgotten story from the lips of those
denizens of the loom, who were ever fond of song and
jest, and, not unfrequently " A Wee Drappie O't."

Being the eldest of the family, young Willox was, at an
early age, sent to work at " Sand Chapping," an occupation
now unknown, and regarding which some little explanation
may be interesting. In those days most of the houses of
the poorer class had earthen, or clay, floors, which were
beaten hard, and when roughly swept and sprinkled with
fine sand were considered clean ; indeed, many of the
wooden floors were treated in the same way. Thus a large
quantity of sand was required. Amongst those who made a
living by dealing in this commodity in Parkhead was a
woman called Kate Haley, and it was in her employment

that the subject of our sketch earned his first money. The sand, having been pounded very fine, was hawked from door to door, and sold at so much per pint, quart, or gallon— sand, in these days, being considered an essential to cleanliness, if not comfort.

In these days a fire was something to be remembered, and Mr. Willox can relate many interesting stories in relation to this. When a fire broke out, the policeman on his beat instantly sprang his rattle, or "clappers," as they were called, also announcing the name of the street and the number of the house in which the fire originated. His companion on the next beat would then take up the alarm, and in this way the intelligence spread over the town. Soon the ancient fire-engines were out, a crowd gathered, and all was excitement, much to the delight of the boys and girls.

It was a common thing to hear the policeman in the early morning calling "Five o'clock! A fine morning. All's well!" Sometimes their intimations were mixed up in a very humorous fashion, as the following: "Four o'clock! A cold morning! An Irishman drowned in the Clyde, and all's well!"

Looking back over fifty years of a lifetime, Mr. Willox can recall many singular and interesting characters, amongst them being Mr. George Honeyman, who owned some property in Parkhead, and was, in addition, a water merchant. In these days of an unlimited supply of the purest water in the kingdom, it is difficult to realise that such a business as that of water merchant flourished. It must, however, be remembered that the water supply at that time depended on draw-wells, dip-wells, and pumps, which were liable to dry up in time of drought, or during heavy rains to become impure. The water supply was, however, augmented by Mr. Honeyman, who carted the Clyde water from the water works in Springfield Road to Parkhead, and retailed it at a farthing a "stoup," a wooden vessel which held about six gallons, or a halfpenny a "gang." which held double the amount. Such a business would scarcely pay nowadays.

Many stories of boyish escapades might be told did space permit, for Glasgow Fair was then in all its glory, being held annually on Glasgow Green; and it almost goes without saying that young Willox sometimes neglected his duties to witness the glories of the "geggie."

Sickness and trouble overtook the family about this time, and Mr. Willox, senior, left Parkhead and went to Torphichen, near Bathgate, where he had a brother, and where he obtained work, his wife and family remaining in lodgings in their native place. After a few months' absence, he rejoined his wife at Parkhead, where he began work again at the loom, and at the same time started to learn his son the weaving. The experiment was not a success, however, for the boy, high-spirited and fond of fun, did not take kindly to his father's tuition.

Previous to this, young Willox had acquired a slight smattering of the rudiments of education; indeed, he had been at three different schools, but only for short spells. One of his teachers, a Mr. M'Auly, better known as "Corky," was a well-known character in the district—a characteristic dominie of the old time. His education was, however, meagre in the extreme, and had to be supplemented in after years, when, as a youth, he found his deficiencies. "Shortly after this," says Mr. Willox, "I went to work in Miller's print works, Springfield Road, where I received the handsome wage of three shillings a week! We were paid at dinner-time on Fridays, and my sister Agnes used to come with my dinner on that day, so as to take my pay home to my mother." While he was working in the print work the place was burned to the ground, and his story of how the fire originated is a singular one: "It was deliberately set on fire by a young man, whose name I do not remember, but who was an assistant at one of the printing machines. Probably his action was due to thoughtlessness, or from a momentary impulse to see a big blaze; at any rate, he tied a cotton string to the strap that guided the cloth up on to the stove, where it went through a process of drying as it left the machine. He might as well have placed a match in a gunpowder magazine. The result would have been the same in all but the explosion, and the place was burned to the ground." The young man, when too late, saw the evil he had wrought, and threatened the boy with worse than everlasting punishment if he should ever breathe a syllable as to how the fire had originated.

Matters in his home were not improving, and, moved by some sudden impulse, the boy left his native village to make his way to Torphichen, where an uncle lived, who was a collier and in comfortable circumstances. It was a cold, frosty day with snow on the ground when he started on a tramp of well-nigh thirty miles, without a penny in his pocket, and with an empty stomach. The road was unknown to him, but he faced it with a characteristic determination which enabled him, in after years, to face difficulties before which many would have quailed. Briskly he started on his journey, and a curious figure the boy must have looked, barefooted and bareheaded, plodding his way over the ice-bound roads. After passing Airdrie he overtook two girls who were carrying a large and very clumsy parcel. The boy frankly offered to assist them with the parcel, which, after some little demur, they agreed to. The natural openness of youth led to their exchanging confidences, and soon a good understanding was established between them. The girls were the daughters of a shoemaker, who pursued his calling in the village of Blackriggs, some six miles from Airdrie, to which place they had been for a supply of leather, and were now returning home. The strange trio continued their journey, the boy explaining that he was proceeding to Torphichen, and his companions informing him that the distance was long and that he would not reach the place before night. He assured them that he did not care, but meant to push on. The darkness of the winter night was falling when they reached the village of Blackriggs, where the youthful wanderer found himself amongst friends. When they heard the service he had rendered their girls, the shoemaker and his wife welcomed him kindly, gave him a good supper, a warm bed, and substantial breakfast before he started, on the following morning, to pursue his journey. With eager steps, the boy for a time pushed rapidly on his way, but soon the frosty road cut his bare feet, and his scanty clothing proved but a poor protection against the keen wintry air. About midday, when passing a row of colliers' cottages, he went up to one of the doors and asked if he would be permitted to warm himself. A kind-hearted woman asked him to come in and sit down by her blazing fire. Observing his forlorn look, she gave him food, and what was equally serviceable, a pair of stockings and a pair of old pit-shoes. The latter protected his feet from the snow and frost, and, having thanked her as best he could, with renewed vigour the wanderer proceeded on his journey. After various adventures he ultimately reached the quaint old village of Torphichen. The difficulty of finding his uncle's house now confronted him, and while loitering near the village well, a voice he knew, namely, his aunt's, accosted him in the words: "In the name o' God, callant, what are ye daein' here? Come in o'er. Lod, ye're an awfu' sicht!" He accompanied his aunt home, where, to his surprise, he found his father sitting by the fire. His father's desire was to take the boy back to Parkhead, but it was finally arranged that he should remain with his uncle and aunt, which he did, and for some time had the benefit of the best teaching the village could afford. After living with his relations for nearly a year, he again returned to his parents at Parkhead, and once more commenced to work at the loom.

About this time young Willox began to develop a taste for reading, and this in itself exercised a strong influence on the formation of his character, and opened up fields of enjoyment and knowledge hitherto unknown.

A few years after this found him in charge of a furnace at the Parkhead Ironworks, where he earned a good pay and devoted his spare time to self-improvement. Says Mr. Willox : "I borrowed books wherever I could get them, and to obtain books I stopped smoking, and saved my tobacco money to purchase more of them." Mr. Willox had also became a total abstainer, at a time when, in the Parkhead Ironworks, there were only three men known to be teetotallers.

About this time Mr. Willox joined the Freemasons, which is fully referred to in another page.

About a year later Mr. Willox took to himself a wife, a step which had a strong influence in shaping his future. He says: "I first met my wife when attending Wardlaw Congregational Church, in Bellgrove Street, and a year after this meeting we were married. 'Marry in haste and repent at leisure' is a saying which has not been true in my case. My married life has been a singularly happy one. During the twenty-six years it has run my wife and I have shared its joys and sorrows, her love and sympathy enabling me to bear up against difficulties, and to come out victorious when ruin seemed to stare me in the face."

For some years Mr. Willox continued to work at the Parkhead Ironworks, and shortly after his marriage was asked to take the post of foreman, which he, after some consideration, accepted. For about six years he remained foreman at the works, Mr. Beardmore, the head of the firm, having the utmost confidence in him. During these years many changes took place, not only in the works but in the process of iron manufacture, in all of which Mr. Willox took his share. On the death of Mr. Beardmore, the new management dispensed with his services. He then, in company with two others, started a small chemical factory, but the partnership did not prove a success. Mr. Willox was unfortunate in his partners and employees, who proved neither honest nor sober. After struggling for some years. Mr. Willox took the business into his own hands, and now can safely say he is in a fair way of making it a success.

A prophet has no honour in his own country, it is said. but so far as Mr Willox is concerned that is not the case. for he is highly respected and exceedingly popular, not only in Parkhead, but throughout the east end of Glasgow generally. The respect in which he is held by his fellow-rate-payers was shown in 1896, when they elected him to represent them in the Town Council of Glasgow.

Mr Willox sits for the Whitevale or 4th Ward, which includes Parkhead, or his native village. as we may call it. During the time he has occupied a seat at the Council Board Mr Willox has proved a most efficient and painstaking Councillor, whose motto is work not talk. The poetic element being rather scarce in such bodies, he holds an unique position, for his fellow-Councillors have unanimously claimed him as the municipal poet.

As an author, but still more as a poet, Mr Willox has attained a considerable literary position, and his poems have been eagerly read by a wide circle of admirers, particularly throughout the Masonic body.

Mr. W. J. Hughan writes—:"I consider that you, Tam McPhail, are a wonderfully good Masonic poet. Few of the numerous Masonic effusions are worth reading, but yours are always good—humorous and breathing the true spirit of poetry."

Alexander Cross, M.P., writes:—"I have read your poems with great delight; indeed, I may say that when returning home by train from the House of Commons the other night I read several of your pieces to some of my fellow-members, who appreciated them very highly."

Just before his death that gifted poet and writer, the Rev. Geo. Gilfillan, wrote:—"I have read Mr Willox's welcome pieces with considerable pleasure. 'The Gift' is very creditable indeed, and the lines on honest Janet Hamilton worthy of the theme, and that is saying a great deal. Would like to see some more of Mr Willox's sketches."

Many of Mr. Willox's fellow-townsmen have spoken highly of his poems; and he has been the recipient of numerous laudatory letters from men of taste and culture throughout the country. Some of his verses on local subjects have attracted much attention in official and other circles in Glasgow. In his humorous sketches, and more particularly his humorous verses, he reaches a high level. This is all the more wonderful when it is remembered that Mr Willox could express his thoughts in rhyme before he had educated himself to the point of writing them down.

The sketches and poems in this volume have been produced at odd moments snatched from a busy life, and are now for the first time published in collected form. Should those who take up the volume find in its pages something to instruct, amuse, or to wile away an idle hour, the book will not have been written in vain.

Masonic Career.

Mr. Willox was initiated into the mysteries of Masonry on the 29th February, 1869, in **Lodge** (Shettleston) "St. **John, 128."** He was passed Fellowcraft **a** fortnight later, **and raised** to the sublime degree of Master Mason two weeks **later still. It may** be mentioned here that his grandfather joined **the same Lodge in 1821,** and remained a member of the **Masonic body until his** death.

For years Mr. Willox had been a Mason at heart, and **when initiated was strongly impressed by the** symbolisms **of the Craft and the** sublimity **of the ceremonial.**

Speaking of those days, Mr. **Willox says : "The majority of Lodges then hold** their meetings in **public-houses.** Now **it is an unusual thing** for one to do so **; indeed,** it is doubt-**ful if a Charter would bo granted to a** Lodge proposing to **meet in. such a** place. **The** ceremonial nowadays is con-**ducted in a** much more **impressive** manner; indeed, the **whole** tone of Masonry has been raised to **a** higher level since then, and consequently **its influence** has become **much** wider and **more** powerful.

Mr. Willox **joined** the Royal **Arch** Masonry **in** November, **1870, so that he lost little** time in being **"exalted," as it is termed. Chapter 87, "Shamrock and Thistle,"** was the **name of the Chapter,** and at present he is a **life** member of **that Chapter. The ceremony of** Exaltation was somewhat **different then from what it is now,** but the enthusiasm for **the Masonic** cause is even greater **than** what it was then. **Becoming a** frequent attender **at** the Lodge meetings, he **was asked to** take office, and for **twelve** years held the post of secretary, only resigning it when he was pressed to take the chair. **Previous to this the Lodge** had been in difficulties; but during the time he occupied the chair it prospered both in membership and financially. Altogether, his rule proved exceedingly beneficial to the Lodge; and when Mr. Willox retired from the chair, on the 4th April, 1894, he was presented by the Lodge with a very valuable gold watch and chain, together with a diamond ring for his wife, as showing their appreciation of his services to the Craft. It was stated, when the presents were made to him, that for the long period of twenty years he had never missed a meeting of his mother Lodge, special or otherwise; and for fifteen years of that time he had held office. Further, he had never been absent from an office-bearers' meeting, and was never known to be five minutes late. He possesses diplomas for various Orders connected with the Craft, and one which he values highly was conferred by the Grand Lodge, England, namely, Membership of Lodge "Clausentum, 1461, Woolston, E.C.," for services rendered to the Craft. The following is a list of the Diplomas held by Mr. Willox, and the dates upon which they were conferred:—

1. Scottish Diploma, Blue Craft, 3rd August, 1869.
2. Scottish Diploma, Red R.A., 30th November, 1870.
3. English Diploma, Blue Craft, 28th February, 1888.
4. Scottish Diploma, Knights Templar, 13th December, 1889.
5. Scottish Diploma, Royal Ark Mariners, 16th January 1890.
6. Scottish Diploma, Order of Malta, 19th June, 1890.
7. Scottish Diploma, Installed Master, 16th December, 1890.
8. Early Grand Orders of Temple and Malta, 25th September, 1893.
9. Eastern Star Sovereign Sanctuary, 7th December, 1893.

10. Ancient and Primitive Ryte, 33, 90, 90, 8th December,
          1893.

In addition to the above, Mr. Willox holds other Diplomas and honours in the Masonic body, amongst which it may be mentioned that he was unanimously appointed Grand Bard to the Early Grand Body, and can count amongst his friends some of the most distinguished Freemasons in Great Britain.

In 1894 it was decided, on the suggestion of Mr. Willox, to start a Masonic Monthly. A company was formed, entitled the Scottish Freemasons' Publishing Company. Mr. Willox was appointed manager, and the first issue appeared in May, 1894. From the beginning it was a success. 800 yearly subscribers were obtained, and large quantities of the paper were disposed of through the news-agents. But, as is often the case with a literary undertaking, started with too many—well, conductors—misunderstandings took place, and ill-feeling was engendered, the result being that Mr. Willox resigned, and shortly afterwards the paper was stopped.

It was in the pages of the "Freemason" that Mr. Willox, under the nom de plume of "Tam M'Phail," contributed many of those poems and sketches republished in this volume, and which are now appealing to a wider public.

Says Mr. Willox: "Through the pages of the 'Scottish Freemason' I have made the friendship of many kindred spirits, which I never otherwise could have gained. Many of them I have never seen, still I value their friendship all the more, though probably we may not meet in this world. I trust I may never do aught to forfeit that love and friendship, and that when this earthly pilgrimage is ended I may meet with those absent brothers in the Grand Lodge above, where all is Peace, Love, and Harmony."

POEMS AND SKETCHES.

LET BROTHERLY LOVE PREVAIL.

Sweet were the notes when Israel's bard
　　Awoke the slumbering lyre,
The tuneful numbers then were heard
　　In pathos and in fire.
But far the sweetest notes of all
　　That wafted on the gale
Were those that bore the plaintive call,
　　" Let brotherly love prevail."

The mountain echoes caught the tone,
　　The valleys far and wide
Re-echoed back and carried on
　　The message full of pride.
The lonely shepherd on the hill,
　　The ploughman in the vale
Were startled, but rejoiced to hear
　　" Let brotherly love prevail."

The warrior checked his fiery steed
　　And quelled his kindling ire,
Nor sought the conquering host to lead
　　With retribution dire.
The sword was sheathed and peace proclaimed,
　　And Conquest trembling, pale,
Heard the refrain again, again,
　　" Let brotherly love prevail."

Far o'er the land from sea to sea
　　The heavenly message swelled,
Proclaiming peace; the bond, the free,
　　Their fiery passions quelled,

And sought in love's fraternal bond
Their fellow man to hail,
Repeating oft, in accents fond,
"Let brotherly love prevail."

Let brotherly LOVE, BELIEF, and TRUTH
Our band forever bind,
And trembling age and vigorous youth
Within our circle find
That love fraternal shelters here,
And wayward passions quail,
And all have learned the precept dear,
"Let brotherly love prevail."

TAM M'PHAIL JOINS THE CRAFT.

I.

DEAR MR. EDITOR,—Some o' your readers'll be wondering wha Tam M'Phail is? They'll ken a' aboot that by-and-bye; in the meantime, it'll be sufficient tae say that I come o' a guid auld Hielan family, am a Burgess o' the ancient City o' St. Mungo, and am a married man wi' two-three o' a family. On hearing that ye were gaun tae start a Masonic paper, I thocht I micht dae waur than let ye ken what ma experience was o' Freemasonry in particular, an a' things in general. Ma reason for daeing this is that the younger members o' the Craft may tak' a lesson frae ma experience, an' no' be o'er ready in letting it be kent that they hae joined the Craft. Of coorse, there's naething to be ashamed aboot in joining sic an ancient an' honourable Order, but some o' us in oor anxiety tae fraternise sometimes fa' an easy prey tae the sharp an' unscrupulous moocher.

At least, this was ma experience, an' I hae nae doot it has been the experience o' a great wheen mair.

Ye ken, when I joined the Freemasons I wasna a'thegither a mere youth. I had been married tae oor Meg for a guid wheen years, and there had been a large increase o' oor family wealth in the shape o' a lot o' wee M'Phails that micht hae put the thocht o' Freemasonry oot o' ma heid. But Meg says I've been naething but "a muckle sumph" a' ma days, an' that I never could think o' onything seriously for five minutes at a time. Nae doot this is the reason she snapped at me like a cock at a grosset that nicht I proposed tae marry her. Indeed, I hae some doots yet whether I proposed at a' or no', but I'll maybe tell you something o' oor courtship by-an'-by. In the mean-time, I've tae tell ye o' ma Masonic experience.

Weel, as I was saying, I wasna quite a youth when I joined the Craft, but I had a' the fire an' enthusiasm o' youth for ma new hobby, and the first thing I did efter being made was tae gang an' buy a new scarf preen, nearly as big as a five shillin' piece, wi' the square and compasses embossed on it, an' a keystane tae hing tae ma watch chain. Of coorse, I learned efterwards that I had nae richt tae dae this, but what, betwixt ignorance and enthusiasm, I wis fairly carried awa'. Losh, bless you, sir! if you had seen the glower oor Meg gied when I let her see the things. She was fair dumfoonert, an' seemed tae lose a' reason, an' the only sense I could mak' oot o' what she said was some-thing like, "wiser-like if ye had bocht bits tae the weans than squander yer siller on sic trumphery as that." Bit, ye ken, women are quite unreasonable at times, an' altho' oor Meg's ane o' the best that ever lived, she seems tae think that I can dae naething richt. I needna say that I didna relish her remarks, especially as she had been bothering me for the last twa months tae buy her a fine brooch she had seen in a sale shop window; an' during a' that time there hadna been a single word aboot bits for the weans. Among the first o' ma Masonic experiences was a tift wi' Meg. Ye ken she has a tongue that wad clip clouts ance she begins, an' I can tell ye she didna spare me for the first twa or three weeks. If I happened tae get a dram she was share tae open on me wi' something like the following—"Oh, aye, awa' wi' yer drucken Masons again"—even tho' I wis jist hame frae a meeting o' oor Kirk Deacons—"a fine job you'll mak' o't; you'll see what the Masons'll dae for ye when the weans an' me are in Barnhill an' yersel' in Gartnavel, whaur ye should hae been lang syne. A fine pirn ye'll wind us, Tam M'Phail! An auld fule like you joining ony sic crew." An' when I wad interpose wi' "Hits, tits, Meg! ye dinna ken whit yer talkin' aboot," she wad reply, "O, it's a' very weel for you, Tam, tae say I don't ken whit I'm talkin' aboot, you that has naething a dae but rise in the morning an' gang tae your wark, while I'm left here wi' the weans, won'ering hoo the rent's tae be payed." Of coorse this kin' o' logic's unanswerable, an' I jist haud ma tongue for fear I micht fare waur. But if Meg wisna pleased wi' ma preen and keystane, I can tell ye they were highly admired by ma brethren the first meeting I gaed tae efter I bocht them.

"Oh, my, Tam! whaur did you get the preen?" "My, sic a beauty!" "It wad maist dae for a shield!" an' sic like exclamations and admiration were bandied aboot on a' sides, while ae ignorant fellow, if I may be excused ca'in' a brither that, asked whaur I got the coffin plate. But I kent it wis jist envy on his pairt, for mine wad hae made half-a-dozen o' his at least. Dae ye ken, I taen a kind o' scunner at that fellow ever since, an' whenever I see him sporting a

Masonic jewel I mak' it a point aye tae get ane faur bigger than his. Ye'll maybe think this is an indication o' vanity, but it's naething but evendoon enthusiasm for the guid o' the Order. But if ma preen took the shine oot o' a wheen o' them that nicht, I can tell ye my keystane fairly surprised them. Ane o' them asked if I had made it masel', an' anither asked if it wis a bit o' the Municipal Buildings. The blockheeds, if they had jist taen time tae think, they micht hae seen that the makin' o' sic a thing wasna in ma line at a'. I'm a weaver tae trade, an' could nae mair hae made sic a thing than I could hae jumped tae the moon. An' as for it being a bit o' the Municipal Building foundation stane, it wasna stane at a', but guid clean solid mother pearl, made oot o' the doup o' an auld snuff-box that belonged to the family. I got Andrew Tyler tae mak' it, wha's kind o' handy at thae kind o' jobs, and I think he made no' a bad job o't efter a'. It's maybe a shade tae the big side, but that mak's it a' the easier seen; an' whit else are sic like things for than tae be seen? They're fine advertisements, especially tae sma' business men like me. Ye ken I'm a "cork" weaver—that means a manufacturer on a sma' scale. But, of coorse, it wasna wi' an eye tae business that I got thae things; it wis jist tae let folk see that I wasna ashamed o' the Order, and that I wis ready tae mak' freens wi' a' o' a like kind.

But maybe I'm trespassing on your space; an' as this is merely an introductory letter, making the announcement that I hae j'ined the Craft, in ma next, if it's agreeable tae ye, I'll gi'e some account o' hoo I wis received by some o' the brethren o' ither lodges. I intend tae tell ye o' a visit I made tae a sister lodge, an' hoo I got on in ma examination.—In the meantime, I remain, yours fraternally,

TAM M'PHAIL.

TAM M'PHAIL VISITS A LODGE.

II.

Mr. Editor,—I wis awfu' weel pleased tae see that ye had thocht it worth while tae publish ma last letter. Ye ken there's aye a touch o' vanity, mair or less, even in grown-up folk like masel'. I think it's Byron that says

> "Ane likes tae see their name in print,
> A book's a book tho' naething's in't."

Nae doot some o' your readers wad look sour at seeing my name figurin' in the pages o' the "Scottish Freemason," but I can tell ye there were ithers wha were in nae way displeased, an' if you had seen the glower oor Meg gied, tho' she pretended no' tae care aboot it, it wad hae dune your heart guid; an' tho' she said something aboot me being "an auld fule," she didna object tae me reading the article ower tae her in the presence o' oor family. Talk aboot throwing oil on the troubled watters, I tell ye it wis like oiling the wheels o' the matrimonial machine.

Baith the Craft an' masel' hae risen fifty per cent. in oor Meg's estimation since the issue o' the last number o' the "S.F.," no' that she's a reader o' the voracious kind, but there seems tae hae been something in't that has taen her fancy. I hae a strong suspicion that her reading propensities hae become largely developed since August the first, this year; and tho' I canna speak wi' ony degree o' certainty wi' regard tae the variety o' matter that she devours. I hae a strong suspicion that it's limited, for pages 40 and 41 o' the "S.F." are the only twa that seem tae be weel thumb'd. Noo, it's a singular coincidence that thae twa pages are the very twa that contain ma letter. But it's aboot time that I should tell you hoo I got on when I visited Lodge 553, Glasgow. Ma certy, if they're as particular aboot letting everybudy in as they were wi' me they'll huff a few, I hae nae doot. But they're quite richt, tho' I didna see things in the same licht then that I see them noo. Ma certy, they're a sharp lot o' chiels in that lodge, and the way they bumboosl'd me that nicht put visiting oot o' ma heid for a long time.

I hadna been a fortnicht joined, an' had only got my first degree at the time o' ma visit but wis anxious tae see hoo things were dune in ither lodges. I hae a fair memory, an' flattered masel' that I could mind a' that wis telt me when I wis made. Sae dressing masel' up in a suit o' guid Scotch tweed o' ma ain manufacturing, an' arranging my preen an' keystane tae the best advantage, I set oot fu' o' hope, fu' o' enthusiasm, an'—will I say it?—fu' o' pride. As I had a guid distance tae gang, I rehearsed in ma mind, as weel as I wis able, the ceremony o' the degree I had got, and mentally pictured tae masel' the rapture wi' which I wad be hailed by the brethren, and resolved tae be as modest as possible under the circumstances, never thinking for a moment o' a refusal.

Having reached the locality in ample time, I daundered up tae the hall, or rather tae what is ca'd the adjacent. The Tyler was busy arranging things, and there was maybe a score o' brethren sitting roon, cracking an' laughing wi' the greatest cordiality. Of coorse, being a stranger, I couldna join in wi' the rest, at least at present, sae I sauntered aboot for a few minutes, and then I ventured tae mak' masel' kent tae the Tyler. He wis an elderly man, maybe aboot 60 or fully mair, and had, apparently, seen better days, as his manner an' speech afterwards indicated.

"That's a guid nicht, frien'," says I, approaching him, as he was selecting frae a capacious kist the articles necessary tae furnish the lodge. "Ou, aye," he replied, eyeing me wi' what I thocht was a look o' enquiry, and finding that he did not look me straucht in the face I thocht that he wantit me tae say something else; but it was ma preen an' stane that had taen his e'e, an' when I noticed this I felt reassured, and thocht I had established ma claim tae his regard at ance. "I'm a visiting brither," I said, stickin' ma twa hauns in ma trowser's pouches, "an' I've jist ta'en a dauner up tae see hoo yer getting on; ye ken, oor Lodge meets on a different Wednesday frae your's, an' I thocht I couldna dae better than jist gie ye a look up." "Oh, we're gled tae see visitors at a' times when they're properly vouched for; an' if there're ony o' the brithren here that you're acquainted wi' you'll be made braw an' welcome, but you'll excuse me the noo until I get the Lodge in order, an' then I'll attend tae ye," an' wi' that he bustled awa' wi' the things he had been selecting. Noo this brief encounter wi' the Tyler hadna been a' that I could hae desired, nor was it onything like what I expectit. I looked for naething else at least than a grasp o' his haun an' the Mason's grip, thereby recognising me as a brither withoot ony mair palaver; but, instead o' that, he answers me in the plainest, matter-o'-fact way he could, besides using an expression o' precaution that was quite new tae me, namely, "properly vouched for." What could this mean? Was I no' a Mason as weel as him? Had I no' got the receipt for the money I paid? An' as guid luck wad hae it, I had it in my pooch at that very moment. If that wisna a voucher that couldna be gainsaid, then ma name's no' Tam M'Phail. But I wad produce it at the proper time.

The Lodge having been a' properly arranged, an' the time, 8 o'clock, being up, some ane gaed twa or three raps, an' a' made intae the hall. Of course, I made tae gang in wi' the rest, but the Tyler body touched me on the shouther an' asked me whaur I was gaun. Sic a stupid-like question, when the thing was as apparent whaur I was gaun as that 3 and 3 are 6. I hinted as much, when he said, "O, but you'll hae tae be examined first." I expected as much, but thocht that the examination wad hae taen place before this. "It's a' richt," I said, "I'll jist wait till ye send somebody oot." Sae I took ma seat in the adjacent room an' waited wi' patience. I had waited maybe aboot ten or fifteen minutes, when twa brithren entered wha I hadna before seen. Ane was a man rather past middle age, stout, and somewhat florid in complexion, named W.B. He had been Master o' the Lodge at one time, an', as I afterwards learned, was considered awfu' weel up. This opeenion I can verify noo, but I thocht him awfu' stupid that nicht. He couldna understan' ma answers at a', tho' I tried tae be as plain as daylicht.

The ither chiel was much younger, and accompanied the elder for the sake o' instruction. The elder ane took up the speakin', an' began by saying it was "A guid nicht." I answered that it was, tho' I could hear the rain batterin' on the window ootside.

"You're a visiting brither," he remarked, eyeing me frae head tae fit, ma preen an' stane comin' in for a guid share o' his attention.

"Whence come you?" and when I answered that I had a vote in the parliamentary division o' Camlachie, I thocht that his een wad hae jumped clean oot o' their sockets, but whither it wis wi' pleasure or disappintment I wasna able tae determine. I thocht I heard the younger ane gieing a cough, as if tae keep himsel' frae choking, an' I'm positive that his face wis flushed wi' smothered mirth, but whit he had got tae laugh at I couldna tell, sae I set it doon tae his inexperience.

"Are you a Freemason?" the auld ane next asked, an' as I had been telt tae be cautious, I answered "Umphum," but this didna seem tae satisfy him, for he asked:

"Hoo dae you ken you're a Freemason?"

"By paying ma siller!"

"Hoo much did you gie tae be made a Mason?"

"Twa pounds, ten shillings."

"Hoo will I ken ye tae be a Mason?"

"I'll let you see the receipt for the siller," I answered, delving into ma pouch confidently.

"Oh, no; never mind your receipt. Answer ma question."

"But what answer dae ye want?"

"That's for you tae decide."

"But I canna tell what ye want."

"I want tae ken hoo I'll ken ye tae be a Mason."

"Oh aye, I see, it's a conundrum. Man, I'm no' guid at thae things, but I'll tak' it hame tae Meg, she'll solve it at ance."

By this time I thocht the young chiel wad choke a'thegither, and he made some excuse aboot gaun for a drink an' left tae get a mouthfu' o' water. I wis michty glad, for I was feart he wad hae a stroke o' apoplexy, his face had become that red, but what wis really the matter wi' him I couldna tell. He cam' back in a meenit or twa, an' by some overlook or neglect on his part, probably on account o' his agitation, he left the door a wee bit ajar, but I had ower much tae dae wi' masel tae draw his attention tae the matter.

The auld ane, no' yet satisfied, resumed his interrogation.

"Ye canna answer the question, then?"

I answered that I gied it up until I consulted wi' Meg.

"Very weel, then; I'll try ye wi' a few mair."

An' then he put some o' what I thocht were the maist senseless questions that it wis possible tae conceive.

"How old is your mither?" he asked.

"She's deid, sir." At this, notwithstanding the solemnity of the tone in which ma answer was gien, I could tak ma oath I heard a titter outside the door, while the young fellow wha wis present coughed louder than ever. I looked frae the ane tae the ither expecting an explaination, but the auld ane just cleared his throat an' begun again.

"Your mither's deid, puir body! We'll no' disturb her memory by referring to the sad event, but maybe ye'll be able tae tell us when you were made a Mason?"

"Wi' the greatest o' ease—exactly a week the nicht."

"Wha made ye a Mason?"

"Tam Morrison, the wabster."

"Why were ye made a Mason?"

"Because I wis weel kent."

"What made ye a Mason?"

"The twa pounds ten that I paid."

"Have you a certificate?"

"I hae," an' I drew forth the receipt, remarking, "If ye had ask'd for that before a' this palavering it wad hae saved baith your time an' mine"; but what was ma astonishment when he merely glanced at the document and handed it back wi' the remark that that wisna the document he wanted tae see. I said that wis a' the document I had got, an' I had never heard tell o' ony ither.

"Oh, but," he said, "ye'll get anither in due time. Ye're hardly entitled tae the ither ane yet; an' when ye get it be sure an' gie us a ca' again."

"An' am I no' tae get in the nicht after comin' a' this gate an' stauning a' this heckling?"

"No, frien'; I don't know you tae be a Mason—I don't

even ken yer name. I've tried to ascertain wha ye are in the simplest way I could, an' ye've failed tae satisfy me. I'm loth tae refuse a brither—as no doubt ye are—but duty compels me tae see that ye comply wi' certain forms, all of which ye have overlooked or have not yet learned.

"Ma conscience! hear tae the like o' this! Ye believe me tae be a brither, an' yet ye refuse tae acknowledge me as such. What strange paradox is this? Ye say that ye don't know my name. At the beginning I wad hae telt it wi' the same readiness that I answered a' your ither questions. Ma name's Tam M'Phail, nephew tae Laughlan M'Phail, grieve tae the Duke o' Sutherland, an' third cousin tae Angus M'Phail, sergeant o' police; but I winna—even for the sake o' gettin' into the Lodge—draw the names o' ma connections in. Ma ain name should be sufficient, an' if ye want tae ken mair aboot me I can only refer ye tae oor worthy minister."

"It's a' richt, Tam; I don't doot your respectability for a single moment; but I want ye tae understand that your present Masonic status does not warrant you in claiming admittance into Lodges beyond the first degree, and, as a frien' an' brither, I wad advise ye tae get better posted up even in what ye hae got. Your enthusiasm has evidently overcome your discretion; and if it hadna been that I saw ye were a well-meaning fellow it wad hae been waur for ye."

"An' sae I hinna tae get in after a'? What will Meg say when I tell her o' this turn-up?"

"Don't tell her ower much, Tam; an' come back some ither nicht."

I thanked him for his advice, and bade him guid nicht, an' cam' awa' a sadder, if no' a wiser, man than I went.

Noo, Mr. Editor, what dae ye think o' that? Or rather, what wad ye hae thocht o't had ye been in ma place? I can tell ye what I thocht o't. I thocht it ane o' the strangest things possible, an' I never felt mair disappinted in a' ma life. As for yon sneevelling chap wi' the bad cough, if it had only been him I had tae tackle, I think I could hae soon dichted him aff; but the auld ane, wi' his senseless queries aboot ae thing an' anither, fairly wan'ered me; an' when he telt me tae come back some ither nicht, it then began tae daun on me that I wisna tae get in that nicht, an' I began tae feel as if ma new suit was too big for me and that ma heart was too big for ma bosom; an' I canna very weel account for onything that took place betwixt the time o' leaving an' that o' staunin' at the bar o' the nearest pub. asking for a glass o' the very best tae droon ma disappintment. It was then that I cam' tae masel' again, an' then—only then—that I realised that I had made an ass o' masel' without kenning it; but it wis a' yon auld ane's faut. He wis that sly and sleekit, and yet sae plausible, that ye wad maist hae thocht he wis gaun tae embrace ye while a' the while he was jist trying tae confuse ane. I was aye waiting tae he wad begin tae examine me, and hardly kent whaur I wis when he telt me tae ca' back again. If he had asked me for the sign, or the word, I could hae gien them richt aff loof, but tae gang beating awa' aboot the bush wi' " Wha made ye?" " Whan were ye made?" " Why were ye made?" and, aboon a', " Hoo auld's yer mither?" I tell ye, at the time, I thocht he wis takin' the len' o' me.

TAM M'PHAIL AT A HARMONY MEETING.

III.

"But ye whom social pleasure charms,
  Whose heart the tide of kindness warms,
  Who hold your being on the terms,
    Each aid the others;
Come to my bowl, come to my arms,
    My friends, my brothers!"

DEAR MR. EDITOR,—The above lines o' oor immortal brither just hits tae a "T" what I felt the first Harmony meeting I gaed tae. I hae a warm side tae everybody and everything, an' altho' ma early fervour has become somewhat modifeed wi' ripening years, I still feel the glow o' fraternal love, an' especially on Harmony nichts.

I don't know that I should hae bothered ye wi' ma experience o' Harmonies, had it no' been that I heard a few original Masonic sangs that nicht which it micht please your readers tae see in the special number of the "S.F." I don't ken what merit they may hae, but I think you'll agree wi' me that they bear the stamp o' sincerity at least.

But I maun first tell ye how it came aboot that I gaed tae a Harmony at a', seeing that it wasna in oor ain Lodge. An invitation had been read at oor meeting frae the S. and T. Lodge, asking a deputation tae attend their "Mark and Harmony," and when twa-three o' oor fellows proposed gaun, as the S. and T. chiels were famous for haeing fine Harmonies, I volunteered tae gang alang wi' them. I was puzzled at first tae understaun what was meant by S. and T., and had mentally concluded that thae twa letters could only staun for Saut and Tatties, but I ken better noo, and I hae nae doot the maist o' your readers can interpret them as weel.

The Lodge was crowded when we got there, and the chap
that sits in the South had jist been placed in command,
so that we were in fine time for the first toast. When I
got time tae settle doon an' look roon' me, I saw a few that I
kent brawly by head mark, and as it was the first time some
o' them had seen me at a Masonic meeting, they seemed
tae be unco weel pleased, and I could see them dunching
ane anither an' nodding ower my way, as much as tae say,
"That's Tam M'Phail." I wasna in ony way put aboot at
this. I expected tae be taen notice o', an' had spent some
time before I cam' oot scourin' ma preen an' polishin' up
ma keystane, wi' the result that they were perfectly dazzlin'.
Of course, I acknowledged their salutations in as affable a
manner as the circumstances wad permit, an' before lang
I felt masel' quite at hame. The kind o' notable characters
o' the Lodge were a' pointed oot tae me, and before the first
sang was ca'd for I was maist on noddin' terms wi' them a'.
"The Queen and the Craft," "The Three Grand Lodges,"
and "The Provincial Lodge" havin' been duly honoured an'
responded tae, the J. W. then called upon the S. W.—
Bro. C.—tae favour them wi' a sang. Bro. C. was a pre-
centor-looking body wi' a gae bauld head, but no' a bad
voice; and when he rose tae make an excuse aboot bein' taen
quite by surprise, we could a' see that he wad just as soon
sing as let it alane, so we gied him a' the encouragement we
could, an' he began wi' "Hail, Light Divine," tae the tune
o' "The Bonnie Lass o' Ballochmyle." As near as I can
mind it ran something like as follows :—

> "Hail! Light Divine, thy gladdening ray
>   We greet with reverence and love ;
> Cheer, kindly cheer our toilsome way,
>   And guide us to that Lodge above

Where Nature's Architect supreme
　The happy Craftsmen will employ,
In praises o' His marks sublime,
　Untiring and eternal joy.

Hail! Light, that cheers the glowing east,
　Dispel the clouds of darkest night,
And call the Craftsmen forth, to feast
　On stores of knowledge, with delight;
The weary toilers then shall sing
　In raptures while the work proceeds;
And every day rewards shall bring,
　Celestial for terrestial deeds.

Hail! Light Divine, diffuse thy rays
　Where ignorance despotic reigns;
Make glad the path and bright the days
　Of all who wear oppression's chains.
Point out that straight, unerring line
　Our Master traced in ages gone;
And shed, oh! shed thy light benign
　In radiant rays mankind upon.

Hail! Light, beneficent thy glow—
　We bask with pleasure in thy beams;
And seek to spread the truths we know,
　Wherever Man thy power esteems.
We mark with pride thy broadening sphere,
　We hail with joy thy light benign,
And Faith and Hope shall ever cheer
　Our labours in thy rays divine.

When the applause and congratulations had somewhat
subsided after this sang, amidst such sounds as "Health
an' song, Bro. C.," "The aforesaid," and such like, the

Maister's mallet was heard ca'ing the brethren tae order, when he announced that Bro. W. L. wad favour wi' the next sang. W. L. is ane o' the sweetest singers ye could desire tae hear, and the way he rendered "My Sweetheart when a Boy" put me in mind o' the time when I courted Meg, and I couldna help shouting out, "Weel din, Wullie," loud enough tae be heard through the hale hall. Wullie and his brither Jock are twa o' the nicest fellows ane could wish tae meet, and baith capital singers. Jock sings "Barlinnie" and "Get up an' Bar the Door," wi' great acceptance, an' he seems tae be a prime favourite wi' everybody. We then were treated tae a fine rendering o' the "Chairge of the Light Brigade" by Bro. B., a member o' St. Mark's, wha fairly carried his audience wi' him, and ane felt himsel' wishing he had been ane o' that immortal band o' heroes. Things were gaun on finely when the J. W. announced that they wad noo be favoured wi' a sang by a visiting brither, wha he was glad tae see present, namely, Brither Thomas M'Phail. Losh, bless me, Sir! I thocht the floor wad hae opened and swallowed me up. I could scarce believe ma ears. There surely wasna twa Thomas M'Phails, an', as everybody looked at me an' clappit their hauns, shouting "Hear, hear," I was forced tae the conviction that it was really me that wrs meant. Of coorse, I felt flattered at getting ma full name, but I get it that seldom that it sounded strange tae me. Naebody ever thinks o' ca'ing me onything but jist plain Tam, an' I must say that I like Tam jist as weel as Thomas. I tried tae put it aff by telling them I was nae singer, and a' that sort o' thing, but they wad tak' nae denial, sae I jist gied them, as weel's I could,

"THE RAISING O' THE DEIL."

"Come a' ye cunning Craftsmen
　　That work wi' plumb and line,
An' join me in a bicker,
　　While oor cares we quickly tine.
I'll sing ye a' a canty sang,
　　In hamely verse atweel,
About the Merry Masons and
　　The raising o' the Deil.

Chorus.

　　The raising o' the Deil,
　　The raising o' the Deil,
　　It's unca eerie working at
　　The raising o' the Deil.

The soldier flushed wi' thochts o' war
　　Forgets the dangers near;
The sailors on the raging sea
　　Hae aye some hopes tae cheer.
But wha can picture half the gloom
　　That settles o'er the cheil,
Wha thochtlissly resolves to see
　　The raising o' the Deil.
　　　　　The raising o' the Deil, etc.

The Statesman losing place and pooer
　　May yet regain them a';
The Lover lives when plighted love
　　Has chill'd like frozen snaw;
The ewe may mourn her wandered lamb,
　　Yet consolation feel;
But wha can lift the drooping heart at
　　The raising o' the Deil?
　　　　　The raising o' the Deil, etc.

> Hearts that hae never quailed before—
>   The bravest o' the brave—
> Hae quaked wi' fear and sought around
>   Some friendly haun tae save;
> But a' in vain. Their helplessness
>   They're ever made tae feel
> Wha wish tae join the Masons
>   At the raising o' the Deil.
>   The raising o' the Deil, etc.

I canna very weel describe the scene that followed the singing o' this sang, no' that I'm a singer, but there was a pawkieness o' meaning in the words themsel' that seemed tae be fully appreciated by the brethren. Indeed, it is only brethren wha can fully appreciate the meaning. "Hear, hear, Tam," "Health and Sang," "Tam, your Health," "What will ye hae, Tam?" "Encore, encore," "Gie's anither, Tam," rang on a' sides. Indeed, I nearly lost ma head, an' I must hae taen a half or twa unintentionally, for I began tae feel a wee uplifted, and thocht what a prood woman Meg wad be could she hae seen the fraca' that was being made. Anither toast was then proposed, and sine anither sang. The singer on this occasion was a Brither R.K., o' the S. and T., no' a bad singer: an' nae doot fired wi' emulation at the reception I had got, he gied them anither Masonic ane, something like this :

"WE'LL HAE NANE BUT LOYAL MASONS."

> "Ye sons o' licht, ye mystic few,
> Wha's hearts are warm, and leal, and true;
> Wha's kindly eye wi' pleasure beams
> On ilka act that kindly seems;

Wha's ready haun, when cares assail,
Gies bounties aye that never fail
Tae brighten woes wi' glowing cheer,
As felt by every brither here.

> We'll hae nane but merry Masons here,
> We'll hae nane but merry Masons here;
> We'll tyle oor doors when foes appear,
> An' hae nane but loyal Masons here.

Nae cowan's daur invade oor biel,
They're fearfu' lest we raise the Deil,
An' envying us oor happy lot
Spitefully say we ride a goat.
But ignorance is bliss, they say,
So let them keep their darksom' way,
We'll aye be blyth, wi' nocht tae fear,
When there's nane but loyal Masons here.

> We'll hae nane but loyal Masons here, etc.

Baith kings and courtiers a' may scheme,
Ambition's but an empty dream;
The highest aim o' life is love,
Tae Man below and God above.
The widows' claim, the orphans' cry,
Command us aye their tears tae dry,
Their woes tae soothe, their paths tae cheer,
Is the task o' every brither here.

> We'll hae nane but loyal Masons here, etc.

Then let the social cup gae round,
Where'er the mystic ties abound;
May want an' woe ne'er crop our door,
Nor jealous care oor hearts explore.

> May charity abiding be,
> An' keep us frae a' envies free,
> An' every tie that's true and dear
> Still bind us tae each other here.
>   We'll hae nane but loyal Masons here, etc.

I felt that some o' the lustre had left ma preen efter the singing o' this sang, an' I saw that there was twa Richards in the field. R. K. took the place by storm, an' I resolved tae hae a copy o' that sang—which I got—an' I've been practising it every nicht since for the next Harmony; but I'm feart I be trespassing on your space tae gae ye ony mair o' the sangs I heard that nicht. Maybe on some future occasion I'll gae ye a few mair that I hae been able tae pick up, but that may depend on hoo ye receive those I hae gien ye here. We had a few ither sangs and toasts, an' a'thegither it was a fine nicht, an' I can bear testimony tae the fact that S. and T. deserve their reputation. By this time it was getting late. I was beginning tae think o' Meg an' the weans when the R.W.M. said that there was ae very important toast that still remained tae be proposed, an' that as he himsel' hadna eloquence enough tae dae justice tae it, he wad call upon the S.W. tae dae sae.

The wee precentor body wi' the bauld heid then got up, an', clearing his throat, asked if the brithren were "a' charged." I began tae ripe ma pouches, thinking it was the price o' the twa or three haufs that I had had that he was referring tae when ane cries oot, "No; we're no' charged in the south!" an' some ithers, "We're no' charged in the west!" an' I could then see what kind o' "charging" was referred tae. After this had been attended tae, Brither C—— continued : "Brethren, if ye're a' charged, I wish ye tae be up-standing an' assist me tae drink the health o' oor visiting brethren. Lodge S. and T. has aye, in the past, been famous for the warmth o' the receptions she has extended tae visitors, an' I hope this will be nae exception. We are pleased tae see visitors on a' occasions, and especially when they come tae share wi' us the pleasures o' oor Harmonies. On this occasion, brethren, we are exceedingly pleased, not only tae see such a large turnout o' visiting brethren, but tae ken that we have with us this evening, for the first time, a young an' talented brither wha bids fair tae be not only an honour tae the Lodge he belangs tae but a credit tae the Craft at large. I refer tae Brither Tam M'Phail, an' when I ask ye tae drink this toast, coupled wi' his name, I'm shure you will do so with right goodwill. The aforesaid, "Count W.'s Count," "Brethren, we'll gie this highest honours, an' send it home wi' R.St.J." An' then sic a carry-on was seen as I hae never before witnessed. Talk aboot a "Royal reception!" I don't know very well what that means, but if it is onything warmer than yon, then it maun be gae hot indeed.

I don't know how I cam' tae be sitting, for I had risen tae ma feet wi' the rest ; but I had either been shoved doon or had fell doon wi' evendoon agitation, and a sting gaed through me like a galvanic shock, leaving me withoot either the power o' speech or motion. The sweat broke on me at every pore an' I wished frae the bottom o' ma heart that I was hame beside Meg and the weans. I had a confused idea that I was expected to say something, but for the life o' me I couldna mak' oot what it was. It is said that Demosthenes, tae overcome some natural defect, practised speaking wi' a stane in his mouth. D'ye ken, although I had had a hale quarry in mine it wouldna hae improved me a bit, but I couldna get oot o't, and wi' "Brither M'Phail's reply!" "Bravo, Tam!" an' sic like ringing in my ears, I rose tae put the best face on't I could.

"Ladies and Gentlemen," I began, wishing tae be as courteous as possible, when, oh, dear, sic a hullaboloo! "Order, order!" rang on every haun', an' the R.W.M. nearly broke the desk wi' his mell. I saw that I had put ma fit in't, tae use a vulgar phrase, an' tried tae recover masel' by saying, "Mr. Chairman and Gentleman," but if the first beginning was bad the second was nae better, for the R.W.M. continued smashing at his desk as if he had a contract for making firewood. I was fair stuck, an' looked roon' entreatingly for some ane tae help me. I don't know what I wad hae done had it no' been for a wee tailor body that whispered in ma ear "Say Right Worshipful Master, Wardens, and Brethren." I did this, and tried as best as I could tae mak' them understaun how happy I was tae hae an opportunity o' thanking them for their kindness. I said that I hadna felt sic a prood man since the day oor wee Tam was born, an' that I was shure a' the rest o' the visitors shared wi' me in this feeling.—Yours fraternally,

TAM M'PHAIL.

———

TAM M'PHAIL GETS THE MARK.

IV.

MAISTER EDITOR.—DEAR SIR AND BRITHER : Some time ago I gied ye a hint that things werena jist as pleasant at hame as I could hae desired—that is, when I cam' frae the Harmony meeting yon nicht. I could see at a glance that Meg had been

"Gathering her brows like gathering storm,
Nursing her wrath to keep it warm,"

an' that there wad be an ootburst if I didna watch what I was aboot.

I own that I was a wee thing late an' had haen a half or twa, but there wasna onything wrang wi' me for a' that, at least I thocht sae, although she seemed tae tak' quite a different view o' things entirely. But she's a deil an' a' for looking at things in a different licht frae me, especially when she thinks I've been tasting. I saw at ance that it wad be ma best plan tae "jouke an' let the jaw gae by," or in ither words that it wad be better tae tak' the saft side o' her. Sae, wi' a' the generalship that I could command, an' steadying masel' as best I could wi' ma twa hauns in ma trouser pouches, I asked, quite concerned like :

"What! no' in bed yet, Meg? Losh, woman, ye needna hae waited up for me! I didna intend being sae late, but I fell in wi' twa-three that I kent, an' ane canna jist rise an' rin." I thocht this was no' a bad beginning, an' was hopefu' that it micht hae the desired effect, but no' a muscle o' her face relaxed, an' I saw that I was in for't. I wish tae guidness she hadna waited up for me, but nae doot she had her ain reason for't.

"You're no' angry, are ye, Meg?" I asked, putting as much concern intae the question as I could, an' indeed, tae tell ye the truth, I was really concerned, for Meg's anger isna common. It's something tae be feart for—the very cat seems tae ken when she's in a tantrum, an' disappears on the very first indication o' a storm.

"You're no' angry, are ye? Losh, woman, it's no' that often that I'm late, an' ye ken brawly whaur I was. I telt ye I was gaun tae a Harmony meeting o' the S. an' T., an'——"

"Did ye tell me ye were gaun tae get fou' when ye gaed oot, an' that I wad be left sitting here hour after hour ma lane waiting on ye while you an' your cronies were a' makin' beasts o' yoursel's?   Did ye tell me that, Tam M'Phail, eh?" an' she gied brushing past me like a modified whirlwind.

The storm had burst, an' burst in such an exaggerated form that I was nearly dumfoonder'd. "Fou'!"   I had it jist on the tap o' ma tongue tae deny the aspersion point blank, but thocht it best tae be cautious an' no' add fuel tae the fire o' her passion. "Beasts o' yersel's!"   Losh, I canna tell ye hoo thae words rankled in my boosom, an' had it no' been that I didna want tae wauken the weans, for they were a' in bed, I wad hae repudiated the imputation at ance.   But, Sir, a consciousness o' the injustice o' the chairge, a hankering regard for Meg hersel', an' an inborn love o' peace an' quietness restrained me jist at the critical moment, an', wha kens, maybe averted a domestic calamity. Sae I interposed wi' "Whist, whist, Meg; dinna be ower severe.   Things are maybe no' as bad as ye think, an' it's a funny body that disna stumble whiles; we're a' fallible, ye ken, we're a' fallible."

"Nane o' your preaching, Tam; nane o' your preaching. Ma certie, if everybody was tae stumble as often as you dae there wad be a gey wheen fa', I'm thinkin'; but it'll no' last much longer. I'm determined on that. I'll bring things tae a crisis afore lang, an' ye'll see what ye'll dae when ye haena a hoose ower yer heid. A fine carry-on for a man cam tae your time o' day, awa' galantin' wi' your cronies tae a' hours at een, as if ye had neither count nor care," an' on she gaed, aff ae thing on tae anither, till I wis nearly dizzy wi' the din. I couldna get a word in edgeways till she had nearly exhausted hersel' an' had emptied the vials o' her wrath on ma devoted heid.

I bore it a' wi' Spartan patience an' let the maist o't gae in at the ae ear an' oot at the ither jist as fast as it wis hurled at me, an' that wisna slow; but, Mr. Editor, there wis ae word that rung in my ears like the tollin' o' a funeral knell, an' swallowed up a' ithers, as the rod o' Moses swallowed up those of the Egyptian enchanters, namely, the word "crisis." Dae ye ken, Mr. Editor, I hae an awfu' horror o' that word, especially comin' frae Meg. I hae an idea that it means something extraordinary at a' times, but when Meg's on the war path, an' comes awa' wi't, visions o' domestic dissolution, anarchy, chaos, an' ruin darken the horizon o' ma married life, an' I feel as if some dreadfu' approaching calamity were castin' its shadow ower ma path. I don't know that even Meg understauns the full import o' the word, or that she has the slightest idea hoo it affects ma nerves, but there's ae thing certain that she never fails tae mak' use o't when she's in her tantrums. Therefore, in dread o' the approaching "crisis," I saw that it wad tak' considerable management on ma pairt tae mak' things richt, an' bring Meg intae a mair reasonable frame o' mind; an' it wadna be very much tae ma credit if, efter some years o' married life, I didna ken hoo tae come roon' her.

She has ae weakness that is said tae be the common inheritance o' the sex, an' in her case it is pretty fully developed, namely, curiosity. Sae when I got an openin' I remarked:

"You're an awfu' body, Meg! Here, when I come hame, jist bursting wi' guid news for ye, ye yoke on me like a day's wark, an'll no' gie a body a chance o' tellin' what took place. Woman, if ye kent a' that happened the nicht ye wad be a prood, prood woman; but it's jist aye the way o't wi' ye, up like a tift o' tow withoot listenin' tae a word o' reason."

"Prood woman, nae doot! I wad indeed be a prood woman if I saw you haeing a wee thocht mair sense. Ye've

your character tae look tae, Tam, an' what wad the neighbours say if they kent ye coming hame at this hour, no'
speaking o' the example it sets the callants?"

"Oh, aye; but what the neighbours disna ken'll dae
them nae harm, Meg; an' there wasna ane o' them saw me
coming in."

"No; but they could hear ye. I kent whenever ye put
your fit in the close that ye had been tasting, an' tae mak'
matters waur ye had tae tumble the claes pole in the lobby
wi' a noise sufficient tae wauken the hale laun."

"Oh, but, Meg, that's an infernal awkward place tae keep
a claes pole. Ye maun shift it or it may get broken some
nicht. I hae nearly fell ower it twa-three times, an' it mak's
sic an infernal din when it fa's. But, Meg, I was gaun tae
tell you hoo I got on at the meeting. Woman, if ye had only
been there ye wad hae been a prood, prood woman tae hae
seen the fracca' that was made aboot yer ain Tam. Losh,
they didna ken what tae dae wi' me, an' naething wad haud
them till I gied them a sang."

"An' a braw job ye'd mak' o't."

"Weel, it seemed tae tak' onyway; an' they were *nearly*
asking me tae gie them anither."

"Weel, Tam, they're no' ill tae please when they seek
you tae sing, for there's jist aboot as much music in ma
pirn wheel as there is in you. I hae nae doot ye could roar
lood enough, but as for singing, Tam, we'll no' argue the
point."

By this time Meg was in a mair amiable mood, an' was
willing tae listen tae a' that I had tae tell her; of course,
I jist telt her what wad fit, an' got her at last tae acknowledge that things werena as bad as she had thocht at first.
Indeed, if it wasna against the rules I believe that she wad
gang tae the next Harmony hersel'; in fact, she hinted as

much, an' said she couldna see what way women couldna be allowed tae share in the pleasures o' the men bodies. I couldna explain the reason very weel masel', but was positive it was against the rules. Hooever, we got oor bit tift a' settled again, an' Meg thinks as much o' the Masons as ever; hence it was that when I telt her I was gaun tae get the "Mark Degree" she was quite weel pleased, for although she likes tae hae mony a dig at me hersel' she thinks there's no' mony like me : an' an additional degree, in her estimation, is additional honour tae the family. But, Mr. Editor, ane o' the main reasons that influenced me in gettin' the Mark was the frequent jawin' that I got aboot ma keystane. Everybody seemed tae admire it, an' it wis occasionally asked if I had got the "Mark," an' when I answered "No," some o' them wad say, "Man, Tam, ye've nae richt tae wear that till ye get the Mark "; "Can ye read the letters that are on it ?" "What way hae ye no' got the Mark yet, Tam?" an' sic like, till I mentally resolved tae tak' it on the first occasion it was bein' wrocht. Of course, I set a guid lot o' this doon tae envy, for among a' the keystanes that I ever saw there wisna ane that wis half as big an' braw as mine ; an', besides bein' hame-made, it had a peculiar yellowish tinge betokening extreme auld age, which made it a' the mair valuable—at least in ma een ; an' though I hadna been wearin' it mony weeks until it had a' the front o' ma waistcoat actually glazed wi' rubbin' against it, I wadna hae pairted wi' it for a guid lot. As for the letters that were on't, I kent as little aboot them as they kent aboot me. They were only put there because keystanes generally hae thae letters. I have often wondered what they meant, an' though I had made several attempts tae discipher them I canna say that I had been successful ; an' even Meg, wha's penetration is something extraordinary, was fairly put tae her mettle tae mak' them oot, an' even when we had dis-ciphered them tae some extent we couldna be sure that we were richt. I made them read at least half-a-dozen different ways, while Meg had quite as mony interpretations as me. Ane o' them especially took her fancy—maybe because it suited her better than ony o' the ithers—an' as there's a touch o' originality aboot it, I micht dae waur than gie ye't here.

The letters were—H.T.W.S.S.T.K.S., an' her rendering o' them wis "Haud The Wean, Says Solomon The King, So," an' she wad jist demonstrate what she meant by clappin' ane o' the youngsters doun on ma knee, as if she intended tae mak' a dry nurse o' me.

Hoo near she was tae the true meanin' o' the letters we had nae means o' kennin', an' as her interpretation an' mine differed somewhat, there wis aye a chance o' us disagreein' whenever the subject was discussed. Ane o' ma favourite interpretations, for I had several, was "Happy The Woman, Says Solomon, That Keeps Silent."

This rendering o' the letters didna seem tae gang weel doon wi' her, an' she maintained that that couldna be it, because Solomon, being a wise man, wadna be guilty o' saying onything sae contrary tae the laws o' Nature. That, as for hersel', were she tae be tongue-tied there wadna be a mair miserable being on earth, an' I can tell ye, Sir, there was some force in her argument; but for a' that I had a particular liking for that rendering, an' stuck tae it in spite o' a' that Meg could sae tae the contrary.

Hooever, the meeting nicht cam' roon' at last, an', resolved tae learn a' that was tae be learned aboot the Mark, I spree'd masel' up an' made tracks for the Lodge, Meg flinging an auld bauchle after me for luck as I gaed doon the stair. It seemed tae be a big nicht, an' there were twa-three there on the same errand as masel'. When I stepped intae the adjacent **room I** was greeted on a' **haun's wi'** "Come awa', Tam"; "**Hoo's** a' wi' ye the nicht?" "**Man, ye're** looking rale weel," **an'** sic like; an' **even** some strangers that were there were introduced tae **me as** brithers so-an'-so. I shook **haun's** wi' them a' **roon', an' said I** was gled **tae mak' the** acquaintance o' ma new relations, an' hoped we wad **get** better acquaint by-an'-by.

"Are ye for the Mark the nicht, Tam?" asked a chiel wha seemed tae be makin' himsel' extra officious in getting things ready. "**There's twa-three** forbye yoursel' for't, an' **you'll no' feel jist sae odd as if** ye were your lane." Noo, tae some **minds this remark micht hae passed** unheeded, but **wi' me it set me** thinking, an' **I began** tae wunner after a' **what kind o' thing the** Mark could **be that ane** "wadna feel **sae odd being in** company." Losh, they surely didna mean **tae disfigure me** in some way! If I was **tae be** branded **I hoped** it widna be aboot the **face.** The Jews, ye ken, **lang** syne received the "mark **o'** circumcision," an' seeing **that** the Masons took a lot o' their symbols frae that ancient people there was a possibility that the Mark, as they ca'd it, micht hae a striking resemblance tae that ceremony. If sae, **I** wad **rather** dae withoot **it.** But hoo was I tae ken **until** maybe it was too late? Thinking thus, I resolved tae soon' the Maister on this **point.** Sae assuming a careless**ness I was far frae** feeling **I** stepped up tae him an' asked **him if there were** mony **forbye me for the** Mark. He said **he** thocht there wad be half-a-dozen at least. "Dae ye think **you'll** be lang in getting through wi't, na?"

"Oh, maybe an' **hour** or sae if a' gaes weel," replied the Maister. "**An'** hae ye **ever ony** bother wi' the candidates **when ye're marking them?** I'm shure there will be some **waur than** ithers whiles."

"Whiles, but we've aye plenty o' haun's tae manage them."

"An' does ony o' them ever gang wrang in your haun's?"

"No; we aye manage it wi' satisfaction tae oorsel's, although whiles wi' enough tae dae."

"I don't suppose you'll disable ony o' us onyway?" I said wi' a carelessness o' tone a'thegither assumed.

"Oh, no; we aye watch that; but it a'thegither depends on the candidate himsel'."

"Oh, I'm no' carin'; but ane's jist curious tae ken. I wis jist wondering if the candidates had ony choice in the matter as tae whaur they wad tak' it."

"Yes; some tak' it ae place an' some anither."

"Then, I wad like tae tak' it whaur it wadna be seen, if it's a' the same tae you," I said, thinking I had fixed him beyond equivocation. But I wis baith surprised and disappinted when he remarked "Weel, weel, Tam, ye're a droll ane. I don't know what tae mak' o' ye; you're neither rogue nor fool, an' yet ye speak as if ye were a mixture o' baith. Ye'll get your Mark tae tak' hame wi' ye, an' ye needna be ashamed tae let onybody see't." An' wi' that he hurried awa' intae the Lodge.

This was somewhat reassuring. It wis a Mark that I wadna need tae be ashamed o' onyway; that was aye so much.

The Mark Maister, I learned, was awful weel up tae the job, an' that wis better, as there wad be less danger o' an accident, an', sae puttin' twa an' twa thegither, or a' things considered, I felt a little mair at ease.

Being weel up tae this kind o' wark, the Mark Maister wis weel kent throughoot the hale province, and even beyond it, an' wharever wark o' this kind was tae be done he wis in great repute. He wis a plain-spoken kind o' man, wi' a pleasant, open countenance; and tae judge frae his exterior ye wadna thocht that there was muckle in him, but on Masonry he was a perfect storehouse, an' in workin' a Degree I was telt could embellish it wi' some o' the quaintest auld-world stories ye ever heard. He had a strong partiality for the Dorio (his mither's tongue), which lent itsel' readily tae pawkiness, pathos, an' humour.

Having entered the Lodge alang wi' the rest, I was asked tae retire tae the adjacent room alang wi' a few ithers wha were tae get Marked alang wi' me. This was still further encouraging. I wad hae company at onyrate, an' I could be nae waur than the rest.

A chiel they ca' the Deacon here made his appearance, an' after a few remarks aboot the weather an' sic like, cautioned us tae be carefu' in a' we said and did. He said it was a very important step we were aboot tae tak', an' it depended a'thegither on oorsel's hoo it micht affect us in after-life. I asked if there was ony danger o' us being disabled or deformed in ony way, because if there was I was half-inclined no' tae tak' it, that I had a wife an' a sma' family depending on me, an' if onything was tae happen me Meg wad be in an awfu' state. He didna seem tae ken whether tae tak' ma remarks seriously or no', an' as the ithers laughed and seemed tae think I was makin' fun, he joined wi' the rest an' turned it intae a joke. I can tell ye I wis far frae joking at the same time, but there was nae use o' undeceiving them, seeing they were a' sae weel pleased.

It was, dootless, because I was a favourite that the Deacon selected me for the place o' honour, an' asked me tae carry a specimen o' ma wark—ma wark, mind ye, though I never saw it before, but it bore a striking resemblance tae the keystane that hung at ma watch chain, but it was maybe a kennin' bigger.

"Noo," said the Deacon, "ye'll jist dae as ye see me daein', an' answer whatever question that's put tae ye."

"It's a' richt, lad," I said; "jist lead the way, an' I'll see tae the questions." An' I gied the chap next me a dunch wi' ma elbo' that, nae doot, had a reassuring effect on him.

Being duly admitted, it wasna lang until we found oorsel's in the presence o' ane o' the Inspectors, an' ma guide havin' advanced a step or twa saluted him in a peculiar fashion. I was a' ears and een tae see what I could pick up. I heard the Inspector asking "Wha comes here?" but for the life o' me I couldna tell what ma guide said, although I streached ma neck as far as I was able. After a short confab betwex the twa I was motioned tae advance, which I did, saluting him jist in the same way that I had seen ma guide dae. "Wha comes here?" he asked in a deep, sepulchral tone, as if he had been speakin' oot o' a tomb. I was a wee surprised at him asking this, seeing that he kent me brawly, but withoot ony hesitation I answered "Tam M'Phail," lood enough tae be heard through a' the hall. An irreverent titter gaed roon' the hale room, sadly oot o' keepin' wi' the solemnity o' the occasion, an' although I was conscious o' haein' telt naethin' but the truth, I felt that some ither answer was required.

Even the Inspector seemed tae be disconcerted an' no' at ease. He didna seem tae ken what tae say next, an' fumbled among some marking tools that he had. Havin' somewhat recovered himsel' he next asked: "What dae ye want here?"

It was ma turn tae be a wee bit disconcerted, because for the life o' me I couldna tell, sae I jist answered: "I dinna ken." Had some o' thae bodies they ca' Anarchists drapped a bomb at his feet he couldna hae gien a bigger start, but it wisna wi' fricht that he started. I could tak' ma

oath on that.   He turned his back on me tae hide his confusion.   But it was nae use.   I could see plainly that he was
agitated in nae ordinary degree ; indeed, there was an apparent restlessness on the pairt o' a' that were there.

I looked roon' thinkin' ma guide wad explain matters,
but he seemed tae hae had a sudden attack o' the toothache
or somethin' o' that kin' for he stood wi' his pocket napkin
stapped in his mouth an' his face was as reed as the fire, sae
he seemed tae hae enough tae dae wi' himsel'; indeed,
everybody seemed tae be put aboot but masel', for altho' I
felt a rising impulse tae ask what was the matter wi' them
a' I kept it doon an' remained as cool as the circumstances
wad permit.

The Inspector having recovered his composure again
tackled me wi' the same question: "Wha comes here?
An' no' wishing tae gie ony cause for annoyance, I varied
ma answer this time by asking : "Man, Jock, what are ye
driving at ? I'm shure ye ken wha I am finely ? I'm
Tam M'Phail, wha was best man at your wedding an'
helped ye hame the ither nicht frae the Bowlers' spree."
"Hear, hear !" "Ha, ha, ha !" "Rale guid !" was distinctly
heard on a' haun's.

There was nae mistaking the indications this time, even
the Mark Master gied an unmistakeable guffa', and the poor
Inspector seemed overwhelmed wi' confusion, an' for a
minute or twa everybody seemed tae forget whar they were
an' indulged in winking, laughing, an' nodding tae ane
anither, as if something really funny had happened.   I
couldna see whar the fun come in, an' I'm shure neither
could the Inspector, tae judge frae his appearance.   I
believe that he an' I were the only twa really serious per-
sous in the room.   I was sensible o' ma seriousness de-
generating intae unholy anger, an' I was precious near send-

ing them a' tae——the lower regions, an' makin' tracks
for the door; but, fortunately for a' concerned, just when
ma anger was at the exploding point the Mark Maister interposed, an' clapping me on the shoulder, says: "Tam, your
an original. Just excuse whatever manifestations o' levity
ye hae seen, an' yo'll dootless see the ridiculousness o' the
answers ye hae gien when you're better instructed." This
quelled the fire o' ma passion at ance, for if oor Hielan'
blood is hot and easily fired it is just as easily cooled by a
kind word. I think I telt ye, Mr. Editor, that I was Hielan',
an' that will account tae some extent for the haste wi' which
I was prepared tae resent ony slight, either apparent or real,
that I thocht was being put upon me. I think it's Dr.
Johnson that said that it required a surgical operation tae
let a joke intae a Scotsman's head, but he said naething
aboot a Scotsman's heart. I ken o' nae mair sensitive
organ in the hale mechanism o' Nature than a guid, true,
manly Scotch heart. Of course, I don't endorse the Dr.'s
epigrammatic remark in the least, an' can only account for
him saying that in a fit o' anger or in ignorance o' the
nation he was talkin' aboot; however, be that as it may,
there's nae denying that Scotsmen are sensitive in a high
degree tae the slightest insult, an' nae class o' Scotsmen
mair sae than the chiels o' the heather, but I mauna
moralise, though I'm strongly tempted tae dae sae. I maun
jist tell ye hoo I got on wi' the Inspector. The W.M. telt
me what tae say, and then ma wark was examined, but
it didna seem tae please the Inspector; indeed, he said that
he didna understaun' that class o' wark, an' referred me tae
anither, wha wis in much the same position. He examined it
very critically, turned it ower, tried his square on it, looked
at his plans, shook his head, an' then asked me if this was a
specimen o' ma wark. I swithered a wee, seein' hoo I had

fared wi' the ither chiel, an' looked first at him an' then at ma guide (a braw guide he was: he jist led me oot o' ae scrape intae anither); an' no' wantin' tae commit masel' beyond recall, I answered "Umphum."

It's a real handy word this, man, an' may staun' for onything—either "Aye," "No," or "I dinna ken." Inspector No. 2 took it tae mean "Yes," an' this very nearly led tae anither scene.

"Aye; an' wha instructed ye tae mak' wark like that? It's neither roon', square, nor oval, although ye've managed tae bring up no' a bad polish on't. Ye've dootless spent a considerable time on its finish, but, altho', I canna pass it."

I was gaun tae explain that I had nae haun' in the finishing o't at a', when he held up his haun' and imposed silence. He said that I micht tak' it tae the Mark Master an' see what ho said aboot it; that as fur himsel' he wad tak' nae responsibility in the matter. Sae awa' I gaed tae the M.M., the same that had interfered in ma behalf wi' Inspector No. 1. I thocht I wad fare better noo, seeing that he had interested himsel on ma behalf before, but ma hopes were a' doomed tae disappintment. He examined ma work wi' the greatest o' care, tried if it was soond, turned it ower twa or three times, an' then wi' a look that wad hae spen'd a foal, asked me if this was a specimen o' ma wark, an' having answered in the affirmative I couldna very weel say No tae his next question, although I don't know that it wad hae made ony difference if I had. "An' this is your mark here?" "Yes; but ma guide telt me tae——" "We don't want tae hear what your guide telt ye. Ye've acknowledged baith the wark an' the mark, an' I've never seen ony o' them before. Staun' aside until I see what can be dune wi' this." "But, sir, alloo me tae explain. I'll mak' it a' as clear as day-licht tae ye if ye jist gae me half-a-minute."

"We haena time fur an' explanation the noo; staun' aside till I see what the Inspectors say."

"But, sir, I want just tae say——" Inspectors arrive.

Then a lang confab was held between the three o' them, the upshot o' which was that nane o' them wad accept ma wark as genuine, an' it was thrown aside. But, Sir, I see that the space I usually tak' up is aboot exhausted, and as I hinna room tae tell a' that took place I'll need tae keep the remainder for anither paper, as I don't want tae keep your readers in suspense. I may say that although ma troubles didna end here I got safely through it a', an' as the licht began tae dawn upon me I began tae realise that I had taen part in a ceremony veiled in allegory and illustrated by symbols.—Yours fraternally,

TAM M'PHAIL.

OUR PLEDGE RENEW.

Written for the Brethren of Tarbolton Lodge,
25th January, 1895.

Ye sons of light, ye mystic few,
  Whose heart the glow of friendship warms;
Pledge once again, again renew
  Our pledge to him whose memory charms.
He ask'd it once midst fears' alarms,
  When frowning fortune scowled fu' grim;
He ask'd it here in tenderest terms,
  That yearly we should pledge to him.

Then pledge his memory ever dear,
  An' dearer aye as years go bye.
When yearly ye assemble here
  Let jealousy nor care be nigh;

Let all who feel the mystic tie
  In louder praise its bonds declare.
He ask'd for this with "brimful eye."
  It was his wish, it was his prayer.

The circling year brings many joys
  To all who keep the unerring line,
And once again bids us rejoice
  In memory of our bard divine.
Our brother bard whose love benign
  Embraced mankind from pole to pole,
Fulfilling Nature's grand design :
  In brotherhood to bind the whole.

Then let us pledge his memory here,
  Where oft he sat in seat supreme,
Where oft his voice, in accents clear,
  Has told the sweet Masonic theme ;
Where hallowed memories ever teem
  And chasten as the day returns
That gave the world that gift supreme,
  A child of genius, Robert Burns.

TAM M'PHAIL'S WELCOME TO THE GRAND LODGE OF SCOTLAND'S FIRST VISIT TO GLASGOW.

30th November, 1894.

Saint Mungo bares his reverend pow,
And welcomes ye wi' mony a bow,
Ye mystic chiels wha keep the lowe
      O Love sae bright ;
Ye Faithers o' the Craft just now,
      Baith Squire and Knight.

Frae east tae west ye often gang
In search o' that that has gane wrang;
Oor wonder was ye were sae lang
    O' searching here.
We'll help ye wi' a goodly thrang
    O' brithers dear.

See, here's St. John's, o' ancient date;
St. Mungo and St. Mark await
Wi' numerous ithers, bauld an' blate,
    But ever true;
A' anxious tae improve your state,
    An' zeal tae show.

We'll thinkna o' the years gane past
Nor let regret oor joy o'ercast;
But noo that ye hae ventured wast
    In kindly mood
We'll shelter ye frae ilka blast
    In Brotherhood.

We'll dae the best we can tae cheer
An' mak' ye blyth as lang's yer here,
While Time, unheeded, on may steer
    His course alang.
We'll pledge ye a' as brithers dear
    Wi' toast and sang.

Lang may your term o' life extend,
Ye few wha mak'—wha patch an' mend
Oor Constitution so tae blend
    Life's weel and woe
That we may ever hae a friend
    Where'er we go.

And you wha fills that honoured chair.
Lang may you reign's oor humble prayer;
Your courtesy and talents rare
    In lustre gleam,
As oft in judgment ye declare
    The Law Supreme.

Quick in decision, firm and clear:
Just, without harshness, void o' fear;
Kind while reproving, always dear.
    Thy name has been
Our Sage, Philosopher, and Seer,
    To Craft and Queen.

DALRYMPLE, justly honoured thou,
Our Patron and Grand Master too.
Could higher honour we bestow
    Than what ye hae
Ye wadna lack it, not, I trow,
    Anither day!

An' thou, the NESTOR of our host,
Grown grey in service, still our boast;
Our beacon light that guards the coast
    When storms appear,
And points the way, when tempest toss'd,
    Our course we steer.

Lang may you live, revered, beloved
By all who have thy counsel proved
So rich in wisdom, so removed
    From ostentation:
A Saul in intellect, approved—
    Our preservation.

Quiet, unobtrusive, active still,
With breadth of mind and strength of will.
To guard our Craft from threat'ning ill
    We can rely on
Calm and clear Secretarial skill
    In MURRAY LYON.

And many more in budding fame
Which 'twere too tedious but to name,
You're welcome here, aye, just the same
    As ony others,
Sae mak' yersel's a' quite at hame
    Amang your brithers.

And now, ae word afore we part,
I wish it wi' my haun' o'er heart,
May every pointed, poisoned dart
    That can assail
Gang swiftly bye some other airt,
    Says
                TAM M'PHAIL.

PREPARING FOR THE FESTIVAL OF ST. ANDREW, HELD IN GLASGOW.

VI.

DEAR SIR AND BRITHER,—Can ye tell me wha it was that said man was a compound o' strange contradictions—or has onybody ventured tae say onything o' the kind? If no', then I, Tam M'Phail, a burgess freeman o' the City o' St. Mungo, for the first time in the East declare that such is the case; and I ask you tae acknowledge it tae be sae. And for the second time in the West, I declare the truth o' the above question, and I ask you to deny it if you can. And for the third and last time, in the South I declare what I hae stated tae be true, an' I ask onybody tae deny it if they can.

That's a challenge tae a' comers: tak' it up wha will.

But, I hae nae doot, like masel' ye hae often proved the truth o' ma question an' hae lang since come tae the same conclusion, therefore we'll no' argie the matter; indeed, whar there is nae diversity o' opeenion there can be nae argument.

The truth o' the above declaration was never brocht mair forcibly to ma mind than in connection wi' the last Festival o' St. Andrew, held in the Queen's Rooms, Glasgow, 30th November, 1894. I'll explain masel' as I go alang, an' you'll be able tae judge for yoursel' whether I be richt or wrang in the declaration I hae made.

For weeks afore the affair cam' off I had been terribly troubled in ma mind concerning hoo I should broach the subject tae Meg, for although I wad face Auld Nick himsel', especially if ma daunder was up, I dinna care aboot haeing an encounter wi' her, because in ony that hae taen place I hinna hain much tae brag o'. Honesty compels me tae mak' this confession; sae when I learned that the price o' the tickets was five shillings each—exclusive o' the wines —ma heart gaed tae ma mouth an' I nearly dispaired o' being able tae get; no' that I couldna afford tae part wi' the money, but ma parting wi't an' Meg parting wi't are twa entirely different things, although it a' comes tae the same thing in the lang run. But I kent the bother I wad hae in gettin' oor ane roon' tae ma way o' thinking, an' as for gaun withoot gettin' her consent I wad as soon think o' trying tae flee in the air. Na, na; catch me trying tae dae ony sic daft-like caper. Catch me trying tae dae onything by stealth or force either whar oor ane's concerned, an' whar by a wee bit o' management things can be far better dune withoot leaving ony sourness o' reflection. It's only your newly-married folk wha wad fa' intae that mistake an' mak' baith themsel's an' ithers miserable ower naething ava. Catch an auld haun' like me daeing onything o' the kind. Here's hoo I managed it. Some o' you young fellows tak' note:

Ma first concern was hoo tae break the subject tae her withoot letting her discover ma anxiety tae gang, for I was michty keen tae be there; in fact, I meant tae be there by hook or by crook. Ae nicht when I thocht she was in a mair pliable humour than ord'nar', I remarked in an offhaun' kind o 'way—jist as if it had occurred tae me quite acci-dentally—"There's gaun tae be a fine turnoot wi' the Masons, Meg." Losh! if you had seen hoo she cocked her ears. A stranger micht no' hae noticed onything oot o' the way, but tae me wha hae studied her every movement the liftin' o' her head an' the glance o' her e'e betokened an alertness an' interest that nearly made me doot whether I wad carry ma point or no'. I therefore added: "An' twa-three hae been at me tae gang, but I thocht it better tae consult you before I wad promise." This, of course, was a peace-offering, an' was meant tae stem the storm that micht otherwise arise. It's wonnerfu' whiles what a few well-chosen words can dae. Women, ye ken, like tae be made o', an' especially in matters o' this kind; therefore it's jist as weel tae humour them, especially when it costs naething but a few saft words.

"Aye, man, an' whar are they gaun?"

"Oh, they're no' gaun ony place at a' in particular; they're jist gaun tae hae a bit spree tae celebrate the anniversary o' St. Andrew."

"Aye, man, an' wha is he? I never heard ye speak aboot

him before. Is he a Freemason tae? I've heard you speak aboot St. John often enough, but I dinna mind o' ye speaking o' St. Andrew. Is he what ye ca' a Fellowcraft ?—whatever that means."

"Weel, Meg, I'm no' shure whether he was a Fellowcraft or no', but it's mair than likely he was a Mason o' some sort ; an', besides, he was, an' is the Patron Saint o'' oor country, an' it's considered patriotic tae celebrate his memory, ye ken. Sae as the Masons are a loyal an' patriotic fraternity, it's fitting they, aboon a' bodies, should celebrate his memory."

"Aye ; an' dae ye no' think there's been enough o' celebrations lately? You've been celebrating something or ither twa or three times a week this while back ; an' at your time o' life it wad be mair sensible were you thinkin' o' something else. You're hardly ever a nicht in the hoose noo, an' the weans are gettin' big an' beginnin' tae tak' note o' things. Jist yestreen, nae further gane, young Tam was asking whar ye aye gaed tae at nichts, an' when I telt him ye were awa' tae a meetin' he wondered what way the meetin's aye took place at nicht. I think ye wad be better tae stay at hame an' let the St. Andrews affair alane for a nicht. Dae ye no' think sae yoursel' ?"

This is jist the point whar mony a ane wad hae erred. Tae hae shown resistance tae her remonstrance wad jist hae roused a spirit o' strong opposition tae ma cherished design, sae I dissembled, as the saying is, an' appeared tae fa' in wi' a' that she said, mildly hinting that she was maistly aye richt—reminding her o' hoo often I had been guided by her advice in the past. I had nae idea, however, o' lettin' her hae such an easy victory as this, especially as I had set my heart upon gaun, sae I replied as if it were a thing o' very little consequence :

"Oh, I didna say I was gaun. I was jist lettin' ye ken that sic a thing had been spoken aboot, an' I wanted tae hear yer mind on the matter. Ye ken twa heids are better than ane."

"That's very true, an' I'm muckle obleeged tae ye for your consideration. But, ye ken, we've haen a lot tae dae this while back, an' things are no' jist that brisk wi' us the noo. I was fear'd ye had made up your mind, for we can ill afford the siller the noo, Tam."

Of course, tae hae let the cat oot o' the pock an' telt her that ma mind was made up, an' had been for some time—in fact, that I had baith paid for an' received ma ticket an' at that moment had it planked within twa yards o' whar she was sitting—wad hae been the hicht o' foolishness, an' mair than likely wad hae led tae ane o' thae things that Meg ca's a crisis! Sae, realising that things were hardly ripe for a development, I, in the language o' the "P.R.," sparred for wind. When it comes tae a real test o' skill 'tween Meg an' masel', I can maistly aye haud ma ain wi' her; an', indeed, no' unfrequently hae the best o't. But when she opens the fire o' her artillery I'm silenced at ance, believing in the guid auld maxim that "Discretion is the better part o' valour." I can at this moment remember only ae occasion on which I was inclined tae retaliate; but we'll let that flee stick tae the wa'. There's nae necessity for opening up auld sairs. Therefore, pairtly wi' a view tae conciliate her, an' mainly wi' a view tae gain ma point, I replied, as if Masonry was ane o' the last things in the world tae think aboot:

"We'll no' bother ony mair aboot that the noo, Meg. We'll maybe fin' a better use for the siller. Indeed, noo that I think o't, I was in asking aboot the price o' that set o' auld china ye took a fancy for the last time we were in the toon, an' I hae nae doot but I'll get it for ye; but I didna want tae let the shopman see that I was anxious aboot it, for fear he micht increase the price. I tried tae prig him doon tae aboot a half o' what he wanted, an' I believe I'll get it yet, though I'll maybe hae tae come an' go a wee bit."

"Man, you're no' that ill efter a', Tam; but I've been thinking since I spoke tae ye aboot the china that we micht put oor heids thegither an' get Maggie a piano. Ye ken she's jist gaun intae her teens, an' if we want oor bairns tae be respected an' like their neebours we maun gie them a liberal education. Ye ken music's ane o' the maist important branches o' a liberal education; indeed, it's ane o' the finest accomplishments a young lady can hae. Besides, I don't think she wad be ill tae learn. She has a fine ear. If you jist heard hoo she can sing 'We're a' Nodding,' it wad dae your heart guid."

Had a 16-inch shell exploded at ma feet I couldna hae been mair startled than by this announcement—no' that I was surprised at the discovery o' ma dochter's musical talent. An announcement o' that kind must at a' times be very gratifying tae the ear o' an affectionate parent, but the thocht o' being landed for a piano was mair than I had bargained for. Was Meg playing a game o' diamond cut diamond, or was it merely an incidental or accidental coincidence? Hoo I managed tae control ma feelings an' disguise ma embarrassment is mair than I can tell. Perhaps Meg's mind being somewhat carried awa' wi' the grand idea prevented, or rather obscured, her usual quickness o' perception. Be that as it may, she didna seem tae notice onything wrang. Or perhaps interpreting ma start o' astonishment as an indication o' newly-awakened interest in the wonderfu' musical precocity o' Maggie, Meg became perfectly eloquent on the advantages likely to accrue frae a musical training, no' only tae the lassie hersel' but ultimately tae the hale family; therefore, realising that everything was tae be gained an' naething lost by a little dissimulation, I fenced the subject, withoot committing masel' in ony way. She dootless noticed a little uneasiness on ma part, but, as I hae said before, she dootless set that doon tae the fervent emotions o' a fond faither's heart. This new idea o' Meg's was the pivot upon which I meant tae turn things tae ma ain advantage—the fulcrum by which I meant tae remove the load o' her objections tae ma gaun tae the Festival o' St. Andrew, an' this is hoo I gaed aboot it :—

"You're a wonderfu' woman, Meg, for discoverin' things, thus early noticin' the musical propensities o' oor bairns. I had ne'er dreamt o' sic a jump for ane o' oors, but noo that ye mention it the thing's worthy o' consideration—serious consideration, Meg—and I'm shure I wad be ane o' the last tae staun' in the way o' oor lassie's advancement. Jist imagine oor Maggie learning the piano! An' wha kens but she micht turn oot a teacher o' music yet, wi' pupils coming frae a' pairts for lessons. Dae ye ken it wad look rale weel tae hae her name painted in big letters at the close mouth 'Miss M'Phail, Music Teacher.' Losh! it wad read like poetry. Your neighbour Lucky M'Phee wad be neither tae bin' nor haud wi' fair envy. I wonder wha she tak's the musical faculty off, Meg—you or me, eh? Ye ken it maun be hereditary, like a' ither things. Jist look at the genius o' young Tam for making mouse traps! He is shure tae mak' a name for himsel' some day, but wha does Maggie tak' her music off o'—you or me, Meg, eh !"

"Onybody that heard you sing, Tam, wad hae nae difficulty in deciding that question," she answered wi' a seriousness that was suggestive; an' seeing that it pleased her tae think that the lassie's musical bent cam' off her side o' the house, I jist let it be that way and tackled the subject frae anither standpoint.

"By jingo, Meg, dae ye ken the mair I think o' this matter the mair I'm taen up wi't. Talk aboot steam-loom weavers, dressmakers, an' sic like! They're like the man wha fell oot o' the balloon: they're not in't wi' music. I'll jist tak' the first opportunity I hae o' speaking tae wee Paddy M'Laughlin the pawnbroker, an' tell him what I want, an' tae let me ken o' the first chance he sees. He's in the second-haun' furniture line, an' nae doot comes across things o' that kind at the sales."

Of course I had nae intention o' daeing onything o' the kind, but diplomacy was uppermaist in my mind, an' I threw this suggestion oot jist tae throw Meg off the scent. Women, ye ken, are said tae be the mischief for takin' notions, an' ma ane is nae better than her neebors in that respect; an' I find it works best jist tae humour her a little til' the tide ebbs. In showing an apparent interest in her suggestion, an' colourin' it wi' some suggestions o' ma ain, I maistly aye manage ma way wi' her afore lang. Thus it was that I secured an opportunity, an' returned tae the original subject —the ane I had maist at heart at this time.

"We'll say naething mair aboot the turnoot in the meantime, Meg, seeing we're likely tae be at considerable cost in getting things for Maggie; but there will be disappintment in some quarters, as twa or three o' them were unco anxious for me tae gang. It's tae be a grand affair a'thegither, an' they'll be there frae a' pairts. The like o't, I believe, hasna been seen in Glasgow afore."

"Oh, I've nae doot it'll be grand, but the expense'll likely be grand tae. What's the price o' the tickets?"

"Five shillings each, Meg. No' much when ye consider the company an' the occasion."

"Jist five shillings! Bless ma heart, Tam, are ye daft !
I could feed ye a hale week for that. An' siller sae scarce
the noo tae! Besides, ye couldna eat five shillings' worth
at ance for your life! Let me see, I could get at least half-
a-dozen o' loaves, three stane o' tatties, twa stane o' meal,
an' ever sae mony vegetables, a bane tae mak' kail wi',
besides tea, sugar, butter, an' cheese. Five shillings! It's
evendoon wasterie, Tam! Man, ye can get as guid a dinner
as onybody needs for aboot fourpence, or fivepence at the
maist; an' tae say that ye wad throw awa' aboot four an'
sixpence, or four an' sevenpence, on a lot o' slisters! The
thing's rediculous, Tam. Your bawbees dinna come sae
easy as a' that, an' there's nae saying when the 'Rainy Day'
may come, when we'll need a' the bits o' bawbees we can
scran thegither. Let us keep oor five shillings, an' let
them keep their dinner."

"I'll back ye against a' the philosophers in creation,
Meg, for takin' an evendoon, practical view o' things,
especially when there's siller concerned ; but, ye ken, some
allowance maun be made for festive occasions like the ane
we're speaking aboot. Variety's the fillip o' life, ye ken."

"Variety! Ma certie, an' there should be a big variety
for five shillings! It's evendoon wasterie, an' sae mony
puir souls wha dinna ken hoo tae get their breakfast."

"But, Meg, we maunna aye be looking at things in that
licht. Ye ken what the guid auld Book says, 'Sufficient
for the day is the evil thereof.' We maun allow something
for association, the exchange o' ideas, the reciprocations o'
kindred feelings, an' sic like ; sae that it's no' a'thegither the
first cost o' the thing that's tae be reckoned wi' but the
efter-effects."

I thocht this wasna bad as a sort o' bait, but she has the
deil's ain knack o' knocking holes in the very best o' ma

arguments, and bringing the maist select o' ma ideas intae ridicule.

"Efter-effects, did ye say? Ma certie, I ken what the efter-effects'll be!" she exclaimed, wi' particular emphasis on the twa words "Efter-effects."

"The efter-effects in your case, Tam'll be your stomach oot o' order an' twa or three days in bed, wi' an occasional drap o' toddy tae bring ye roon'. It's no' the dinner a'the-gither that I'm feart for, it's the efter-effects as ye ca' them, wi' the slockening that tak's place. It's the slockening, Tam; it's the slockening! Ye've aye been fully waur tae water than corn, an' I've nae doot your drouth wad be in keeping wi' the occasion that's tae be sae grand, an' wad be unco ill tae droon', but jist please yoursel'—as you're likely tae dae onyway, an' you'll no' dee in the pet."

Wi' some this micht hae settled the hale argument, but I kent Meg better than that. There were ither fish tae fry.

"Lo'd bless me, Meg! tae hear ye ane wad think I was naething but a drucken ne'er-dae-weel. I never made a fool o' masel' yet, an' it's no' likely I wad dae sae on an occasion o' this kind. If I dae whiles spend a bit hour or twa ower a dram it's only for the sake o' the com-pany, an' I ne'er forget ma ain hoose; besides, the company on this occasion wad be quite sufficient tae keep onybody within due bounds. They tell me it's gaun tae be something extraordinary."

I kent this wad awaken her curiosity, if no' her interest, an' ance that point was gained the battle was half won.

"Aye, man; an' wha's a' gaun tae be there?"

"Oh, there's tae be ever sae mony Lords, Dukes, an' Earls, an' what not; an' it's jist possible the Prince o' Wales him-sel'll be there! Ye ken, he's the Grand Master o' England, an' tak's a deep interest in a' that concerns the welfare o' the Craft in general."

I admit this was what is ca'd "laying it on," but then there was a lot at stake, an' I kent whar I was working an' wha I was working wi', as the saying is, and I had every hope that it wad o'ercome ony remaining scruples she micht hae; in short, I thocht that the end justified the means in this case.

"It maun shurely be an awfu' grand affair. Will there be ony ladies there?"

"Weel, no, I hardly think it. Ye ken, it's tae be a meeting o' Grand Lodge in the first place, an' it's no' likely: at least, I've never happened tae see ony ladies at a meeting o' Grand Lodge. The Festival, ye ken's jist a sort o' Harmony meeting on a big scale. A sort o' killing twa dougs wi' ae stane—business first, an' harmony efter."

"O, aye, I see; but it'll tak' five shillings tae buy the stane that kills the doug in your case, no' speaking o' the efter-effects—a pretty expensive stane battle, I'm thinking, afore a's dune."

"Hits, woman; there's mair things than siller tae be looked at. It disna dae tae be aye looking at the siller side o' things."

"No; an' if some folk had their way they wadna hae much siller tae look at."

"But, Meg, jist imagine if the Prince o' Wales was tae be there, an' was tae tak' notice o' me! Losh, woman, our fortune wad be made! There's no' a customer we hae but wad look up tae us, especially if he was tae order the makin' o' a suit o' tweeds frae us. 'Patronised by the Prince o' Wales an' Royal Family' wad sound fine! It wad be the makin' o' us, an' wad gie us sic a lift in oor business that we could look wi' unconcern on a' aroon'. Jist imagine yoursel',

Meg, being ca'd 'Leddy M'Phail' an' me 'Mr. Thomas!' Go, I wad hardly ken masel'! And as for the piano, we wad send a' the weans tae a boarding school."

"But, Tam, dae ye think there's ony chance o' him takin' notice o' ye?"

"Nae doot o't; at least, it wadna be ma faut if he didna."

"Oh, but I wadna hae ye mak' yoursel' ower cheap, Tam. I wad hae ye tae be kind o' reserved like, an' he wad think a' the mair o' ye. Mind the auld saying that 'The water's aye wersh that's flung at ye.' Don't gie yoursel' awa' for naething. Of course, if ye had a chance o' speaking tae him, ye could let him understaun' that he could count upon oor support when he comes tae be king, an' there's nae doot he wad appreciate the importance o' that."

It will be seen that by this time Meg had become, or was becoming, as interested in the Festival matter as I was; and, indeed, seemed tae be fully as anxious that I should gang as I was masel'. The rest was a mere matter o' detail. Ane o' the questions, however, that cropped up exercised baith o' us for a considerable time. This had reference tae the matter o' dress. I hae a strong antipathy tae black claes, especially tae the full, or evening, dress cut: an' seeing that it's some years—we'll no' say hoo mony—since I had ma measure for a suit o' this kind, ma suit doesna fit me wi' that degree o' perfection that it ance did, hence I hae a strong repugnance tae blacks in general, an' tae ma ain suit in particular.

A new suit, of course, was oot o' the question at the present time; because, had I suggested onything o' the kind, she wad hae reckoned the cost o' the spree at the price o' the new suit, plus the price o' the ticket, etc., etc., an' the chances are the Grand Lodge wadna hae seen me at a'.

"I wonner hoo they'll be dressing for the occasion," I remarked, as if dress were only a matter o' secondary consideration. "Dae ye think it'll be a full dress affair, or will it be a gang-as-ye-please sort o' thing? I wadna like tae mak' a fool o' masel' if I were gaun, especially in sic company an' on sic an important occasion."

"Oh, it'll be a full dress thing, Tam, ye may depend on that. Every ane'll be in their best, frae the Prince doon: an' if ye're really gaun you maun put on your best tae, an' no' hae them a' laughing at ye."

"Ah, weel, I think I may jist mak' up ma mind tae gang: because, if I werena, some o' them micht think I hadna the things tae gang wi'. Dae ye no' think sae yoursel'?"

"Well, maybe ye micht; an' five shillings are no' sic a kill-the-bill efter a'."

Thus it was mutually agreed that I should attend the Festival o' St. Andrew. Thus was the battle lost an' won, withoot muckle loss o' dignity on either side.

The subject o' dress is in itsel' a simple ane, but in ma case it's quite different, as it involves issues o' considerable importance. Meg will persist in ca'ing full dress—even that belies its character—ma "best" suit, even though the trousers barely reach ma buit-mooth, efter gieing them a' the length o' gallows I daur, an' ma coat and waistcoat (vest) only meet on me under considerable compulsion. The sleeves o' the former seem tae come tae an understanding wi' the legs o' ma trousers that the ane'll no' mak' a fool o' the ither, neither o' them being ower big for their age; indeed, their growth seems tae hae been inversely proportionate tae the length o' their existence.

"Oh, ye maun put on your 'best,' Tam. It wad never dae for ye tae be an 'O' among the figures. If you're gaun tae be hobnobbing wi' Royalty an' sic like ye maun dress for the occasion. They wad jist think ye hadna a decent suit tae put on, an' you hae three or four guid suits; at least, the ane ye hae on, the ane in the kist, an' your best ane that's jist lying in the kist, tae, wasting for want o' wear."

I inwardly groaned at this decision, but there was nae help for it. Talk o' the laws o' the Medes and Persians! Whaever made them maun hae been something efter Meg's turn o' mind if they are as unchangeable as they are said tae hae been, for when she has fairly made up her mind on ony subject there's nae use trying tae change it; ye micht as weel try tae sweep back the Atlantic wi' a hayfork as tae dispute wi' her on ony subject on which she has fairly an' squarely decided.

In the present instance I maybe had masel' tae blame for being condemned tae wear the inevitable best suit, having overdrawn the picture o' a possible interview wi' the Prince o' Wales, wha's presence had only been mentioned for the purpose o' touching Meg on a saft place. So ma best suit was forthwith fished oot frae the bottom o' the kist, jist tae gie them the air an' tae tak' oot the wrinkles, as she said.

Every time I looked at thae claes I wished frae the bottom o' ma heart that something wad happen tae put them oot o' sicht; but no, there they hung, whiles in ae place, whiles in anither, the very sicht o' them making ma flesh creep an ma soul sin itsel'.

But the eventfu' nicht cam' roon' at last, an' oh! what a blessing it was that there wasna onybody in the hoose but Meg an' masel' when I began tae squeeze masel' inta that everlasting "best" suit! I'm thinking had there been ony ithers near they micht hae heard things that wadna hae been guid for their moral development, especially, aye, when

Meg's back was turned or when she gaed ben the hoose—
things that micht jar a wee on a refined ear, however ex-
pressive they micht be at the time o' ma state o' feelings.
But a' things come tae an en' sooner or later, an' 'efter
sundry tugs an' draws, wi' a threatening rent here an' there,
I got masel' bandaged at last in black, an' was ready tae set
oot for the place o' meeting.

Meg couldna let me awa' withoot expressing her satisfaction at ma improved appearance since she saw me first an'
a warning as tae hoo I should behave masel'.

"Noo, Tam, jist be as mensfu' (mannerful) as ye can, an'
you'll be the mair thocht o'; jist let the big anes see that
there's something in ye—neither be ower blate nor ower
forward, be easy an' affable in your manners, treating everybody wi' due respect an' earning the same regard for
yoursel'. Don't be led intae ony scrape, either in eating or
drinking, even in sic company; an' aboon a', Tam, don't
be led intae the temptation o' gaun hame wi' ony o' them;
if they ask ye tell them you're sorry ye canna gang, an'
they'll respect ye a' the mair for a polite refusal. When
dae ye think you'll be hame? Will ye tak' the check (key),
or will I jist sit up for ye?"

"Meg, you're a born philosopher. I dinna ken what I
wad dae withoot ye. What a pity there wasna free education in oor young days! I'm thinking if there had ye wad
hae held your ain wi' the best o' them. Jist wait up for
me. I'll no' stay ony langer than I can help—say aboot
nine o'clock; but ye ken you'll hae tae mak' some allowance for an occasion o' this kind, for although I hae nae
intention o' gaun hame wi' ony o' the nobility, if they were
tae ask me tae hae a half wi' them it micht be bad manners tae refuse; an', of course, if they were tae staun ane
I couldna think o' pairting wi' them withoot stauning

anither, a saxpence wad be ill hained in a case o' this
kind, sae you'll be as weel tae gie's a check wi's, an', I
say, Meg, something tae keep ma pouch wi."

"O, I was shure that was coming, Tam. Hoo much will
ye need?"

"Maybe a croon or sae, I can hardly tell. It a' depends
on the company ane keeps, an' I dinna ken wha I may fa'
in wi'; but I'll spend nae mair than I can help."

"A croon for your pouch an' anither for your ticket!
Jist what I said; there's aboot ten shillings already! A
dear enough dinner it'll be, I'm thinking, even including a
chance acquaintance wi' some o' the nobility!   It wadna
need tae happen often; but, as ye say yoursel', there's nae
saying what may come o't. There ye are. Noo, see an'
mind a' I've said tae ye. I'll look for ye hame aboot nine."

Thus, wi' Meg's blessing an' best wishes, an' nae less than
five shillings in ma pouch, I started for the Queen's Rooms,
tied up in ma "best" suit.

TAM M'PHAIL AT THE FESTIVAL O' ST. ANDREW,
30th NOVEMBER, 1894.

VII.

MAISTER EDITOR.—DEAR SIR AND BRITHER: Besides
being a burgess o' the City o' St. Mungo I'm part proprietor
o' a large carriage-hiring concern. Thus it happened that
instead o' walking, as I micht hae dune, for I had plenty
o' time, I jist hailed ane o' oor ain machines an' telt the fitman
(some ca' him guard) that I was gaun tae the Queen's Rooms,
an' asked him tae put me doon at the nearest point tae that.
He promised tae dae sae, an' I took ma seat in ane o' the
far awa' corners o' the carriage (next the driver), for I

wanted tae be oot o' the road as much as possible o' those entering an' leaving. You'll be astonished at this manifestation o' modesty on ma pairt; but, tae tell the truth, I had a reason for't—a guid ane tae: I didna want tae be taen notice o', for I had an inward feeling that I didna look quite at ma best in ma best suit o' claes, for reasons which I hae already explained. I had put ma feet ower far through ma trousers, an', in spite o' ma best efforts tae hide it, a considerable margin o' ma socks was seen between ma buit-mouth an' the extremity o' ma trouser leg. This condition o' things was considerably emphasised when I sat doon, an', although at a considerable sacrifice o' comfort, I planted the tips o' ma taes at the bottom o' the machine, below the seat I was sitting on, I felt there was still room for improvement in ma appearance. The fitman was unco civil, an' although the drive should only hae cost three bawbees, in a fit o' generosity I telt him tae keep the odd ha'penny (I had gien him tuppence). Ane doesna mak' much by being niggardly, an' a bit tip judiciously dispensed whiles brings a world o' comfort. I was landed at the very place I wanted, and after a short walk reached the hall. Among the first tae salute me as I entered the side room, whar everybody was busy tying on their aprons and preening on their jewels, was a wee body wi' a sandy-fair moustache. His face was the very picture o' guid nature, an' he seemed tae be on extra guid terms wi' himsel' an' every ither body. He had a large pile o' blue envelopes beside him, which he was handing tae everyone that cam' in, remarking that it was "a present frae the Editor o' the 'Scottish Freemason.'" It looked mair like a lawyer's letter, an' I was half-dootfu' whether I should tak' it or no', but thocht I could be nae waur than the rest, sae I thanked him, and put it in ma pouch.

I learned that this was your advertising agent, an' I can testify tae his industry. I don't know what salary ye gie him, but I can tell ye he wasna idle. He seems tae be pretty weel kent, wi' a strong tendency tae mak' himsel' mair sae—no' a bad fault in a public man, if it's no' pushed too far. Learning that he was in authority, as the saying is, I asked him if the Editor was present, for I fully expected tae see ye, as I wanted tae get better acquainted wi' ye. He said that he hadna seen ye yet, but had nae doot ye wad turn up shortly. Wad he say wha was asking for him? "Oh, aye, he micht dae that. He could jist say that Tam M'Phail wanted tae see him on business o' importance, and that I wad be on the look-out for him, an' dootless wad ken him by his likeness in the 'Freemason'."

"An' are you Tam M'Phail?" he asked, lookin' at me openly, his gaze resting on ma lower extreemities, an' a mischievious twinkle kindlin' in the corners o' his een. "Bless ma soul, I micht hae kent ye withoot askin'! He'll be awfu' pleased tae see ye, I'm shure. I've heard him talking aboot ye twa or three times, and wondering if ye were gaun tae be here the nicht."

"A' weel, if ye see him before me ye can tell him that I'll be on the look-out for him."

"Wad ye no' care aboot seeing the Manager? He's here, an' I'm shure he wad be mair than pleased tae mak' your acquaintance."

"No; ma business is mair wi' the Editor than wi' him. But I'll maybe see them baith when the thing's a' bye."

I needna say that this expectation wasna realised, as ye didna turn up at a'. Wi' that I left your Advertising Agent distributing his envelopes, and seemingly michty weel pleased at something or ither—if ane micht judge frae his readiness tae laugh ootricht, but evidently controlled by some extraordinary effort.   Maybe if the legs o' ma trousers had been twa or three inches langer there wadna hae been sic a strong temptation for him tae be hearty.   But if he tak's Tam M'Phail tae be a saft ane he micht fin oot his mistake some day.

Having entered ma name on the slips ready for that purpose, I made ma way intae the Lodge alang wi' a young freen'—distinguished baith as a Mason and a Doctor o' Medicine.   It still wanted a few minutes o' the hour o' beginning business, sae I had time tae look roon' and tak' stock, as the saying is.

Maist, if no' everybody, were dressed in their best—that is, if swallow tails an' an ample display o' shirt fronts is the best—an' there were some that I thocht jist a wee over-dressed, in so far as their breasts were literally covered wi' jewels, squares, compasses, levels, seyments o' circles, medals, stars, crosses, an' what not, a' jumbled thegither wi' the utmost disregard tae time, place, and arrangement.

Some o' the office-bearers o' the Grand Lodge struck me, so far as appearance gangs, an' ane o' the first tae attract ma attention was the Grand Marshal.   Nature had blessed him wi' no' a bad figure an' seems tae hae cut him oot for the office he hauds, an' although tae ma untrained ears there was a touch o' harshness in his commands an' an apparent militarism in his manner that bespoke a drill instructor, I was rather pleased than otherwise wi' his appearance, an' I thocht I occasionally detected in the twinkle o' his e'e a latent fund o' humour and guid nature.   I was pleased tae learn afterwards that ma estimate o' his character wasna far wrang, an' that under his ample vest there beats a genuine an' manly heart, kind, sympathetic, and genial.   The Master o' Ceremonies is maybe no' a bad soul in the main, but if he wad jist let an occasional smile play ower his features it wad greatly enhance his appearance. Maybe it was his newness tae the office that made him sae fearfully earnest looking. It's no' a bad faut, an' nae doot he'll get easier as he gets aulder. But maybe I'm tiring you wi' these sketches o' character, an' it's jist probable that you are better acquainted wi' the Grand office-bearers than I am; an' as I afterwards learned that you had the misfortune no' tae be there, I jist want tae gie you an outline o' things as they appeared tae me.

The Grand Lodge was opened in ample form (I think that's the term), an' the office-bearers were a' installed. I never was in the company o' sae mony lords in a' ma life—there was nae less than three o' them present—an' what seemed strange tae me was that they were as plain-lookin' chiels as ony that were there. There were several baronets an' ither chiels wi' a handle tae their names, an' a'thegither it was a brilliant gathering, an' ane lang tae be remembered. Sir Charles was ushered in wi' great fraca, an' efter a few indispensable formalities took the throne. He seemed tae be deeply affected by the heartiness o' his reception, an' thanked us a' for the honour we had done him. A few other formalities having been gone through, Grand Lodge was closed, an' we a' made tracks for the banquet room. What a sicht! I never saw the like o't in a' ma life. I never conceived o' sic a grand thing, an' was fairly mystified wi' the display o' crystal, linen napery, decanters, bottles, glasses, plates, knives and forks that literally covered the tables frae ae end o' the hall tae the ither. The tables were a' marked off according tae some understood arrangement, an' were set for aboot 500. Maist o' the big wigs were on the platform, an' a splendid appearance they made. I made ma way as near tae the plat-form as I could get, an' took up a position at the table

"G," near tae ma freen' Bob MacDonald an' his brother John, an' it was then that ma real embarrassment began, even in sic company. A blessing having been asked, everyone called a menu card tae see what was what. I picked up ane alang wi' the rest, for Meg had telt me before leaving hame jist tae dae as I saw ithers daein', an' no' mak' a fool o' masel; but, Lord bless ye, Sir, I micht as weel hae taen up a Greek Testament! Imagine the following presenting itsel' tae a plain, unlettered soul like me :—

MENU.

Hare Soup.   Barley Cream.

Salmon Moyonnaise.

Fillets of Soles a la Mirabeau.

Game Pie and Madeira Sauce.

Haggis and Mashed Potatoes.

Gelatine of Capon.

Roast Turkey and Ox Tongue.

Roast Chickens and Ham.

Roast Beef.   Corned Beef.

Potatoes.

Carmel Pudding.

Apricot Tartlets.   Pine Apple Jelly.

Assorted Creams.   French Pastry.

Cheese and Celery.

Dessert.

WINE LIST.

Sherry.   Rudesheimer (Hock).

Sparkling Hock.

Dentz and Geldermann Champ.

Ch Heidsieck (Vint. 1887).

Dunning (1884).   St. Julien (Claret).

Chateau Palmer (1884).

Old Port. Whisky. Brandy. Caracoa.

Ales.   Stout.   Ærated Waters.

Cigars.

I rubbed ma een, dichted ma specks, drew a lang breath,
an' then tried it again, but it was no go. There it was, as
unintelligible tae me as the hierogliphics of an Egyptian
monument. I threw it doon in despair, and seized on a
bottle o' whisky, thinking that it micht wauken ma wit.
I swallowed ae hauf in sheer desperation, an' turnin' tae the
doctor wha was at ma left asked if he was for a dram.
He said he preferred a little sherry, an' wad I jist pass
the bottle? I never looked at the menu card the hale
night again until the toasts began; but I had a sair time
o't before that. There wad be maybe five or six plates a'
heaped up on the tap o' ither, three or four knives an' forks
o' different sizes, an' as mony spins a' similarly assorted
as if tae accommodate a' sizes o' mooths, but apparently
they were intended for different dishes. Having spread ane
o' the towels (wi' which everybody there was provided)
across ma knees, I waited a meenit or twa till ane o' the
waiters cam' roon', and, acting on Meg's advice, I determined no' tae commit masel'. He mumbled something
aboot what wad I hae, an' mentioned unintelligible things
that I couldna understaun'. Ane doesna like tae show his
ignorance in affairs o' this kind, sae I remarked that I wasna
in a hurry; he could see what ma freen' on the left wanted,
an' I wad jist tak' the same—it wad be a' the ae bringing. This wasna a bad stroke, an' wrocht weel as lang as
I stuck tae it. It was only when ma curiosity led me tae
deviate frae this rule that I nearly let the cat oot o' the
pock. For instance, I was michty keen tae ken what barley
cream was, as I had never heard tell o' ony sic cream. I
had heard o' ice-cream, but as for barley cream, that was
an article I had never tasted tae ma knowledge. Sae, efter
we had had twa or three dishes o' ae thing an' anither,
I ventured tae suggest tae ane o' the waiters that he micht

bring me a little barley cream. "Yes, sir," he said, an',
reaching ower the table, he lifted the whisky bottle frae
ane that was sittin' opposite and planted it doon before me.
I saw through the swindle at ance, but made nae remark,
an' flattered masel' that the incident had passed withoot
observation, an' determined no' tae be caught again. Sae,
keeping ma eye on the doctor, I resolved tae fa' back on
ma auld rule, an' jist dae as he did. Things gaed on finely
for maybe an hour, but, of course, we werna eatin' a' the
time. I was quite satisfied wi' masel', an' thocht I had dune
brawly, when I asked the doctor if we were nearly finished,
for ye ken I had never looked at the menu after the first
attempt tae discipher it. He answered that we were aboot
hauf through, an' the best was tae come. Imagine this,
and imagine, if you can, ma condition between what I had
eaten an' ma ticht claes! But, no' tae be beaten, I jist
lowsed a button or twa an' set masel tae the task before
me, an' it wasna a cannie ane, I can tell ye! Plate efter
plate was handed roon' wi' a mechanical regularity that
suggested clockwork, an' every ane seemed tae be better
than anither, till I concluded that it was a' a vile conspiracy
tae gar folks burst themsel's, an' resolved tae cry " a barley" (parley), an' leaned back in ma chair defeated for
ance, but by nae means disgraced, for I had shifted a pile
o' stuff. I looked roon' tae see hoo ithers were gettin'
on, and noticed that some were in the same condition as
masel, while ithers stuck tae their guns wi' a determination
that wad hae honoured a forlorn hope. But everything
comes tae an end, and the dinner was ower at last, everyane
seemingly better pleased than anither, an' anxious tae hear
the toasts, speeches, an' sangs that were tae follow. The
toast list embraced a number that are familiar tae Masons,
but the way o' gaun aboot them on this occasion was differ-

ent frae onything I had ever **seen**. **The** Master o' Ceremonies had a position immediately in **the rear o'** the Grand Master, an' **aye when onything was tae be dune** he nodded tae a chiel in the gallery at his richt **haun' wha** gied a few notes on a bugle, or some instrument o' that sort, an' then the Master o' Ceremonies announced what was tae be next. The toasts were, as **a rule**, very well put an' heartily responded tae, an' the replies in some instances were humorous an' interestin', **an'** everything cam' aff like the skin o' a new tattie, easy an' clean. There was only ae wee bit jar in **the hale** affair an' that was at **the** end when the heads o' the deputations **were** asked **to** reply. Through some **overlook, quite unintentional, I believe, the** R.W.M. o' Glasgow's auldest lodge wasna called upon, an' he, feeling **hurt at the** overlook, injudiciously made **use o' a** phrase that in his **calmer** moments **I** hae nae doot **he** regretted. The **Grand** Master rebuked him for it, **an'** there was nae mair **aboot** the matter.

You'll see that I'm hurrying **ower things a wee.** It's no' for the want o' material, **but I** feel tae be takin' up the space o' your valuable paper when you've dootless matter o' much greater importance tae chronicle; but, man, ye've been sae indulgent **wi' me in the past** that I'm half induced tae trespass **baith on** your space an' patience, an' wad hardly be daein' **justice tae a** few were **I** no' tae mention ane or twa **bit things** that cam' tae ma knowledge an' that micht be a benefit **tae some** ithers **in the** future.

I telt ye that the dinner **was** 5s., withoot **wines.** Weel, **that was the** first announcement, but what think ye o' the **spirit an' generosity** o' some o' oor Glasgow brethren when **they resolved tae** provide the wines free, thereby adding tae the comfort an' convenience o' a' that was there? Among **those deserving o' this credit are** Bros. Graham, M'Naught, an' Galletly, as worthy a trio as ever donned an apron, a' craftsmen o' the real sort, big-hearted an' open-haunded. But, bless me! here I'm at the end o' ma letter again, an' I havena telt the hauf o' what happened. What a pity ye werena there! Ye wad hae been able tae describe sae much better than me, an' I'm shure your readers wad hae been delighted wi' a description o' sic a grand affair.

Tae say that we a' enjoyed oorsel's is an awfu' puir way o' expressing oor pleasure. Ye can rest assured that I wasna hin'most either in eating or drinking, an' wi' the exception o' a bit blunder or twa ma share o' the pleasure wasna the least, and, if I may tell the truth, the hale truth, an' nae-thing but the truth, I didna get hame at nine o'clock, as Meg expected.

TAM M'PHAIL AFTER THE FESTIVAL.

I didna get hame at nine o'clock, as Meg expected, an' as I fairly intended masel' when I set oot for the festival, but then ye ken that

> " The best laid schemes o' mice an' men
> Gang aft agley,
> An' le' us nocht but grief an' pain
> For promised joy."

So sang ane who had guid reason tae ken, as he had plenty experience in his short lifetime o' baith pain an' pleasure.

Had I foreseen what was gaun tae happen that nicht baith before an' efter I got hame the Queen's Rooms wad never hae seen ma face, that nicht at ony rate. An' a' through ane o' the simplest incidents, or rather a series o' incidents, that ever happened tae an unlucky soul. But I manna anticipate events, sae you'll get them a' in due course. I had enjoyed masel' rale weel at the dinner, for although I was in complete ignorance o' what I had been eating an' supping that didna in ony way detract frae ma relish o' the feast. Na, na! it wad tak' far mair than that tae spoil the appetite o' Tam M'Phail, especially when he's in guid form. I hae a fair appetite as a rule, an' when it's encouraged by onything tastie, as on this occasion, it fairly surprises masel'.

I canna say hoo mony plates I cleaned oot, but I was aye ready afore the waiter cam' roon' wi' anither. In fairness tae masel', however, I may mention that the plates werena a' fou tae begin wi', an' I couldna help askin' the waiter if he had scaled ony o' them on the way. You should hae seen the glower he gied me. However, 'tween sups an' bites I managed tae get ma fill, which, wi' the halfs I had as a slockener, I was quite weel pleased wi' masel', an' ye may tak' ma word for't, I didna throw much ower ma shouther.

Weel, efter it was a' ower—that is, the guzzling pairt o't —I was jist in the act o' gettin' ma coat tae come awa' hame when I got an infernal slap on the shouther, accompanied wi' a voice in onything but a minor key that I kent brawly, shouting: "Hallo, Tam; whaur in a' the world hae ye been? Whaur was ye sitting? Man, I hae been lookin' for ye a' nicht! Dod, man, there'll be nae speakin' tae ye noo! Ye've made a rare hit wi' that 'Welcome' o' yours! Everybody's speakin' aboot it; an' those wha dinna ken ye are wondering whaur in a' the world Tam M'Phail is, an' if he's here." This ootburst o' natural eloquence was frae an auld freen' o' mine wha styles himsel' the "Rough Ashler." An' when I had somewhat recovered frae the surprise o' seeing him, no' tae speak o' the shock frae his heavy haun', an' could draw ma breath freely, for he had nearly

knocked the wind oot o' me, I seized his ootstretched haun'
an' gied it a squeeze he'll no' forget in a hurry.

"What! you here a' the way frae B——? Wha wad
hae thocht it? Are ye for hame the nicht; or are ye
comin' ootbye tae see oor guid wife? Man she'll be
delighted tae see ye. Hoo's a' at hame wi' yoursel's?"

"Real weel, Tam, real weel; but Im afraid I'll no' can
go ootbye wi' ye the nicht. I maun gang straucht hame;
indeed, that was ane o' the conditions o' me getting here;
an' anither condition was that I should be T.T."

"It strikes me the last condition is the hardest o' the
twa tae comply wi', an' I'm far cheated if ye haena broken
it already, an' wha can blame ye under the circumstances?"

"You're jist aboot richt again, Tam; but tae mak' amends
for violating the last condition I maun try tae fulfil the
first."

"Oh, there's nae harm in that, Roughie; but we're
shurely no' gaun tae pairt withoot haeing a doch-an-doris.
It's no' every day you and I meet, an', ye ken, when freen's
meet hearts warm."

"I see you're aye the same auld saxpence, Tam. Dae ye
think we could staun' a half?"

"A half! Aye, maybe twa o' them."

"Come on then, Tam. I'm jist bursting tae hae a twa-
handed crack wi' ye for auld lang syne."

Noo, wha could resist an invitation o' this kind, especially
coming frae an auld acquaintance, an' ane o' the Rough
Ashler stamp? It wad hae been evendoon bad manners
tae hae dune sae, an' I'm no' ane wha wad lightly insult
a freen'. Besides, he's nane o' your stuck-up sort o' chiels,
nane o' your staun'-aff-if-ye-please sort o' fellows, but ane o'
the open-handed, warm-hearted callans wha adorn the Craft
in a' climes an' wad adorn ony society they wad join, ane

that ye're happy tae meet wi, sorry tae pairt wi, an' happy tae meet wi' again—a Rough but a soun' Ashler. Sae aff we set tae the nearest pub., airm in airm, discussing baith oor ain an' oor neighbours' affairs, an' those o' the Grand Lodge, wi' a relish an' eloquence peculiar tae oor twa sel's.

"But tell me, Tam, when did you write yon bit 'Welcome' o' yours? It's aboot the best thing I've seen you hae for a long time. Did ye hear Sir John Stirling Maxwell quoting it frae the platform? Dod, there will be nae haudin' o' ye in efter yon!"

"Did I no' hear him! Had it no' been that there appeared tae be plenty on the platform as weel as before oorsel's I could maist hae asked him oot tae hae a dram. It was a' written, printed, an' published in aboot twa days, an' I'm rale gled it took sae weel. I micht hae mentioned a few ithers in it weel worthy o' notice, but that wad hae made it too lang, although I micht hae a try at that some ither time, for there are mony o' them weel worthy o' a better muse than mine. But hoo are things daein' wi' yoursel'?"

Thus the crack gied on, until he had barely time tae catch the last train for B——, an' we

> "Each took aff his several way,
> Resolved tae meet some ither day."

By this time it was fully half-past ten—I'll no' say hoo much. An', of course, ma mind turned hamewards, "jist as naturally as the needle turns tae the pole," an' for fear that I micht fa' in wi' somebody else, an' no' wantin' tae be ony later than I could possibly help, I thocht I wad jist tak' a car, as that wad land me within twa or three minutes' walk o' ma ain door, an' by that time it wad be efter eleven o'clock. Ma conscience, eleven o'clock! an' I ettled tae be hame aboot nine. I wad likely get a fine keel-hauling frae Meg. But I had sic glorious news for her the nicht that I felt shure I wad be able tae pacify her wi' little bother. She wad likely be in bed though by the time I got hame, even wi' the car, having, nae doot, come tae the conclusion, quite pardonable under the circumstances, that I had gane awa' hame wi' Lord Haddington or some o' the ither big wigs, an' wadna be thinking o' ma ain hoose the nicht. But catch me breaking ma word wi' her in that way! It wad tak' far mair than an invitation even frae an Earl tae induce me tae forego the pleasures o' ma ain hame. However, it was time I was there, at ony rate, an' every passing moment only made things waur, sae the car was the thing. An' as guid luck wad hae't, jist as I cam' oot o' St. Enoch's Square there was ane passing. Noo, the cars, as ye dootless ken, are a' distinguished by different colours on the different routes. Those on oor route are green, an' as I hae ne'er been fashed wi' colour blindness, I had nae difficulty in making it oot. There could be nae mistake. There's naething like certainty in the matter o' cars. Wasn't it a wonderfu' foresicht on the pairt o' oor City Faithers tae sae arrange it! So darting efter this ane, like a fielder efter a crickit ba', I boarded it withoot askin' the conductor tae stop, an' plankin' masel' doon in a corner I began tae ruminate ower the events o' the evenin', especially those o' the last twa or three hoors.

I hadna been mony minutes in the enjoyment o' this blissfu' pleasure when the guard came roon' for the fares, an' no' wanting tae be interrupted in ma train o' thocht I haunded him a threepenny bit, telling him tae keep the change, an' put me doon at the terminus. That was a penny mair than ma fair came tae, an' was three bawbees I had gien awa' that nicht on tips, but they hae a deil o' a

thankless job, thae guards, an' a bit tip o' this kind nae
doot lichtens the cares o' their situation, an' lets them see
that everybody's no' o' a sordid disposition ; an', besides,
ane can aye depend on getting the full value o' his generosity in extra attention an' respect frae those upon whom
it is bestowed ; indeed, it wadna dae if everybody was alike
hard an' withoot consideration for ithers. The conductor's
remark was sufficient reward for my kindness, an' his
deference tae me was maybe an object lesson tae those wha
were witnesses. The respect that accompanied the words
"All right, sir," was something tae remember an' be prood
o' tae your dying day ; at least, it set ma mind perfectly
at rest for the time being, and gave me such a feeling o'
security that I fell into ane o' thae dreamy kind o' dovers
that ane whiles enjoys sae much, when visions, dimly-oot-
lined, come crowding upon the mind, an' ye hae neither
the power nor the desire tae interrupt what's gaun on—
"car dreams" I micht ca' them. Wha hasna enjoyed
them ? Nae doot ye hae hain your ain "car dreams," like
ither folk, an' can understand better than I can explain
the joys an' pleasures o' a few minutes' pleasant reflection,
even in the corner o' a crowded car. Indeed, so pleasant
were my reflections on this occasion that I maun hae fa'en
fast asleep, an' didna wauken until someane shook me
by the shouther, saying, "Hurry up, sir. Here you are.
The terminus, sir. All right. Mind your feet on the
step." etc., etc.

"A' richt. I'll be there the noo."

But it was only the guard.

"Here you are, sir—the terminus."

Being thus suddenly awakened, and the word "terminus"
ringing in ma ears, I was baith dazed an' startled, an' sae
I got up wi' a vague idea that I was hame at last. Of course,

I was half sleeping and half wauken, sae, mumbling a word
o' thanks tae the guard, I scrambled doon aff the fitboard
an' made tracks for the house, concocting the most plausible story I could think o' tae pacify Meg, an' account for
ma being sae late, thinking ower this thing an' that,
an' calculating the result wi' an inward feeling o' satisfaction that made me perfectly oblivious tae a' else: at
last, it began tae dawn upon me that I should be in the
neighbourhood o' oor close-mouth, sae I paused, jist tae tak'
soundings, as it were, when, on lookin' up, I was stunned
tae discover that I was in the wrang street a'thegither, but
it wad be a' richt directly. I had dootless jist turned doon
ao street instead o' anither. I wad jist turn back tae
whaur I had left the car, an' tak' proper bearings, an' the
mistake would be rectified in a minute. But this a' meant
a loss o' time; but there was nae help for't, so I maun
gang if I meant tae get hame at a'. Sae back I gaed, but
only tae get still further confused. What was the matter?
Was I dreaming, or what was wrang?—or rather, could
there be onything wrang? The green licht o' the car I had
jist come in was vanishing in the distance, on its return
journey. That seemed tae be a' real enough. There could
be nae mistake aboot that, at ony 'rate; but everything
else seemed tae be an infernal nichtmair. Everything
aroon' was strange an' new. I looked at ma watch. It was
ten minutes past eleven. There was nae mistake aboot
that; but some confounded transformation had shurely
taen place wi' a' else. There wasna a building in the hale
neighbourhood that I kent; big four-storied lands had taen
the place o' ane or twa storey anes, an' what I hadna taen
notice o' before was that the buildings were a' of a superior
class tae those in oor neighbourhood. I glowered roon',
dazed an' dumfoundered, only tae realise that the very

names aboon the shop doors were strange an' unfamiliar
tae me. "Change" seemed tae hae been written on the
face o' everything aroon'. I was a stranger in a strange
land shure enough; an' besides, there were very few folk
moving aboot, an' what few there was were hurrying alang,
in the semi-darkness o' the lamp licht, like phantoms o' the
nether regions. Guid gracious! what had happened? I
shurely hadna landed there! Time was passing. The hour
was late. Whaur was I at a'? I kent nae mair whaur I
was than the man i' the moon—if there be sic a being there.
Had I fa'en intae some trance, only tae wauken, like Rip-
Van-Winkle, a spectacle o' curiosity tae the present genera-
tion? It shurely wasna a dream! I minded fine o'
parting wi' the "Rough Ashler," an' hurrying tae the car,
bent on being hame as soon as possible, tae retail a' the
tit-bits tae Meg an' the weans; an' yet here I was, guid
kens whaur, in ane o' the awfu'est fixes that ever befell a
puir, harmless, well-meaning soul. This was awfu'. What
should I do? I couldna staun' there like a stookie an'
glower frae me until somebody took me by the haun' an' led
me tae ma ain door. Guid be thankit, here was a policeman. He wasna "changed" at ony rate—the same slow,
measured tread, as if every foot he put doon was, like Rab
Roy's wife, saying:

> "My foot's upon my native heath,
> And my name's MacGregor."

This ane, like maist o' the Glasgow policemen, was mair
substantial than shadow-like. I wad jist ask him tae put
me richt. He wad be able tae set me on the correct tack
shurely, and the mystery wad be a' cleared up in a jiffy.
Sae, stapping up tae the stalwart guardian o' the peace, oor
lives and liberties, I asked him if he could tell me hoo I
cam' herenawa'.

"What's that you'll say?" demanded this guardian of the peace, in a tone that caused me tae start.

"Can ye tell me hoo in a' the warl' I came tae be here?" I asked, in a tone of innocent enquiry.

"Hoo the teevil will I ken hoo you'll come here? Maype you'll pe fou, an' no' ken yoursel', whateffer."

"Weel, no, guidman; but that's no' exactly what I mean. I want tae ken whaur I am. I've lost ma reckoning somehoo."

"If you'll tak' me for a tam greenhorn you'll pe far wrang. She'll see the likes o' you afore ta-day, so shist move on, an' no' interfere wi' me in ta discharge o' ma duties."

"But, ma guid sir, I'm really no' what ye tak' me for; an' if ever you did a duty in your life it wad be in setting me richt. I want tae get hame, an' I dinna ken hoo tae go aboot it."

"Aye, an' you'll maype no' ken whaur you'll pe gaun."

"Weel, I ken whaur I wad like tae gang tae, if I only kent hoo tae go aboot it."

"An' whaur will that pe?"

"Weel, I think if I were in Camlachie I wad fin ma way hame."

"Hooly, hooly! an' what the teevil are you daein' here at this time o' nicht?"

"That's ane o' the things I dinna ken."

"O! she'll see fine what'll pe wrang. You'll get fou, an' ye'll wan'er, that's a'."

"No, sir; I deny that I was fou. I was seein' a freen o' mine awa' in the train tae B——, an', coming oot o' St. Enoch's Square, I saw ma car passing, an' jumpit intae't, an' here I am."

"Man, the thing's as clear as ma lantern. The car's peen

ooming the ither road, an' instead o' gaun hame, as ye should, you pe here."

"Dod, that maun jist be aboot what has happened; but hoo am I tae get back?"

"Let me see. It'll pe half-past eleven noo, whateffer, an' you'll shist pe in time tae get the last car pack. See, there it is shist coming in. If ye look sharp ye micht get hame aboot twelve."

"Guid bless ma soul, this is an awfu' job! I'll get the house aboot ma ears when I dae get hame, if I ever got there. I'm muckle obliged tae ye, an' if ever I meet ye when you're no' on duty you'll no' regret the advice ye hae gien me. I'll no' forget this in a hurry. I wish I saw the end o't. I'll mak' shure wark this time," an' wi' as warm a grip o' the haun' as I ever gied a livin' mortal, an' wi' thae remarks, I made for the car, an' took ma seat, thankfu' that the end o' ma troubles were noo within measurable distance, an' wondering what kind o' reception I wad get frae Meg.

Oor ane wad likely be in an awfu' state by this time, if she wasna in bed; an' it wad require carefu' management on ma pairt tae avoid a crisis, as she ca'd it. An' yet hoo simply it had a' happened. But hae ye ever noticed hoo frequently oot o' the maist trifling incidents some o' the maist momentous events arise, perhaps changing the hale efter current o' a life? But these reflections are only for the philosophical—they're no' for the like o' me. Wha wad hae thocht o' that car gaun the wrang road, an' landing me at the ither end o' ma journey? Certainly no' me. Dod bless me! if folk are tae gang through life wi' the continual dread o' stappin' intae the wrang car, then I, for ane, hae nae hesitation in saying that "life's no' worth living." It wad be a miserable business a'thegither, an'

yet hoo mony o' us dae get intae the wrang car efter a'!
It's a very important thing this, look at it ony way ye like,
an' wadna mak' a bad text for a guid preacher; indeed,
onybody wi' a smattering o' learning, a gift o' the gab, an'
a little imagination could mak' a fine thing o't. There's
oor minister, for instance, wha has a taste for a' oot-o'-the-
way subjects, he could han'le it finely. He could picture
baith men and women a' crowding intae the wrang car an'
drivin' tae the wrang end o' life's journey, jist as I had
dune here, only realising their mistake when they landed
intae the place they hadna bargained for an' didna want, wi'
no' anither car tae tak' them on the return journey—cars
whaur there wad be nae tippin' o' the guards, an' whaur
they didna stop tae change the horses. Efter a', I wasna
as bad as that, although I was bad enough; this ane wad
land me near tae ma ain door before lang, an' I wad be
hame aboot half-past twelve, at the latest. I had been as
late mony—well, ance or twice before, an' had aye managed
tae bring oor ane roon' tae believe that the thing couldna
be helped. I wad jist tell her hoo it had a' happened, an',
nae doot, she wad be as ready as ever tae forgie me ma
shortcomings; indeed, on the present occasion I felt as
if I deserved her sympathy—that I needed it there was nae
doot. I could picture tae masel' the look o' surprise an'
bewilderment that lit up her sonsie face as I rehearsed incident efter incident o' the strange chapter o' events that
had happened, an' in imagination could hear her saying——

"Fares, please."

This was a vulgar interruption indeed tae ma pleasant
train o' thocht, an' jarred terribly on ma ears. It was the
guard, wha, like a' ither guards, seemed tae be quite
oblivious tae the fine sensibilities o' human nature, wi' nocht
tae care for but hoo tae "gather the siller, man, gather the
siller."

"Here ye are. When dae ye think you'll be at P——?"

"Not to-night, sir."

"O! I ken that it's efter twelve noo, but ye needna be sae miohty smart. It strikes me you're far too clever for the job ye hae. Ye maun learn tae be civil tae ratepayers, or there's a danger o' ye being reported. Civility and guid manners wad dae much tae adorn even your station o' life."

"I beg your pardon, sir. I didn't mean tae be uncivil. This car's only going to the stables."

"Guidness gracious, you don't say sae?"

"It's a fact, sir. This is oor last run, an' we only go the length o' the stables."

"I think it's I wha should beg your pardon. I thocht you were trying tae mak' fun o' me. There's your fare. God knows what's tae come ower me this nicht!"

Guidness gracious! whaur an' whan wad ma adventures hae an end? The stables wad be a mile at least frae hame, an' at this time o' nicht—or rather morning, for it was morning noo—what was I tae dae? What could I dae? Jist, as the Yankee says, "Grin and bear it." I think Auld Nick himsel' maun hae been at the bottom o' the hale affair; an' wi' a grin that I don't want photographed, I handed the guard his fare, an' resigned masel' tae ma fate—for Fate seemed tae be written on the face o' everything that had happened the nicht.

The guard was richt, the last car only gangs the length o' the stables, an' the few belated travellers wha, like masel', were left tae fin' their way hame as best they could seemed quite reconciled tae their lot.

I had aboot a mile tae gang, wi' hardly a single reflec- tion o' pleasure tae keep me company, because the enjoy- ments o' the early pairt o' the evening were a' overshadowed by the misfortunes o' the last hour or twa, an' the dread o' what was tae come broke upon me wi' increasing vividness at every step.

Meg wad be in bed lang syne, there could be nae doot aboot that ; an' as ill luck wad hae't, I had neglected tae tak' a check wi' me, sae confident had I been that I wad be hame in reasonable hours.

There was nae possibility o' gettin' in withoot her kennin', an' hoo was I tae wauken her withoot waukening the hale family ? This was the problem I had tae solve, an' I set masel' tae the solution o't wi' a' ma power. I hae nae doot less troublesome problems hae puzzled the heids o' some great men before ma time. Ah, cricky! jist the very thing. A splendid idea evolved itsel' frae the seemingly chaotic mass, which I'll noo explain tae ye, wi' its attendant results.

By the time I reached hame it wad be fully ane o'clock, an', jist as I expected, a' was as quiet as the kirkyard, an' as dark as the grave itsel', save ae wee glimmer o' licht in the kitchen window. Meg aye leaves the gas peeping, simmer or winter, as she says ane disna ken what may happen through the nicht, so I didna think it onything unusual tae see the bit glint in the window. Noo was the time for putting ma grand scheme intae operation, i.e., tae wauken Meg withoot waukening the rest.

Getting richt under the window, I put ma fingers tae ma mouth an' gied ane o' thae low, plaintive whistles that resemble the cry o' a cat mair than that o' a human being—ane o' thae whistles, low, but clear, an' penetrating, that often force themsel's upon the attention o' those they're intended for, without disturbing the uninitiated—one o' those signals often made use o' among the worshippers o' Cupid when they want tae draw the attention o' their sweethearts,

without disturbing the echoes o' the parental ears. I was
a past-master in this airt, an' could perform the trick tae
perfection. I had brocht Meg oot o' the house a hundred
times wi't when we were courtin'. Tae be courtin's ae
thing an' tae be wantin' tae steal intae your ain house is
anither, as I found tae ma cost. There was nae response tae
ma first call, so I tried again, and waited patiently. Still
nae response. She shurely couldna be sleeping efter that;
but a' was as silent as ever, except the short, shrill burrel
o' a policeman's whistle, dootless hailing his neighbour tae
gie him a haun' tae dae naething. I waited a few moments
tae see if I had made ony impression wi' ma second whistle,
but everything was as quate as before. I was disappointed,
but not disheartened. My plan o' operations wasna exhausted, yet I had failed in the preliminary. But the grand
"coup" had yet tae be tried. He's a puir general that has
only ae plan o' campaign an' canna adapt himsel' tae a
change o' circumstances, an' it jist shows the genius o' a
man when he can rise tae ony occasion, an' has originality
sufficient tae convert apparent obstacles intae real stepping-
stones tae success. I micht be excused if, on the present
occasion, I felt as if there wasna ane in a hundred could hae
planned an' put intae execution the scheme I was jist aboot
tae try, an' I chuckled tae masel', wi' a feeling o' conscious
greatness, as I thocht o' the result. "But what was ma
plan?" you're askin'. Weel, it was jist tae throw up a bit
haun'fu' gravel at the window. "Oh!" you say, "there's
naething in that." Granted. Isn't simplicity the dis-
tinguishing feature o' maist a' great discoveries. It was an
easy matter for the grandees tae gar an egg staun' on end
efter Columbus had shown them hoo it was dune; but it's
no' ma business tae haggle wi' ye aboot the greatness o' ma
conception, but jist tae tell you hoo it resulted; an' as the

result fully demonstrates the principle for which I'm contending, I leave it tae the unprejudiced reader tae decide. Lifting a bit haun'fu' o' gravel, I threw it wi' medium force against the window. There was a distinct rattle on the panes, but no' a sound frae within followed in response. This was extraordinary. She was shurely soond asleep. I kent she was a gey soond sleeper—but I had tae get in. I couldna staun' there a' nicht, an' the longer I stood only made things waur. I wad try again, an' failing this time, there wad be naething for't but jist tae chap her up, an' tak' the risk o' waukening the hale house. But she wad shurely hear me this time. I wad throw wi' a little mair force. Sae, stooping ance mair, I lifted anither haun'fu', an', aiming direct for the middle o' the window, I let drive wi' as much force as David did at Goliath. The result passed a' ma expectation; it fairly dumfoun'ered me. Great Scott! there maun hae been some " stanes " in that last haun'fu', for instead o' the former patter there was a crash o' broken glass, mingled wi' screams o' "Murder, murder! police, police!" a rumble o' owerturned furniture, an' ither sounds, that made the night hideous an' troubled ma soul.

In the name o' a' that's guid will the misfortunes o' this nicht never cease? Was I dreaming? Was it an infernal nichtmare? But there wasna room even for this shadow o' consolation. There was the fact o' Meg's voice—I wad ken it among a thousand—pitched in a key far aboon high " Doh," ringing throughoot tho stillness o' the night. an' burning holes in ma very heart.

"Tam, Tam! Will, Jock, Maggie, rise! There's somebody breaking intae the house; we'll be a' murdered afore morning! Rise, I tell ye, an' rin for the police! Chap through the wa' on Sandy M'Phee! Oh! whaur's your faither the nicht, weans? We'll be a' deid afore he comes hame!"

"What's wrang, mither? What's the matter?"

"Matter?   I tell ye somebody's breaking intae the house, an' we'll be a' killed directly.   I heard them coming through the window.   Can ye no' see for yoursel's?"

On this, someone—young Tam, I believe—ventured near the window, an' it was only then I could mak' masel' heard amidst the din an' confusion.

"Open the door, Meg, an' let me in, for God's sake, before I gang wrang in the mind."

"It's ma faither wanting in. I ken his voice. He's gane oot an' shut the door on himsel'."

I mentally thanked him for the unintentional suggestion, an' he dootless spoke as he thought.

On this, Meg hersel' approached, an', lifting the window —or rather, what remained o't—demanded, in tones o' onything but affection, "Wha's there?"

"It's me, Meg ; let me in if ye dinna want me tae dee."

"It's you, you auld fule!   An' what are ye daein' staunin' there smashing the window for, an' frichting folks oot o' their wits?   Rin awa' tae your beds, weans, oot o' the gate, an' no' get cauld.   Your faither's jist gane oot an' sniket the door on himsel'.   I'll let him in.   Aff ye go."

This was maist considerate an' wise on Meg's pairt, for wi' a' her bits o' faults she has aye sense enough no' tae let the youngsters ken too much.   She had evidently taen in the situation at a glance, an', acting on the lucky remark o' young Tam, wanted tae keep the young anes in the dark wi' regard tae the true state o' affairs.

In reply tae her enquiry I begged her tae open the door an' let me in.

"It's a' an accident, Meg, it's a' an accident!   I'll tell a' aboot it ance I get in."

The next moment the door was thrown open, an', thankfu'

tae see the inside o' ma ain house anoe mair, I sank intae a chair utterly prostrated wi' the excitement o' the last few hours. My admission was not a moment too soon, nor did it save me the humility o' hearing several other windows in the neighbourhood thrown up, from which peered as many curious heids. A general illumination had taen place in the surrounding windows as the result o' ma attempt tae wauken Meg withoot waukening onybody else.

"Meg, Meg, this has been an awfu' nicht! I think I've been bewitched since I left hame. See if there's onything in the press. I'm fairly upset. I've never haen sic a nicht o' misfortunes since I was born."

"What's the matter wi' ye? Whaur hae ye been tae this hour i' the morning? What made ye smash the window? A lunnie ane couldna hae dune ony waur."

"Whisht, woman, an' I'll tell ye a' aboot it. That was a pure accident, the climax o' a hale series o' accidents. I'll explain a' tae ye by-an'-by. In the meantime, gie's something tae settle ma nerves."

She wasna slow tae comply wi' ma request, for she saw that something by-ordinar' had happened tae put me sae much aboot.

Having recovered some o' ma usual composure, I related the events o' the evening frae the time I left her, an' had the questionable satisfaction o' hearin' her say:

"Weel, weel, jist like ye. You're ane o' the stupidest men in creation. It's a wonner ye've managed hame at a'. Could ye no' see the car was gaun the wrang road? Ye can hardly be trusted tae yoursel', Tam. Something'll happen some day that'll put an end tae't a'. I wonner what some men wad dae if they hadna their wives tae look efter them! But hoo did ye get on at the spree? Ye haena telt me that yet. Ye wadna gang far wrang there."

"Grand, Meg; an' grand's no' a name for't. I'll hae tae look up the dictionary for words tae describe it. I never saw the like o't in a' ma life. I wadna hae missed it for a guid lot."

"No even for a smashed window, eh?"

"We'll let that flee stick tae the wa'. Jook Shavings, the joiner'll mak' that a' richt, an' it'll be nane the waur."

"An' hoo did ye get on wi' the big haun's? Was the Prince kind o' nice wi' ye, na?"

"Oh, he didna manage tae get; but there were ever sae mony o' the nobility there, a' as sociable as could be."

"Was ye speakin' wi' ony o' them? What like are they in company?"

"Weel, I wasna jist exactly speaking tae them, but I was awfu' near't. They're jist like ither folk in the main, wi' what they ca' a little mair refinement o' manners than some o' us. But, mind ye, I'm a marked man efter the nicht, for a' that. I believe oor fortune's made, or in a fair way o' being made, altho' ane hasna time tae mak' a fraca aboot onything at a thing o' the kind. A nod's as guid's a wink. Tae mak' a fraca wadna be in yon big folks' line; it wadna dae tae let everybody see what they think, but the thing's moleskin for a' that. Dae ye mind yon twa-three verses o' a 'Welcome' I wrote tae the Grand Lodge? Weel, they had a reception I ne'er dreamt o'. Everybody's speaking aboot them, an' nae less a personage than Sir John Stirling Maxwell quoted them frae the platform, in presence o' the hale assembly, when proposing the health o' the Grand Master."

"Never!"

"It's as true as you're there. There's something shure tae come oot o' yon or ma name's no' Tam M'Phail."

"Hits! it'll jist be like some o' the rest o' the haivers

you've written : it may fill their mouths for a wee, then
there'll be nae mair aboot it."

"Nae fears o' that, Meg. I tell you we'll be gettin' a
ca' frae some o' the big haun's afore lang ower the heid
o' yon. Jist imagine, if Lord Haddington was tae drive up
tae oor door—what would ye sae tae that, eh? You wad
be looking at Luckie M'Phee an' a' the rest o' your neighbours as if they were common washerwomen, eh? Wadn't
that be rare?" an' I gied Meg a dig wi' ma elbow by way o'
emphasising what I was trying tae mak' her believe.

"I'm thinking it wad, Tam ; but it's no' likely."

"Likely or no', there's something bound tae come oot
o't at ony rate."

"Don't fash yoursel', Tam ; you'll hear nae mair aboot
it."

"Nae mair aboot it? As shure's you're living there'll
be mair aboot it. I tell you oor fortune's made, an' I wadna
be surprised if we had a ca' frae some o' the big folk in
the morning, an'—'Rap, tap, tap!'—Guid gracious! there's
somebody at the door. I telt ye, Meg ; I telt ye what it
wad be. That's no' an ordinary chap. Bless ma soul ! I
had nae idea they wad be here already—'Rap, tap, tap!'
Run an' open the door, Meg. It doesna dae tae keep
thae big haun's waiting. That's the chap o' authority, or
I'm mistaen. Don't show you're elated, Meg. Let us tak'
oor honours wi' becoming modesty. Run an' open the
door, an' show them intae the best room. It's maybe Lord
Haddington, the Earl Roslin, or Lord Saulton, or some o'
the sma'er gentry ; it's somebody o' note at ony rate.
Hurry up. There, they're getting impatient. It doesna dae
tae keep thae fellows waiting—they'll no' be denied. Tell
them I'll be ben in a jiffy."

Meg, throwing a shawl ower her heid, hurried tae the door,

an' I, trying tae look as unconcerned as the circumstances wad permit, waited the entrance o' ma noble guests, straining baith neck an' ears, however, tae catch what was said.

The following is a summary o' what I heard, on the door being opened :—

"Will that pe your ain sel', Mrs. M'Phail? Wad there pe onything wrang at all, at all?"

"Guid help me, Dougal', is that you? What in a' the worl' brings ye here at this time o' the morning?"

"She'll jist want tae see if things'll pe a' richt, whateffer."

"In the name o' a' that's wonnerfu', Dougal', what puts that intae your heid?"

"Weel, jist apoot five or twenty minutes ago, or maype less, she'll hear a mysterious whistle gie a plaw, an' there'll pe a noise o' proken gless, an' she'll think tae hersel' it'll pe gey strange, an' maype a case o' hoose-preakin', sae she'll jist call her neepour, Tonal, here, an' we'll come roon' tae see, an' your window pein' lichtet, we thocht we'll jist speer."

"Thank you, Dougal', for being sae thochtfu'."

"Oh! ton't mention it at a', at a'; it's jist oor tuty, ye ken. There's peen a lot o' hoose-preakin' lately, an' we canna pe too carefu'."

"You're quite richt, Dougal'. Tam'll explain a' tae ye himsel' the first time he sees ye. Guid nicht."

"Guid nicht, Mrs. M'Phail; it's a guid thing that there's naething wrang," an' wi' that Dougal' an' his neighbour departed, an' Meg shut the door wi' a slam. Having shut the door, Meg returned tae the kitchen, wi' an ominous look on her face an' sarcasm an' reproach on her tongue.

"O' a' the fules on God's earth, Tam M'Phail, you're ane o' them!" But there are incidents in married life that are too sacred tae be made public : moments o' conjugal bless that are no' tae be intruded upon, moments when the heart's innermost emotions are laid bare an' poured out in language too sublime for repetition here. So I will not attempt tae disclose what followed. Suffice it tae say that I hae never mentioned ony o' the noblemen's names above referred tae since that nicht.

BROUGHT TO LIGHT.

IN THREE PARTS.

PART I.

MY FIRST DEGREE.

I have sometimes laughed since I joined the craft,
    When I think of my first degree,
I felt so queer, 'twixt doubt and fear,
    Though I many friends could see.
But they seemed so strange, as if some revenge
    They intended to carry out,
And some passed by with a lear in their eye,
    As I thought, but my heart was stout.

For long in my mind I'd been well inclined
    To the mystic social band,
And the friend of my youth, when I told the truth,
    Gave an extra grip of the hand.
He said that I might, on the meeting night,
    To their Lodge Room then repair,
And that he and those who were there would close,
    And settle the whole affair.

Whether false or fact, in the course of crack
  With those of the Masons I knew,
Strange hints, at least, of a bearded beast
  That often outrageous grew,
I had heard, but, of course, it was nothing worse
  Than the chaff of a social lot,
And yet I'll admit I couldn't get quit
  Of a dread of that awful goat.

It was pictured so grim, so fierce tho' slim,
  And with horns so fearfully strong,
That the fiercest shock had never yet broke
  A piece from their tips so long.
'Twas said he grew wild should a woman or child
  Dare to approach his den,
And strange in a beast, in a goat at least,
  He couldn't abide some men.

I smiled at this chaff and joined in the laugh
  With the rest when their stories were told,
And made it appear that no craven fear
  Of my heart or mind had got hold.
So come weal or woe, I settled to go,
  A particular night was named,
And my friend and I, feeling somewhat dry,
  O'er the matter a measure drained.

When the night came round my nerves I found—
  An unusual thing for me—
Were quite relaxed, though I had not taxed
  Their strength by work or spree.
But somehow or other I began to swither
  If I really were doing right
To tempt my fate by being late
  On this particular night.

I felt quite strong, but something was wrong,
  I was quite unsettled in mind,
Perhaps 'twas the bile, however, meanwhile,
  No rest or peace could I find.
Anxiety whiles our pleasure spoils,
  I was anxious, that was all,
And if I must own, had rather not gone
  That night to the Masons' Hall.

But I'd promised my friend that I would attend,
  And he might think it rather queer
If I made an excuse, it would be no use,
  They would say it was naught but fear.
So I took one nip—I don't often sip
  Of brandy when it's old—
But I thought in this mood it would do me good,
  And at least keep out the cold.

The Lodge Room, I found, was away from the ground,
  In part of an upper flat,
Where none could intrude, if they meant no good
  To the Lodge that within it sat.
I was welcomed, of course, but this made me worse,
  In my present condition of mind,
Though I made it appear to my friend, who was near,
  It was all as I hoped to find.

I was asked by a few of this social crew,
  In a bantering sort of style,
If I had no fear in coming here,
  And I answered No, meanwhile.
But my heart beat fast, and I cautiously cast
  A glance round the smiling lot,
As I heard one say, in an off-hand way,
  Has anyone fed the goat?

They asked me to tell, though they knew me well,
  My name and my age and trade;
And the notes they took were put into a book,
  To certify all that I said.
Then one of them there bade me quickly prepare,
  And assured me no harm would come;
But I felt in my heart I would never depart
  From that place as I'd left my home.

In this terrible plight I fairly lost sight
  Of what was transacting around,
And dreaded the shame that would cling to my name
  If I shrunk from the task I had found.
I could not withstand the half-coaxing command
  To be bold; so I tried all I could
To comply with good grace, and adjusted my dress
  In a half-forced and resolute mood.

Well, perhaps it was fear, but my collar felt queer,
  And I fain would have taken it off,
And had I but known I should not have gone
  Dressed up like a modern toff.
They all were so plain, without blemish of stain,
  That I felt I was oddest of all,
And everyone scanned my apparel so grand,
  That I felt in my shame I would fall.

But too late to change, or my dress re-arrange,
  I was led by my guide to the door,
Who knocked once or twice, or it may have been thrice,
  When a voice that I'd ne'er heard before,
Inquired from within the cause of the din,
  Which added somewhat to my fear,
And when he was told, he added quite bold,
  "What on a' the earth do you want here?"

I answered in brief that I had the belief
  They would make me a Mason right free,
And he just gave a roar, as he banged tae the door,
  "Just stay where you are for a wee."
I then wished to go, but my guide whispered "No;
  He'll be back in a minute or two,
And you'll certainly find him attentive an' kind,"
  And all this I found to be true.

I was told to advance, but had dagger or lance
  Been stuck in my breast, I am sure
I could not have moved had my dearest beloved
  Been present my path to allure.
I felt such a pain, but it vanished again,
  And my courage once more gained command,
An' my guide, pawkie chiel, wha stuck tae me weel,
  Took a grip of my trembling hand.

We came to a halt, when I'm certain I felt
  That sting in my breast once again,
And I gave such a start that I near lost my heart,
  And my guide asked if I were in pain.
I owned, 'twas as well, I was scarce at mysel',
  But was hopeful I soon would be,
Then a voice, low and sweet, in my ears did beat,
  Imploring a blessing on me.

This gave me relief, for I hadn't been deaf
  To the voice of instruction in youth;
And I knew very well every word as it fell
  On my ears was a message of truth.
Three times I went round, no objections were found
  To my bearing, when all like a shot,
A thunderous din made me shake like the win',
  And think once again of the goat.

All seemed dark as the grave, so my body to save
  I groped with my guide all around,
When soft to my touch, which I wondered at much,
  An obstruction I speedily found.
Then a voice in my ear said, "What seek ye here?
  Go round a wee bit tae the west;
Ye're all right, I see, but we all must agree
  Before you are suffered tae rest."

So onward we gaed, the same things were said,
  Then off we were sent tae the east,
Where the Master himsel' was prepared to dispel
  All my fears of that terrible beast.
Having pledged me quite, he restored me to light,
  When, oh! such a sight I beheld;
It filled me with pride, and I scarcely could hide
  The love in my bosom that swelled.

The great lights, he said, were designedly made
  To instruct all the morally blind;
And the lesser ones, too, had a meaning quite new,
  As he told me I shortly should find.
He said in the Lodge I should aye wear a badge,
  And he gave me one spotless an' white,
Symbolic of peace, and wished me long lease
  Of life to enjoy it aright.

I was led by the hand, at the Master's command,
  And the fountain of knowledge I saw,
Where seated around, in silence profound,
  The brethren studied the law.
The Master severe, like prophet or seer,
  Then expounded, reproved, and warned
All present to mark the spots that were dark,
  And the passions within that burned.

The token and word I had both seen an' heard,
  Though I cannot repeat them just now;
And the signal so droll was impressed on my soul,
  But I cannot explain to you how.
The tools then I gained, they were fully explained,
  I was taught how to handle them well,
And to measure with care all works of repair,
  Till my task should in beauty excel.

Three jewels most dear were then made appear,
  So precious, no wealth could secure
Even one of the three, so I'll keep them with me,
  Through life, though I'm ever so poor.
They then had me placed where I felt so distressed
  That I fain would have shown I was kind
To the poor and despised, but I soon realised
  I had left all my money behind.

I searched, but in vain, and I searched yet again,
  I was sure I had money somewhere,
But in my distress I was forced to confess
  In which pocket I couldn't declare.
I was told not to fret, as I doubtless would get
  It all right when my trouble was o'er,
But I'm bound to declare that never elsewhere
  Had I felt so exceedingly poor.

The Master enlarged on the symbols, and charged
  Me my duties always to perform,
Being honest an' true in whatever you do,
  He said would aye weather the storm.
Aye study with care the lights that are there,
  They will guide you aright in the world,
And lead you to fame an' a glorious name,
  Though slander against you be hurled.

I then was invited, and felt quite delighted,
  To sit by the Master a while,
Observed by them all in that well-filled hall,
  In my pride I could not but smile.
I was vain, I admit, and had not learned yet
  All the precepts that I had been taught;
At least, quite a few from my memory flew
  On that most prominent spot.

I was asked to note, which I did on the spot—
  I am somewhat expert with the pen—
So I jotted it down, it was handed round,
  And returned to me again.
I thought it was right, and tried to indite,
  In my own peculiar style,
A letter or two which everyone knew,
  But my hand quite shook the while.

I tried once again, no use, such a pain
  Had come into my writing hand,
That had I been shot I could not have got
  Of that pen a right command.
The room seemed to swim, and things grew dim,
  And with shame my features burned,
And a smile I could trace on everyone's face,
  Wherever my eyes were turned.

I owned then at once I had been a dunce,
  And my mind was not always clear,
And the Master smiled, I thought he'd been riled,
  As he whispered a word of cheer.
Then a short address on the sacredness
  Of fraternal love he gave,
Exhorting us all, when our duties call,
  The fallen to succour and save.

I have pondered well the precepts that fell
  On my listening ears that night,
And deep in my heart I have treasured each part
  That then filled my breast with delight.
To the precious store I have added more
  Of the knowledge I then acquired,
And drinking still from the sparkling rill,
  In my journey I've never tired.

I felt reconciled when the Lodge was tiled,
  And we all quite attentive stood,
With listening ear to the Chaplain's prayer,
  I was one of the brotherhood.
I felt I was one, and though years have gone
  The impression but deeper grows,
And the light Divine which that night did shine,
  Shall cheer me till life shall close.

MY SECOND DEGREE.

Ye wha hae got the first degree,
An' anxious are mair licht tae see,
Jist haud yer breath an' follow me,
     But, mind, don't tell,
I'll ilka secret let you see
     I got masel'.

Weel tutored in the first I'd been,
Could mak' the signs a' neat an' clean,
An' Jock, ma ever trusty frien',
     Wha tutored me,
Admired ma wark wi' glancing een,
     Quite fou o' glee.

He felt quite shure I wad be past,
Nae doot o' that had e'er o'ercast,
His sanguine mind frae **first tae last**
      Was calm an' **clear**.
He answered questions quite as fast
      As I could speir.

Ane likes tae ken, **ye ken,** before
Whatever's like tae **be in store,**
An' whiles wad **glean the hidden lore,**
      'Gainst common laws,
But Jock wad never tell me more
      Than he had cause.

I pressed him aft tae tell me noo
That I was made, if it was true,
Or jist the talk o' some **half-fou,**
      Half-drucken **chiel,**
That fellow-crafts, **ere they got through,**
      Aye **met the deil.**

He whiles **wad** lauch, but **ne'er** wad tell
Hoo he had fared when made himsel',
I thocht **it** strange, **but** 'twas as well,
      I **kent nae** better,
Sae thus ma feelings rose an' fell
      Aboot the matter.

The **nicht cam' roon',** as nichts aye wull,
Tho' **days** be e'er sae bricht or dull,
When I was tae get quite ma full
      O' square **and level,**
An' learn tae snod **wi'** cunning skill
      Wi' mall and chisel.

I reached the hall in ample time,
Where a' was orderly an' prime,
An', as it was a venal crime
      Tae overlook
The lowest or the most sublime,
      Or tyler's book,

I wrote ma name in letters large,
In keeping wi' a former charge,
Got dressed thereafter an' emerged
      Frae the adjacent.
Towards the tyler, then I verged
      Wi' smile complacent.

He scanned me closely richt an' left,
Was satisfied ma fit was deft,
Seemed pleased, but still o' powers bereft
      Tae let me pass,
Till certain knocks, baith slow an' swift,
      Disclosed ma class.

The door wis opened jist a wee,
An' something said I weel could see,
But couldna hear, 'twixt you an' me,
      They spoke sae low.
I wondered much what it could be—
      Was't Aye or No.

Whate'er it was they seemed tae ken,
For tho' the door was shut again,
It opened shortly wide, an' then
      A voice, fou clear,
Said "Brither, welcome, come ye ben,
      Come enter here."

I entered boldly then an' there,
In Faith an' Hope, an' on the Square,
An' satisfaction everywhere
    Was manifested
By all when told they should declare
    I had been tested.

Frae West tae East, wi' prudent tread,
I then was by the wardens led,
Wha telt me hoo tae haud ma head
    An' mind ma feet.
I marked wi' care a' that was said,
    An' was discreet.

Wi' head erect an' feet set square,
I ventured forward tae declare
Ma readiness tae tak' a share
    In a' their dealings,
An' was assured that naething there
    Wad hurt ma feelings.

I said I had nae thocht o' fear,
Was quite prepared tae pledge an' swear
By a' I held in memory dear:
    I wad be steady,
An' signified in language clear
    That I was ready.

"Then, draw in ower," the Master said,
"An' grasp the lichts before you laid,
They will yet greater brightness spread
    Than ye hae seen,"
I followed a' he said an' did
    Wi' mouth an' een.

Ma body being squarely set,
An' something said I'll ne'er forget,
My brightening vision ance mair met
    The three great lights,
Clearer, brighter, fuller yet
    Wi' new delights.

Ma apron then was altered quite,
Tho' still remaining spotless white,
An' then at angles left or right,
    . I hardly min',
I was instructed at first sight
    Tae mak' the sign.

Tae speak the word I then was telt,
But aye tae watch hoo it was spelt,
Lest enemies wha knew nor felt
    Its true import
Should seek wi' it ma heart tae melt
    In wanton sport.

An unco word it is, an' queer,
For tho' familiar tae the ear,
It's ill tae speak, distinct, an' clear,
    By some at least,
Especially when danger's near,
    An' fear's increased.

This very word, I've heard, had been
Before a test 'twixt foe an' frien',
An' when the vanquished, baffled clean,
    Were put tae flight,
They got the chance, but none, I ween,
    Could speak it right.

The word I managed tae get thro',
Wi' help, but this is naething new,
Ane's awkward aye at first, an' few
      Can mind it weel,
Besides, tae rattle't aff, its true,
      Micht raise the Deil.

The grip, of course, I brawly mind,
Was of a very curious kind
O' grip that aye as brithers bind
      A' that can gie't,
An' tells the searchers aye tae find
      A something wi't.

Tae mark the progress I had made,
I then was tae the south-east led,
When bountiful Instruction spread
      Before ma view,
A' kinds o' learning, living, dead,
      But ever true.

The Plumb, the Level, and the Square,
Were a' explained while staun'ing there,
I could dae nocht but gape an' stare
      At what was telt,
In drinking a' an' wanting mair,
      Ma thirst tae melt.

But wha can satisfy the soul
Aye thirsting tae contain the whole,
An' aye denied an' telt tae thole,
      Wi' patient care,
While Wisdom ladles, dole by dole,
      A little mair.

The mind anticipates, an' fain
Wad rend the veil o' Time in twain,
An' snatch frae Nature o'er again
                Her hidden laws,
An' demonstrate, in language plain,
                Effect an' cause.

Weel feasted here wi' truths sublime,
An' precepts tried by flicht o' time,
I onward gaed, intent tae climb
                That winding stair,
Devised by architect supreme,
                An' built wi' care.

I reached the porch in safety, where
Twa brazen pillars made me stare,
I wondert hoo they had got there,
                Sae strong an' stable,
Tae match their beauty onywhere
                I wasna able.

A Chapiter, five cubits long,
Roon' which was wrocht a network strong,
Ilk pillar graced, an' frae them hung
                Pure lily work,
While pomegranates shone among,
                I did remark.

Fit emblems these o' power Divine
Tae mak' the licht in darkness shine,
Protecting Israel's chosen line,
                In days of old,
When forth they marched, in grand design,
                As they were told.

Still onward seeking ma reward,
I passed, but found ma passage barred
By ane wha said a certain word
      He there should get,
Ere I could pass, as I desired,
      Still further yet.

I looked the chiel frae tap tae tae,
An' scarcely kent what I should say,
An' swithered long, an' wondered aye
      What he could mean.
Quoth he, "Hae ye the pass-word, pray;
      It maun be gi'en."

Quoth I, "Ma frien', an' your no' blate
Tae challenge me in sic a gate;
I've got the word, but daurna say't
      Till you begin,
Sae gin you're willing help me wi't,
      An' let me in."

Quoth he, "You're cautious quite, I see;
That's richt, an' cautious ever be
Wi' strangers, but wi' such as me
      You've nocht tae fear;
I'm here tae ask, an' no' tae gie,
      While staun'ing here."

"Oh! then," quoth I, "an' that be sae,
I winna langer here delay,
Sae gie's your haun' an' listen, pray,
      I'll dae ma best,
Your scruples a' tae brush away,
      An' set at rest."

I whispered in his listening ear
That word significant and queer;
Nae further questions did he speir,
  But stood aside,
An' bade me pass: the portal near
  He opened wide.

I passed, an' lo! I could but glower,
Sic wonders saw I there in o'er,
It baffles yet ma outmost power
  Tae comprehend.
The mysteries o' that solemn hour
  Hae ne'er been penned.

Before me rose, in cunning art,
That stair, symbolic every part,
 Replete wi' meaning frae the start,
  An' thrice divided,
Tae mount I scarcely had the heart,
  But soon decided.

Then upward, step by step, I rose.
My admiration stronger grows,
As knowledge richer store bestows
  On all ascending,
Than schools or colleges disclose,
  Tho' much pretending.

The moral laws an' rule o' life,
Wi' sage-like precepts true an' rife,
Point oot the path that's clear o' strife,
  An' blessing brings
Tae a' that travel't, man or wife,
  Or doughty things.

Wi' muckle toil I reached the tap,
But scarce had gained the hindmost stap,
When, lo! another watchfu' chap
    Ma errand speired.
I wondered could it be a trap,
    An' muckle feared.

Quoth I, "Ma frien', ye needna speir,
I've come tae get ma wages here,
An' I've been telt tae hae nae fear
    O' being wranged,
Sae gin ye winna let me near,
    May you be hanged.

"Ma work has matched the very best,
An' stood the overseer's test,
Sae what I've earned I ne'er guessed
    Wad be denied,
Come, put your doots an' fears at rest,
    An' staun aside."

"Na, na," quoth he; "that may be true,
But certain tokens ye maun show,
Ere ye can manage tae get thro'
    This guarded door,
Wi' them the Middle Chamber you
    May then explore."

Wi' cautious care I then bestowed
The tokens which by right I owed,
He smiled approvingly and bowed
    Wi' muckle grace,
Then showed me in in kindly mood.
    O sic a place!

On every haun' rich treasures lay,
A' labelled genuine, need I say?
Nae gaudy show or vain display
      O gowden gear,
But gems o' pure an' matchless ray,
      Tae Masons dear.

Here Faith an' Hope sat cheek for chow,
Like twins celestial, sleeping now,
While Chastity, wi' steady glow,
      The place made bright,
An' Fortitude, wi' knitted brow,
      Seemed fit for fight.

Mil'l Temperance, chastened an' refined,
Wi' modest mien, stood close behind,
Reproving like, but looking kind
      On a' aroon',
While Justice, wha I thocht was blind,
      Towered high aboon.

Love, crowned wi' diadem, was there,
In robes o' state an' jewels rare,
And Peace an' Joy, that happy pair
      O' laughing queens,
Tho' auld's the worl', seemed nae mair
      Than in their teens.

Truth, ever candid, whiles severe,
Looked quite at hame wi' kindred dear,
While a' aroon', baith faur an' near,
      I could behold
Sma' groups o' kindred spirits here,
      Baith young an' old.

Far in the East my wandering een
Beheld a sioht before unseen,
But what it was, or may have been,
          I canna tell.
I wondered much, was baffled clean,
          Its sense tae spell.

Some characters o' common mould,
That could some hidden truth unfold,
Were they but kent, but young an' old
          Jist guessed their meaning.
Such is the story I was told,
          While there that e'ening.

But why prolong this lengthened tale,
When a' ma efforts maun but fail
Tae half describe the very wale
          O' what I saw?
I got ma wages free an' hale,
          An' that was a'.

Nae further progress, I could see
Was to be made in this degree;
I'd got it a', an' yet I'm free
          Here tae relate;
The greater part remained for me
          Tae contemplate.

Ah! contemplation, fruitful child
Of truth divine, wi' lessons mild,
You've schooled ma heart when passions wild,
          Hae fired ma blood
Tae staun' unshaken, undefiled,
          In Brotherhood.

Oft, oft, since then, I've pondered o'er
The many truths unknown before,
An' yet, alas! wi' a' ma power
      O' penetration
I've failed tae reach the inner core
      O' information.

A few bright gems, but jist a few,
Wi' lustre sparkling ever new,
I've managed tae possess, an' through
      Life's chequered ways
I'll bear them wi' me, guided to
      The brighter days.

But cease, ma Muse, nor longer dwell
On themes sae far beyond thy spell;
Let others, abler far tae tell,
      These themes extol,
In measured verse that passions quell
      Within the soul.

Past Fellowcraft thus I hae been,
An' wondrous things hae heard an' seen,
Wi' brightening mind an' gladdening een
      I've felt their power,
An' prized them aye the mair, I ween,
      I've pondered o'er.

Then fear ye na' wha's born free,
An' hae got through the first degree,
If mair o' licht ye want tae see,
      Congenial, saft,
Jist persevere, become like me,
      A Fellowcraft.

Respectfully Dedicated to
BRO. D. MURRAY LYON,
Secretary of the Grand Lodge of Scotland,

In recognition of his literary genius as a historian and man of
high character as a Mason, from whom the Author has received
many marks of kindness, and considers himself still his debtor.

Revered, beloved, respected, honoured friend—
　　To thee I dedicate this humble lay;
A tribute to thy worth, unask'd, I send
　　My Muse's offering—spurn it not, I pray.
Though lack of learning and of polish may
　　Bespeak her poverty of power of song;
With generous impulse, strong and bright as day,
　　She hails the Nestor of that mystic throng,
　　Whose lineage runs through generations long.

Thy worth, thy merit, and thy labours claim
　　Far higher tribute than I can bestow;
But when the Craft reveres thy honoured name,
　　Why not an humble member of it also show
His deep regard for thee, whose worth to know
　　Exalts our thoughts into a higher plain,
And swells the virtuous currents as they flow
　　Through beating heart, and through the throbbing brain,
　　With impulse strong, a purer sphere to gain?

No mercenary motive guides my lyre,
　　Nor prompts the theme I seek in verse to sing;
My inspiration is my heart's desire,
　　In clearer light our mystic art to bring,
That it perchance may firmer, closer cling
　　Around our hearts, and guide our heavenward way
In purer paths of life, where all may fling
　　Aside the ills that grieve us day by day,
　　Impeding in our march to destiny.

MY THIRD DEGREE.

Hail, a' ye cunning, crafty chiels,
Wha's mystic art alone reveals
The love that southers a', an' seals
      In britherhood :
Lang may ye boast, o'er flowing creels,
      Wi' ilka good !

I've pondered lang, since last in rhyme
I sought Parnassus' hill tae climb ;
The auld excuse, aye want o' time
      Tae settle doon
Has fashed me sair, but noo I'm prime
      Wi' a' aroon'.

Sae, gin ye promise no' tae tell,
An' keep it snugly tae yoursel',
I'll let ye ken a' that befell
      Puir helpless me,
When searching after Truth hersel',
      Ma third degree.

Ma first degree, as I hae said,
Had dootless a foundation laid
O' moral principles, that gaed
      Far doon within,
An' taught me, tae, whate'er I did,
      Tae look abune.

Ma second, still advancing on,
Had taught me much tae muse upon
In Art sublime, and brighter shone
      The intellect,
When taught tae love an' reverence yon
      Great Architect.

Still further truths, I had been told,
Increasing light would yet unfold;
I had ma doots, but wasna bold
      Enough tae say't.
Ane's whiles as weel their wheest tae hold,
      An' learn tae wait.

Wi' anxious mind I hailed the nicht
When a' was tae be settled richt,
An' ilka cloud, dispelled wi' licht
      Abundant free,
Shed o'er me dazzling—sic a sicht,
      Ma third degree.

Prepared, of course, as weel's ane could,
Enquiring at the door I stood.
Ma guide advanced, an' chapping loud—
      Baith fast an' slow—
As if he were in angry mood.
      But 'twas not so.

The door gied gee, an' deep within
A voice enquired, "What's a' the din?
What seek ye here, whaur ilka ane
      Maun be weel kent?
Ye look like strangers.   Say what in
      Your time's been spent."

Ma guide replied, an' I was gled,
"This is a brither o' oor trade.
He's served his time, a 'prentice bred
      Tae maul an' chisel;
An' a' wha ken him oft hae said
      He's unco civil.

"I'll vouch for him masel', off haun',
A better 'prentice isna gaun.
An' here I pledge ye, whaur I stan',
          He's safe an' fast.
For merit, ye maun understaun',
          He has been past.

"An' noo he hopes by dint o' skill,
An' persevering strength o' will,
Tae maister what's remaining still
          Unknown to him;
An' vows he winna rest until
          A's trig an' trim."

"His claims are gude, but something mair
Maun yet his worthiness declare,
Before he can expect tae share
          Oor rites sublime,
Perhaps the compasses an' square
          'Ill dae this time."

"E'en they themsel's'll hardly dae.
Has he the password, did you say?"
"No; but I'll gie ye't right away.
          Incline your ear."
He whispered—be it what it may;
          I didna speir.

"A's richt, sae I'll acquaint the East,
An' rest ye there the noo at least;
I'll soon return." Wi' that he ceast,
          An' shut the door.
Ma heart gied dunt against ma breast,
          As ance before.

Some twa-three minutes dragged alang,
An' a' the time ma brain was thrang,
Recalling if ocht could be wrang
            Tae cause delay,
When back the door gied wi' a bang,
            I'm blythe tae say.

"Come, enter, brither, enter here,
In name of the Most High an' dear,
An' though you've little skaith tae fear,
            Be careful still,
Lest dangers, though unseen, be near,
            Tae work ye ill.

ADMONITION.

"Ye mind, when first ye were admitted,
How pained ye were an' badly fitted,
An' how your bleeding conscience twitted
            A' thocht o' guile;
How meekly ye tae a' submitted,
            An' bore the while?

"An' then, when next brocht in ye were,
How hard ye pressed upon the square,
An' promised ye wad aye be fair
            Wi' a' mankind.
Nae doot ye mind it a' an' mair
            That lay behind.

"An', noo, mark this, an' mark it weel:
As lang's within your heart ye feel
Life's vitals glow, be true as steel
            Tae the oppress'd;
The compasses extended, hele
            Frae breast tae breast.

" As circling round the eternal Sun,
Our earth revolves, an's never done,
So do oor duties constant run
      In circle wide;
Unceasing from the point begun.
      Our course we guide.

Ecclesiastes xii.—1*st*.

" And, now, remember in thy youth
Thy Great Creator, source of Truth,
Ere age infirm, and mien uncouth
      Thy lot befall;
When thou shalt say, in tears, forsooth,
      " All pleasures pall."

Eccles. xii.—2*nd*.

" ' While yet the sun's refulgent light,
Nor moon, nor stars be darken'd quite,
An' floods outpour, both day an' night,
      In drenching showers,
Destroying all that cheers the sight
      With blighting powers.

Eccles. xii.—3*rd*

" ' Ere yet the keepers of the house
Shall tremble like the cowering mouse,
An' strong men sink, their vigour loose.
      An' grinders few,
· An' darken'd windows, all obtuse,
      Obstruct the view.

Eccles. xii.—4*th*.

" ' When ilka door in ilka street,
Fast closed, the weary eye shall meet,

And music's daughters sadly beat,
  With trembling blow,
The weeping harp, once soft an' sweet,
  For they are low.

Eccles. xii.—*5th.*
"'When fear shall haunt both night an' day,
Like shadows cast upon the way,
An' almond trees, in foliage gay,
  Shall flourish rare,
An' the despised grasshopper may
  Increase despair.

"'When fond desire shall cease to flow,
Because men surely, swiftly go
In myriads to that home below,
  Death's mansion's seat,
An' mourners move, despairing slow,
  About the street.

Eccles. xii.—*6th.*
"'Ere yet the silver cord unbound,
Shall fall, unheeded, to the ground ;
E'er yet, in fragments, may be found
  The golden bowl,
Or shattered pitcher scattered round
  Betray the whole.

"'Or e'er the wheel in fragments lie
Beside the cistern, parched an' dry,
An' thirst, unquenched, despairing, cry—
  'Alas, undone !
No longer hope, here let me die,
  Since all are gone.'

Eccles. xii.—*7th.*

"'Then shall the dust to kindred dust
Return, inanimate—it must—
An' soaring high in faith an 'trust,
    The spirit calm
An' free shall seek the good an' just—
    The great I Am.

"'Fear, then, thy great Creator's name
In reverence, still His counsel claim,
An' let it be thy constant aim
    To keep His laws,
Immutable as whence they came,
    The great First Cause."

"So mote it be," low, solemn, clear,
Broke then upon my listening ear.
I bent in reverence an' fear,
    With awe inspired,
Imploring the Most High to hear
    What I desired.

Thus fortified I forward went,
While all around, with eyes intent,
The careful brethren closely bent
    Their gaze on me,
To satisfy themselves anent
    Propriety.

All satisfied, they marked it once,
Clear an' emphatic they pronounce
My bearing proper, and announce
    Their will at least,
That I should challenge the response
    Towards the East.

With solemn steps, like captive led,
Towards the East I onward hied,
Expectant, hopeful, yet afraid,
          I knew not why,
Whilst music soft and sweetly shed
          Its halo nigh.

With outstretched hand I challenge gave,
When one, with voice and manner grave,
Inquired of me what I would have,
          And whence I came;
Ma guide the information gave,
          All but ma name.

" Your answer sets all doubt at rest,
So place oor brither in the West,
The wardens will, at your request
          An' ma command,
Instruct him to approach the East,
          An' how to stand."

Wi' muckle care an' due regard
To ancient form, both fast an' hard,
The wardens taught me how, when squared,
          Tae place ma feet,
That e'en one step would bring reward,
          An' light complete.

Then, placed in humble posture near
The three great lights, in accents clear,
I promised, with a heart sincere,
          I wad be true
Tae a' that's held by Masons dear
          Life's journey through.

Then, by a friendly, kindly haun',
The gloom that shrouded was withdrawn,
And bright effulgent light, as dawn
          In summer morn,
Burst on ma wondering vision, an'
          Within was borne.

Here, retrospective vision cast
Its view o'er all that I had passed,
An' clearly showed, from first tae last,
          Progression made.
I listened with attention fast,
          But nothing said.

Each moral, luminous an' clear,
Was made in order to appear
That I might gather how they bear
          Each on the other,
An' how the whole combined would cheer
          Each toiling brother.

I saw how first, quite as a child,
I was admitted, wayward, wild,
An' how, when taught by precept mild.
          I might be free,
And claim with those, tho' Princes styled,
          Equality.

An' next when passed, maturer grown,
The force of intellect was shown
Ascending to the very throne
          Of God on high,
Almost omnipotent when prone
          Its power to try.

The secret stores of hidden Art
And Science, bared in every part,
Were thrust upon my brain and heart
       In grand profusion,
Enriching from the very start,
       Without confusion.

Yet, to the mind thus fortified
By moral truths and Art supplied,
Dame Nature other methods tried,
       By contemplation,
Ourselves to know, and nothing hide
       In meditation.

So that through life's much-chequer'd way
Our paths be pleasanter each day,
An' all more hopeful, cheerful may
       Still heavenward hie;
Man, living in integrity,
       Knows how to die.

Of this great truth our ancient roll
One bright example gives, whose soul,
Undaunted, stood, tho' murder foul,
       Surrendered quite,
Just e'er the Temple's beauteous whole
       Appeared in sight.

"Like him, let thy fidelity sustain,
Through threatened danger, fear, and pain,
Nor seek dishonoured peace to gain
       By trust betrayed;
An' now, let memory clear retain
       All I have said.

Ma fortitude, by trial severe,
Was tested then in manner queer,
But resolute, and void of fear,
    I all withstood,
Resolv'd, tho' it should cost me dear
    Life's purple flood.

Twice heckled, as by foes assailed,
I persevered an' never quailed
Nor shrank, when lastly I was hailed
    By Jubalum,
Who vowed that now, tho' others failed,
    Ma end had come.

"Forbear, rash man, thy murd'rous threat,
Wait till the Temple is complete,
And when the three Grand Masters meet,
    Thy wish make known;
I cannot, dare not, shall not treat
    With thee alone."

"Then, never shall the widow's son
See finished what he has begun,
While others strike an' only stun,
    By trembling blow,
I seal thy fate e'er I have done,
    An' lay thee low."

As prone before the raging blast
The stately oak is prostrate cast,
Or levelled with the deck the mast
    Of labouring barque,
Methinks I fell, an' I had past
    Death's portal dark.

Swift, then, as thought's unmeasured flight
Methinks I rose in ærial height,
Whilst guardian angels, left an' right,
    Ma chariot bore
To lands were earth and air delight,
    Unseen before.

O'er spreading plain, in verdure gay,
O'er stream, an' lake, an' mountain grey,
O'er ocean wide, far, far away,
    Was our design;
Nor ceased our flight till bid to stay
    In Palestine.

Fair land of promised rest an' bliss,
Reward of faith an' holiness;
When from the weary wilderness
    The chosen band
Emerged triumphant o'er distress,
    At God's command.

Fair land of temple, grove, an' shrine
Where Aaron's patriarchal line,
Extolling Covenant divine,
    Devotion led;
Where olive an' the spreading vine
    Abundance shed.

Here, on Moriah's towering brow,
Methinks I rest untended now,
Near to the Temple, where, somehow,
    Confusion reign'd,
I marvelled, an', that I might know,
    My ears I strained.

A voice, as if of one in power,
I heard demand what was the hour,
And why confusion all out o'er
      The works prevailed;
High twelve had struck, and what was more,
      The plans had failed.

"The plans had failed, and Hiram fled?
Search ye at once: he may be dead;
And instant let the roll be read,
      That I may tell
If all are faithful to their trade,
      And doing well."

"Alas! great King, this has been done,
And three are missing, whither gone
No one can tell, we feared to own
      Desertion here,
Where peace and harmony have shone,
      Our task to cheer.

"Assemble, then, in Lodges three,
And search all round unto the sea:
I fear some great calamity
      Our grief may swell,
And sorrowful the news may be
      You have to tell."

Full many days, in anxious thought,
The King himself for Hiram sought
In vain, till time and fortune brought
      The searchers home
Successful, but, alas! their lot
      Was cast in gloom.

"Hail, you who mark meridian sun,
Haste! tell me how your search has run."
"Great King, our labours, once begun,
    Untiring sped,
Until, at last, we met with one
    Who, questioned, said :

"He had that morning, near the sea,
Encountered weary travellers three,
Who, by their dress, he took to be
    From Temple here,
And who had vainly tried to lea'
    The country clear.

"But an embargo, lately placed
Upon the shipping, had distressed
Their weary hearts, so they retraced
    Their steps inland ;
We also inland quickly paced
    As by command.

"For many miles, o'er hill and dale,
We closely followed in their trail,
Until at last a mournful wail
    Of grief and woe
Came floating on the evening gale
    From cavern low.

"Full well the wretches there we knew,
Our cause was just and valour true ;
We overpowered them, and to you
    Have captive led
The three, that justice may pursue
    Their guilty deed."

"'Tis well; let justice then declare,
In answer to their guilty prayer,
The punishment for crime so rare
    And unprovoked
Must be extreme; 'tis only fair,
    And self-invoked.

" And you, good Warden of the West,
Make known the outcome of your quest;
You seem with grief and woe oppressed,
    What is your pain?"
"Alas, great King! I am distressed,
    Our Master's slain.

"Long had we searched, but all in vain,
And were returning home again,
Footsore, and weary, and with pain
    In saddened breast,
When, to refresh our toil-worn train,
    I called a rest.

"One of our band, in spot obscure,
On rising to resume our tour,
Caught by a shrub to make secure,
    But quickly found
The promised succour was but poor—
    It left the ground.

"This caused him to inspect with care
The cause of this, a thing so rare;
When lo, he found, but lately there
    It shadow gave
And marked a spot proportioned square—
    A new-made grave.

"He hailed his comrades quickly round,
And, pointing to the little mound,
Expressed his fear that underground
    Their labour lay.
'Twas so; on further search we found
    Great Hiram's clay.

"We've marked with reverential care
The lonely grave of Hiram, where
On Mount Moriah, bleak and bare,
    His ashes lie;
And haste our labours to declare
    To thee, most high."

"Thus far thy labours I approve,
But let us now his dust remove
With reverence, respect, and love,
    To Royal tomb;
He ranks with princes now above
    All earthly gloom."

"Thus slow methinks the mournful train
Passed on to music's heavenly strain,
While swelling heart and throbbing brain
    Inhaled the tone
In ecstasy, while once again
    I reasoned on.

Where, Death, was now thy venomed sting,
The terror both of clown and king?
I felt it not, nor can it bring
    The righteous pain,
Who wisely walk in virtue's ring,
    Like Hiram slain.

Where, Grave, thy victory can it be!
When, soaring high, the soul set free
Wings onward to eternity
      Of love and light;
Fair creature of Divinity,
        Unsullied, bright!

Thus reason sped, untrammelled quite,
Tho' shrouded in the shades of night;
I seemed to lie where day and night
      Are all as one;
Nor pomp nor passion can delight,
      And life is done.

But raised at last by cunning art,
With breast to breast and throbbing heart,
I stand once more to take a part
      In all around,
Whilst love and wisdom both impart
      The mystic sound.

Low as a whisper of the gale,
That wafts the fragrance of the vale,
When flowerets all their sweets exhale
      O'er dewy sward,
The listening ears in wonder hail
      The mystic word.

'Tis thus all Master Masons free
Are raised to new vitality
On points of friendship, two and three—
      Peculiar band—
Our love we pledge in secrecy,
      As close we stand.

Instruction then directs the view,
In darkness visible, 'tis true,
And marks how vain to pierce it through
        All efforts are,
Unless when rays celestial shew
        And shine afar.

Yet e'en this cheerless, darksome gloom
Can not obscure the yawning tomb
That silently proclaims thy doom
        When life shall cease,
'Twill clasp thee, though in youthful bloom,
        In cold embrace.

MORTALITY.

And, now, behold these emblems here,
Which bid mortality appear,
And stir the heart with awe and fear,
        And pride rebuke,
Nay, start not, let us venture near,
        And closer look.

Behold, can aught in Nature wide
Than these more justly warn and chide
Unbridled passion, greed, and pride,
        Pomp and display,
Or yet by pointed moral guide
        From day to day.

Can aught in Art in form excel
The structure of this mouldering shell,
Or Science, wide in range, dispel
        The wonder here,
On which our tear-dimm'd eyes now dwell
        In awe and fear.

Can aught of Art in Greece or Rome
Compare with this most wondrous dome,
In Nature's school designed—the home
    Of intellect,
Divinely formed and perfect from
    Its Architect?

Can column of Corinthian mould
Compare with these you now behold,
Proportioned just in line and fold,
    Art's model still?
No sculpture rivals, howe'er bold,
    Nor ever will.

These other emblems—scythe and glass—
Time symbolise and teach how pass
The golden moments which, alas!
    Are oft misspent
In paths where care and grief harass
    Our best intent.

WARNING.

Be careful, then, while yet 'tis day,
And reason, unimpaired, holds sway,
Whatever task allotted may
    Be thine to do ;
Do ere the light has passed away,
    And night ensue.

Continue still with conscious ear
That voice of Hope within to hear,
Which says, a "life immortal dear,
    But refuge claims
Within these tabernacles here,"
    Our mortal frames.

PRIVILEGES.

And, now, thy fortitude and zeal
Demand we should those arts reveal,
Whereby all brothers hail and hele
　　　The world o'er,
And recognise in woe and weal
　　　The mystic power.

First let this badge, by princes worn,
In proper lines thy front adorn,
And symbolise, both night and morn,
　　　Thy right to teach,
Less favoured those, in darkness born,
　　　Within thy reach.

WORKING TOOLS.

And let these implements of art,
In full significance, impart
The Golden Rule that guides—the chart
　　　That never fails
To guide aright the wavering heart
　　　When doubt assails.

The "Skerrit," with extending line,
Points out that path, by law divine,
Prescribed for us; let it be thine
　　　To walk therein,
Tho' all companionship you tine,
　　　Of kith and kin.

The pencil faithful to record,
Obedient as our thoughts afford,
Remind us that in heaven our Lord
　　　A record keeps
Of every action, thought, and word,
　　　And never sleeps.

The compasses unerring will
Remind you of His justice still,
Encircling all, both good and ill,
  Impartially,
And marking with infinite skill
  Our destiny.

The trowel, emblem of our trade,
Will teach love's soft cement to spread
Unsparingly in one deep bed
  Throughout the land,
Uniting all till all have said,
  As one we stand.

Moral.

Thus symbolising, you will see,
The working tools of this degree
Point out that path, from trouble free,
  To peace above,
Where all are bound eternally
  In filial love.

Signals.

And, now, receive these tokens grand—
I give thee them with outstretched hand;
They kindred sympathies command
  Wherever shown—
In desert wide, or coral strand,
  Or lands unknown.

Our working sign, on centre shown,
To Master Masons only known,
Will guide thy mind to dwell upon
  Thy pledge sincere,
And indicate thy rank, when thrown
  To Brothers dear.

And should e'er horror move thy heart,
A further signal will impart,
Its full significance by art
   Unknown to others,
Than those we hail by hand and heart
   Acknowledged Brothers.

Should further anguish move thy soul,
Too strong to master or control,
A further signal shews the whole
   Distress within,
In language clear as written scroll
   Has ever done.

And further yet your care bestow,
If other signals you would know,
And mark aright the waning glow
   Of fleeting breath,
As death steals o'er the clammy brow—
   Sure sign of death.

And, finally, I would impress
Upon thy mind the sacredness
Of this grand signal of distress
   Ere I have done;
'Twill succour bring in wretchedness
   To widow's son.

CHARGE.

And now, concluding, let me briefly say,
 Thy merit claims this privilege at our hands.
No other title, though assuming, may
 Petition here, or with success commands
 The privileges that bind enduring bands,

Outliving life itself in ties of love
  Conferred by kindred, strong outstretching hands
And hearts, desirous and aglow, to prove
How strong and true the feelings are that move.

Now high thy rank, let virtue be thy guide
  In all life's crowded manifold concerns;
Let thy example lead, reprove, or chide,
  And show the rich reward true manhood earns.
  Unshaken faith, with hope illumined, discerns
The blissful haven of the promised land,
  And fortifies the trembling soul that learns
The righteous counsel, the divine command,
  "Be thou prepared before My throne to stand."

MASONIC CEREMONIAL.

[The following lines were suggested by the laying of the Foundation
  Stone of Glasgow Bridge (with Masonic Honours) on October
  8th, 1896, by Bro. Sir James Bell, Hon. Lord Provost of
  Glasgow, assisted by Bro. John Graham of Broadstone, and
  other office-bearers and members of Provincial Lodge, and a
  large turnout of Brethren.]

Ye craftsmen a', wha deftly draw
    Wi compasses an' pencil,
Attend to-day, in grand array,
    Wi' banners trimmed wi' tinsel.
Oor Provost, Brither Jamie Bell—
    Weel worthy o' his title—
Has wark in haun' for square an' mell
    He means this day tae settle,
        Be't wet or dry.

Sae busk yoursel's, put on your best,
  Hae a' your jewels shining,
An' tosh an' trig let a' be dress'd,
  Harmoniously combining
Tae lend a haun' wi' richt guid will,
  An' mak' the wark fu' stable,
Wi' a' your mystic art an' skill,
  As weel as ye are able
      Tae dae't this day.

Oor city's commerce, north an' south,
  Continuously expanding,
Has lang declared its growth, forsooth,
  Was better care demanding
Than it o' late had had frae some
  Wha ocht tae hae kent better,
When lood it cried, "Mair elbo' room
  Tae get across the water
      Wi' ease ilk day."

Oor brig, the "Broomielaw" by name,
  For years has been complaining,
An' vow'd it was a cryin' shame
  Its arches tae be straining
Wi' loads enormous, nicht an' day,
  An' yearly aye increasing,
An' threatened it wad fa' away
  Unless the toil were ceasing,
      An' that ere lang.

The protest reachéd George's Square,
  Whaur sit the City Faithers,
An' caused nae sma' commotion there,
  As it had done wi' ithers.

Some Councillors glower'd, wi' specs on nose,
  As gloomy as December,
An' wonder'd hoo the polls might close
  Wi' them come next November
    Should they refuse.

Some, tim'rous, thocht they should delay
  Discussion o' the matter,
For fear the public voice micht say
  They should hae managed better;
But ithers, kennin' what was what,
  Wad hae the matter settled
Richt off-hand, whaurin they sat,
  Tho' voters should be nettled
    At what was done.

A new brig, there an' then they vow'd,
  Should soon replace the auld ane;
The undertaking, a' allowed,
  Was something o' a bauld ane.
But auld Saint Mungo's sons are famed
  For schemes that are gigantic—
Some few o' which, when firstly named,
  Maist drove some bodies frantic
    Wi' fricht that day.

"But wha should lay foundation stane?"
  Was next a kittle matter,
An' ere discussion far had gane,
  Was settled—"fa wha better
Than Provost Bell, the good Sir James,
  A Maister Mason—shairly
Nae ither chiel had better claims
  Tae lay it snod and squarely
    Wi' 'maul' that day."

His skill nae "Cowan" could dispute,
  His worth nane could deny it,
An' a' the Lodges roon' aboot
  Wad come tae see him try it.
"The function wad be grand," they said,
  "Baith solemn and imposing,
An' then! oh, my! the after spread
  Wad be a glorious closing
    For some that day."

Thus it was settled. Word was sent
  By circular, inviting
The Lodges a', wi' best intent,
  Tae wark they wad delight in.
An' tae assist the maist were fain,
  Though gusty winds were blawing,
An' drenching showers o' chilly rain
  Fu' frequently were fa'ing—
    Fu' cauld that day.

But what can damp the Mason's zeal
  When corner stane is laying?
Or mak' him frae his duty wheel,
  A craven heart displaying?
The elements may rant an' roar,
  The driving blast may bluster;
The rain in torrents doon may pour,
  But he'll attend the muster,
    Let come what may.

His best are waled frae oot the kist,
  Whaur lang they've lain unshifted,
An' if his black coat should be *missed*,
  He kens fine whaur tae lift it.

For whiles it's lent oot tae a frien',
  For sma' consideration,
Wha rolls it up tae keep it clean
  For some sic like occasion
    As this to-day.

A sash an' apron, if he's nane,
  He e'en maun beg or borrow,
Wi' promises, renewed again,
  He'll send them back to-morrow.
To cheat or steal he daurna try,
  Sae his request is granted,
An', dressed wi' them, he'll blithely hie
  Just tae the place appointed,
    Fu' proud that day.

Some do get dressed in faultless fit,
  Wi' cosy twilted linings ;
Some daurna stoop tae tie their bit,
  For fear they burst the joinings.
Some coats are plush o' downy hair,
  Their newness thus bespeaking ;
Some glazed wi' wear, an' gey threadbare,
  An' much in need o' steaking
    ' Wi' thread this day.

Some look like lovers gaun tae see
  Their sweethearts, blithe and jauntie ;
Some blate an' modest as can be,
  An' some a wee thing cantie.
Some step alang wi' martial stride,
  Wi' head on high uprearing ;
Some sloutch alang, as if tae hide
  Frae public gaze an' jeering,
    Wi' shame this day.

See here's oor Marshal, Tailor Will,
  On big bay horse careering;
Like " Quixote" charging some windmill,
  He'll set us a' a-steering.
He marks wi' pride the motley thrang,
  An' points oor proper places;
The order's passed the ranks alang,
  An' smiles flit o'er oor faces,
     Amused this day.

He's evidently ill at ease,
  His horse will be contrairy;
He tries his best the beast tae please,
  An' cause it quietly carry.
But deil ae bit—it will uprear,
  Near emptying the saddle,
While, dootless, mony an inward swear,
  An' wish for't in the stable,
     He gies this day.

Whiles gently pattin't on the neck,
  Wi' kindly haun' caressing;
While in its ribs his heels are set,
  Wi' painfu' dig distressing;
Whiles wi' a jerk the reins get loose,
  Then aff wi' speed 'twill clatter;
An' some remark, " A tailor's goose
  Wad fit his haun' much better
     Than reins this day."

Next, mark ye weel that pompous chiel,
  His name we needna mention,
Wi' jewels decked frae head tae heel,
  Just tae attract attention.

He's sprung frae nocht, he's naething yet,
  But bumptious as a bantam;
He's fawned an' favoured lang tae get
  That gilded, gaudy phantom—
      His rank—this day.

He's high in rank, nae doot o' that,
  An' higher still he's aiming;
He sits whaur better men hae sat,
  Wi' far mair merit claiming.
He's got a wee bit gift o' gab,
  An' kens who wi't tae flatter;
But, as fur wark, the plainest slab
  Wad test his skill tae better,
      I'm sure this day.

That ither chap, wi' visage sour,
  Was aince a poor inspector;
In Lodge debate he's stern an' dour,
  In fight a very "Hector."
For lang he made the air tae ring
  Wi' matters controversial;
But Grand Lodge quietly drew his sting
  By making him a Marshal,
      Wi' power this day.

The ither chiels, unknown tae fame,
  Unless what check procures them,
Are oor *superiors* a' the same,
  As lang's Grand Lodge endures them.
But hoo they e'er attained sic rank
  Is mystery past divining,
Unless it were by quirk an' prank,
  Or better men declining
      The post that day.

There's ane o' them at least I ken,
    Unmatched for bold presumption,
Who's speech betrays him now an' then
    As unco scarce o' gumption.
He talks fur talkin's sake, it's said,
    No' that his style is pleasing,
An' rules o' grammar a' are laid
    Aside wi' coolness freezing
        Ilk time he speaks.

But here comes Daddy Graham himsel',
    Oor Grand Provincial Master,
An' by his side Lord Provost Bell,
    Wha's gaun tae spread the plaster.
A weel-matched pair—for worth, I mean—
    Tho' differing in stature;
Men are alike when hearts are clean,
    An' gentlemen by nature,
        Tho' e'er sae poor.

We canna a' be lords an' dukes,
    Wi' menial trains attending;
A few o' wha are moral flukes,
    An' guid for nocht but spending.
Wha's hale concern's o' themsel's,
    Debauch their highest pleasure;
Whose heart-throbs beat like cracked bells,
    Wi' uncongenial measure,
        Quite musicless.

The test o' worth's an *honest* heart,
    Wi' warm impulses throbbing,
An' scorns tae act that meanest part—
    A fellow-creature robbing.

The heart that prompts tae help distress,
　An' starts the tear o' sorrow,
When gloom surrounds like wilderness
　The prospects of to-morrow
　　　Wi' dread an' fear.

The State may show its sense o' worth,
　Reward wi' rank an' honour;
But canna gie real merit birth
　That Nature takes upon her.
She stamps her hall-mark in the breast
　At birth, unseen by ony,
An' leaves tae Faither Time the rest—
　The setting o't sae bonny—
　　　As time goes on.

Thus Graham an' Bell are rank'd sae high,
　Oor best respect commanding;
Let's doff our hats as they pass by,
　Tho' in the rain we're standing.
They're surely worth a drookit pow,
　If they're what I've been saying—
There, noo they've passed, let's follow now
　An' see the stane a-laying,
　　　Fu' snod this day.

Guid save us, sic a blast o' rain,
　It mak's a body shiver;
I hope it hasna blawn the stane
　An' a' intae the river.
No, there it is by *Lewis* hung,
　O' rain an' wind a scorner;
Hurrah, hurrah! with pith o' lung
　Richt i' the north-east corner,
　　　Fu' safe as yet.

Noo, mark wi' care a' that's gaun on—
    The band's just started playing
"God Save the Queen," lang may her throne
    Show nae sign o' decaying.
Next come the choir.   Their voices blend
    In praise wi' "Hail Eternal."
An' then the chaplain's words ascend,
    Enjoining love fraternal,
        As long's we live.

Next forward step, wi' jaunty air,
    Provincial Scribe and Treasurer,
Wi' casket fu' o' relics rare,
    An' coins o' various measure there,
Which soon are placed in hollow stone.
    The workmen next are wanted;
But e'er the labour's entered on
    "Auld Hundred" has been chanted
        Richt earnestly.

An' while the choir their voices blend
    The upper stone's in motion;
It's stopped *thrice*, but i' the end
    Is laid i' proper fashion.
The Master then stan's i' the east,
    Tae see the stane's adjusted
According tae oor rules, at least.
    Nae random wark is trusted—
        Be't e'er sae grand.

Ane tries his plumb on ilka side,
    To see it's justly bearing;
An' when the level has been tried
    The square's applied for squaring.

The Master then, wi' mall in haun',
  Expressing satisfaction,
Knocks fast the stane, again, again.,
  Pronouncing benediction
    On's wark this day.

Three cheers by a', again the choir,
  Their tunefu' voices raising,
Sing "God of Light," with pith an' fire,
  His flowing bounties praising.
An' then the corn, wine, an' oil
  Are sprinkled o'er unsparing,
Solicitous that nocht may spoil
  The structure we're upraising
    Wi' care this day.

The band aince mair oor anthem plays,
  The choir ance mair hae chanted;
The Provost's words o' thanks an' praise
  Are gien whaur maist they're wanted.
An' "Rule Britannia" swells the air,
  Oor loyal hearts inspiring
Wi' thochts o' hame an' comforts there,
  Sae let us be retiring,
    Weel pleased this day.

Some straggle hame as best they can,
  Through miry dub and puddle;
Some, blithe tae meet their fellow-man,
  Remain tae hae a fuddle.
But a' are pleased an' proud at heart,
  An' gled that they consented
Tae tak', though 'twere a humble part,
  In wark sae weel cemented
    As this to-day.

LINES SUGGESTED BY A VISIT TO LODGE "BEN CLEUCH," AND ADDRESSED TO THE GRAND LODGE.

Ye may weel be prood o' your wean, auld wife,
  Ye may weel be prood o' your wean,
For a healthier bairn I've seldom seen,
  And never may see again.

Sae plump an' steerin', tae, for her years,
  Sae mannerly, tae, beside,
An' sae pawkie an' droll the things she speirs,
  Her knowledge sae varied an' wide.

She's a wonnerfu' wean, jist three years auld,
  Tae crack sae glib o' sic things
As morals, religion, heat an' cauld;
  An' tae hear hoo she prays an' sings

Wad tickle the heart o' a saint divine,
  Tho' he leeved in the darkest cell,
An' had vowed he would shun a' womankind
  An' spurn their charming spell.

Her very name is strange—an' it's rare,
  For a lassie, at least, you'll say;
"Ben Cleuch," what a name tae adorn so fair
  A bairn, as blithesome as May!

An' her very manners are a' sae fine
  That you'd say she'd been years at schule;
But they're natural gifts that glist'ning shine,
  An' mak' her a favourite still.

OUR PLEDGE RENEW.

[Written for the Brethren of Tarbolton Lodge,
25th January, 1895.]

Ye sons of light, ye mystic few,
  Whose heart the glow of friendship warms;
Pledge once again, again renew
  Our pledge to him whose memory charms.
He asked it once midst fears' alarms,
  When frowning fortune scouled fu' grim;
He ask'd it here in tenderest terms,
  That yearly we should pledge to him.

Then, pledge his memory, ever dear,
  An' dearer aye as years go by.
When yearly we assemble here,
  Let jealousy nor care be nigh,
Let all who feel the mystic tie,
  In louder praise its bonds declare.
He ask'd for this with "brimful eye,"
  It was his wish, it was his prayer.

The circling year brings many joys
  To all who keep the unerring line,
And once again bids us rejoice,
  In memory of our bard divine.
Our brother bard, whose love benign
  Embraced mankind from pole to pole,
Fulfilling Nature's grand design,
  In brotherhood to bind the whole.

Then, let us pledge his memory here,
  Where oft he sat in seat supreme,
Where oft his voice, in accents clear,
  Has told the sweet Masonic theme.

Where hallowed memories ever teem,
　　And chasten as the day returns
That gave the world that gift supreme,
　　A child of genius, Robert Burns.

AULD MITHER KILWINNING.

A venerable body is Mother Kilwinning,
　　Tho' still she is stately in form,
Her sons they are numerous, sturdy, an' cunning,
　　In craftship a' tasks tae perform, perform,
　　In craftship a' tasks tae perform.

Her age I'll no' tell, for it's never been kent
　　Exactly the year she was born in,
But every ane owns that her time has been spent
　　In the best o' a' causes, adorning, adorning.
　　In the best o' a' causes adorning.

Langsyne, when the auldest among us were young,
　　An' glaiket, as cullans will aye be,
We heard o' her worth, and her praises were sung
　　By oor sires when they met o'er a drappie, a drappie,
　　By oor sires when they met o'er a drappie.

We wonder'd at times, tho' we couldna mak' oot,
　　The sense o' their sang or their crack, aye,
Wha the auld body was that they spak' sae about
　　Wi' sae mony braw sons at her back aye, her back aye,
　　Wi' sae mony braw sons at her back aye.

They were said tae be this, an' were said tae be that,
　　They were said tae be sonsie and bonny,

An' sae fond o' the place where the auld body sat
  That they ne'er could forget it for ony, for ony,
  That they ne'er could forget it for ony.

It was said she had sons in a' parts o' the laun,
  An' some were exalted in station,
Tho' ithers were poor they could aye lend a haun'
  Tae relieve the distress o' the nation, the nation,
  Tae relieve the distress o' the nation.

The widow an' orphan hae never in vain
  Besought their assistance in trouble,
An' a' are sae plumblike that never a stane
  Has been cast at their name tae gie trouble, gie trouble.
  Has been cast at their name tae gie trouble.

It was said when she gathered her family aroon',
  Tae teach them their lessons sae trying.
The doors were secured an' the blinds were drawn doon
  Jist tae keep the ootsiders frae prying, frae prying,
  Jist tae keep the ootsiders frae prying.

It was said that a stranger ne'er darken'd her door,
  An' she hated a' clyping an' clashing ;
Was pack wi' the rich and was kind tae the poor,
  An' cared nae a preen for the fashion, the fashion,
  An' cared nae a preen for the fashion.

Lang may the auld body—she's aye leeving yet—
  Continue her ways ever haimly,
An' watch o'er her bairns ilk time they are met,
  A thriving, affectionate faimly, faimly,
  A thriving, affectionate faimly.

OOR TEMPLE'S STATELY FORM APPEARS.

[An Address to the Masonic Craft.]

Ye craftsmen, a' wha gauge an' rule,
An' deftly han'le ilka tool
That beautifies baith kirk an' school,
  Wi' cunning art,
Nae langer noo be dow an' dool,
  Wi' saddened heart.

At last, an' efter mony years,
Oor Temple's stately form appears;
An' noo, as ilka arch uprears,
  In graceful lines,
Oor auld reproach, oor doots an' fears,
  Ilk Mason tines.

Nae langer shall we look distress'd,
When travellers frae the Sooth or West
Come tae oor toon, an' fain wad rest
  Their weary feet,
Whaur kindred spirits please them best,
  An' Masons meet.

E'en auld St. Mungo marks wi' pride,
An' joy he doesna try tae hide,
Ane mair amang his Mansions wide,
  Baith braw an' grand;
An' vows it will compare beside
  Ocht in the land.

"Hurrah!" he cries, his heart fu' fain,
"Hurrah! hurrah! hurrah again!
Nae langer noo my sons complain,
  As I'm a saunt;
I often had remarked, wi' pain,
  There was a want.

"Till ane, Jock Graham (excuse me, John),
Beheld oor want, an' heard oor moan,
An' vowed he wad see ilka stane
   Should be prepared;
Though a' unaided an' alone—
   If he were spared.

"Hale be his hide, his heart aye soun',
Wi' nocht tae vex him up or doun;
An' as the circling year gaes roun',
   O, Time, be kind!
Anither Graham in a' the toun
   We mayna find.

"Had I the lease o' temporal power,
An' could on him fresh honours shower,
I'd change his name this very hour,
   An' make it known,
Baith far an' wide the country o'er,
   As now Sir John.

"A worthier baronet, I'm share,
Ne'er buckled sword or carried spear,
Than he wad be; but, oh, I fear—
   Yet wha can tell
What honours are in store tae cheer
   His worthy sel'?

"As Patron Saint, Saint Mungo, I
Wi' heart sincere an' glowing eye,
Bless thee an' thine! May the Most High
   Thy Guardian be,
John Graham, should danger e'er be nigh,
   Tae menace thee."

"Hear, hear," say I, plain Tam M'Phail,
Wi' heart as warm an' wish as real;
May he ne'er want for brose or kail,
    Tae clead his wame;
An' routh o' claes tae pick an' wale,
    For ilka Graham.

"May poverty, that gruesome chiel,
Ne'er cast his shadow owre thy biel!
May ye ne'er want for maut or meal,
    A groat tae spend,
Or trusty cronie, true an' leal,
    A sterling friend.

"Wide o'er the lan', frae pole tae pole,
The Craft thy labours will extol,
Rehearsing oft, as onward roll,
    Year after year,
The peerless worth that moved thy soul,
    An' oentred here.

"Here hame o' Art, an' future shrine
O' mystic lore an' love divine,
Whaur ties fraternal shall entwine
    Each beating heart;
An' sage-like precept shall ootline
    Life's better part.

"Here, Gracious Architect Supreme,
Preside, an' guide the work sublime,
Till a' hae ser'd their lawful time,
    However frail,
An' nearer tae perfection climb,
    Prays TAM M'PHAIL."

THE SONS OF THE MYSTIC TIE.

Tune—"The Old Brigade."

Here's to the Brethren of 128,
　And all other sons of light ;
Here's to the Craft and the mystic state,
　And the cause for which we fight.
Here's to the Three Great Lights still seen
　Shining so brightly, where
The Sun in his glorious golden sheen
　First gladdens the earth so rare.

　　Then happily, happily together,
　　　Sons of the mystic tie,
　　Join in the song steadfast and strong,
　　　With the Three Great Lights still nigh.

Here's to the Temple built sublime,
　And the three great Masters there ;
Here's to the Light in the East Divine,
　The Compasses, Plummet, and Square.
Here's to the Level truly laid,
　And the Mallet in Master's hand ;
And here's to the love and attention paid
　When the Master gives command.
　　　　Then happily, happily together, etc.

Here's to the Three Grand Pillars all,
　And the ladder with rounds so few,
And the Rule that proportions the time to all,
　And the Chisel that cuts so true.
Here's to the Word and the Grip of Hand,
　And the silent Mystic Sign
That unites the noblest in every land
　In the bonds of a Love Divine.
　　　　Then happily, happily together, etc.

Here's to the dangers we all have passed,
   And the death we are taught to die,
And the silence that over our Craft has cast
   A grandeur so great and high.
Here's to the heart that is taught to conceal,
   And to glow with that mystic love,
And the Temple that only the light can reveal,
   That is shed by the Master above.
       Then happily, happily together, etc.

ADDRESS TO MR. HUGH M'COLL ON THE OCCASION
OF HIS SILVER WEDDING.

28th June, 1895.

Lang may you live, my auld freen' Hugh,
The whale o' cronies tried and true;
May future years wi' joys aye new
      Your heart aye gladden,
An' happy memories glisten through
      Your silver wedding.

Your silver wedding! blissful year,
What memories crowd, what scenes appear!
What hopes, still rising, warm and cheer
      Thy toilsome way,
Sustaining still the load you bear
      From day to day.

Reflection backward points wi' pride,
An' marks when first your bonnie bride,
Wi' love and joy she scarce could hide,
      At Nuptial shrine
Gave thee her pledge, whate'er betide,
      She would be thine.

Through years of hope, wi' cares beset,
Unwavering love, without regret,
Still constant clung, and, glowing yet,
            Sedater grown
Perchance! but, as when first you met,
            'Tis still thy own.

Thy children's love—what greater joy?—
Has been thy bliss without alloy;
May Envy ne'er that love destroy,
            Nor cause thee tears,
And peace and harmony employ
            The coming years.

How blessed the home where filial love
Abides, and would its value prove,
By reverence stamped in every move
            Of budding youth,
And parents guide to life above,
            By love and truth.

Such bliss be thine for years to come,
A loving wife and happy home,
    And children blessed wi' heathful bloom
            Tae help and cheer
Their parents' hearts through ilka gloom
            For many a year.

THE BOWLING GREEN.

Air—"Come, Sit ye Doon, my Cronies."

When the summer sun is shining,
    And the fields are looking fair,
And the little warblers singing
    In the woodlands everywhere.

When the westlin' breezes gently
  ·Waft the fragrance of the bean,
I love to meet my cronies
    In a game upon the green.
    In a game upon the green.
    In a game upon the green.
I love to meet my cronies
    In a game upon the green.

Now, in throwing up the "Kitty"
  Oor first player's quite a card,
But in playing tae't he seldom
  Ever gangs within a yard.
While oor skip cries : "Throw them up, man ;
  What the devil dae ye mean ?
Losh, I never saw sic playing
  Since I joined a bowling green."
  Since I joined a bowling green.
  Since I joined the bowling green.
Losh, I never saw sic playing
  Since I joined a bowling green."

But oor second plays to order,
  An' he's aye about the jack ;
His first ane draws tae guard it,
  An' his second's at the back.
. Then oor third draws in a besom,
  Wi' his first bool in between,
While his second fills the only port
  Through which the "Kitty's" seen.
  Through which the "Kitty's" seen.
  Through which the "Kitty's" seen.
While his second fills the only port
  Through which the "Kitty's" seen.

Oor opponents seem dumbfoundered,
  But their skip, the sleekit wretch,
He plays his first a " Rider,"
  And dings " Kitty " in the ditch.
Then there's sic a burst o' cheering,
  An' sic a chaffing tae, I ween,
That gloomy Care gangs swearing
  He'll ne'er join a bowling green.
  He'll ne'er join a bowling green.
  He'll ne'er join a bowling green.
That gloomy Care gangs swearing
  He'll ne'er join a bowling green.

Oor skip then scans the end a wee,
  To see what can be dune,
We're lying second, sae tae win
  A bool's tae turn in.
His first he draws a kenning wide,
  His next'll tak' it clean ;
It does ! an' then if you but saw
  The capers on the green.
  The capers on the green.
  The capers on the green.
It does ! an' then if you but saw
  The capers on the green.

Ane throws his bonnet in the air
  An' capers o'er the lawn ;
Anither cries oot loud and clear :
  " Come 'ere, I'll shake your haun !"
While oor opponents, looking blue,
  Declare by open Book,

O' a' the shots they ever saw,
  There ne'er was sic a fluke.
  There ne'er was sic a **fluke.**
  There ne'er was sic a fluke.
O' a' the shots they **ever saw,**
  There ne'er **was sic a fluke.**

Thus goes the game, **an', win or lose,**
  Oor friendship's aye the **same,**
And cheerfully they tak' defeat
  Who know the fickle game.
To-day we lose, to-morrow win,
  'Tis the rule, I've often seen,
But pleasure ever present is
  When playing on the green.
  When playing on the green.
  When playing on the green.
But pleasure ever **present is**
  When playing on **the green.**

IN MEMORIAM.

Lowly, lowly,
  Ah! how lowly,
Is the spectacle of death;
  When some **loved one**—
  Dearly loved one—
Faintly draws the fleeting breath;

  When life's fleeting—
  Breath retreating—
Tells too truly death is nigh;

When despairing
Friends, tho' erring,
Weep in anguish, mourn and sigh.

Ah! could sighing
Save the dying,
Life for ever would extend;
And for ever—
Dying never—
Would we live while lived a friend.

Never ending—
Life extending;
Farewell, then, that bliss above,
Which we sigh for—
Wish to die for—
Living such as Lizzie Love.

Lizzie, youthful,
Meek, and truthful,
In the virgin bloom of life,
Tender hearted,
Now departed
From this scene of sin and strife.

Unrepining,
Still reclining
On the Christian's couch of Faith;
Drawing nearer—
Ever clearer—
She beheld the angel Death.

But how meekly,
Calm, and sweetly,
Like the Christ so lowly born,

She, unfearing,
Saw Death nearing,
But of all his terrors shorn.

Friends were near her—
All to cheer her—
And her smallest wish supply;
But, aspiring,
Her desiring
Soul sought comfort from on high;

Comfort, gracious,
Ever precious,
Comfort by this world unknown;
Comfort, truly,
Yet how freely,
Given by One, and One alone.

Tears were falling,
Grief, appalling,
Overshadowed every heart;
All were sighing
Save the dying,
Who of sorrow knew no part.

"Hush!" she murmurs;
But ye mourners
Think not 'tis in fretful mood.
See how sweetly—
Calm completely—
Smiles the maiden, pure and good.

"Come, dear Saviour,"
She, with fervour,
Sighs, "O, take me to Thine home;

How I weary!
Earth is dreary;
Here no more I wish to roam."

Thus confessing,
And addressing
He who hears the prayerful cry;
She the peerless,
Trusting fearless,
Sought her Saviour's presence nigh.

O, what treasure!
Who can measure
Half the bliss that prayers bring,
When the lowly,
Christlike holy,
Fondly to their Saviour cling?

Dim, yet dimmer,
As when summer
Twilight darkens all around,
Grew those beaming
Eyes, once teeming
With a holy light profound.

Near, yet nearer;
Hark! dost hear her
Voice, like softest sighing wind
When it lightly
Stirs, and slightly
Leaves the faintest sound behind?

Nearer, nearer;
Hark! dost hear her
Voice, in supplication's tone,

Sounding sweetly,
Faint and meekly,
"Gracious Lord, Thy will be done "?

Thus, life ended,
Prayer ascended,
With her last expiring breath
Plainly telling
Faith was dwelling
In the lamb who conquered Death.

AULD RITCHIE'S DEID.

[In Memory of the late Mr John Ritchie, who died on the 5th of
March, 1896, at 91 Gray Street, Parkhead, in his 82nd year.]

"Death! could ye no' yet langer spare
A heart sae kind, sae true, sae rare?
Could ye no' gang some ither where,
Wi' a' yer dreed,
Than here tae kill, wi' dirk an' snare,
Auld Ritchie deid?

"Hae ye no' quenched yersel' wi' gore
Wi' what's gaun on, an's gane before—
Whaur Turkish tyrants lord it o'er
The bleeding slave,
An' thoosands gang for evermore
Tae early grave?

"Ye ken yersel', grim-visaged loon,
A cantier cock in a' the toon
There wasna; yet ye steal aroon',
Wi' subtle art,
An' stab at him, wi' siccar stoon,
Richt through the heart.

"Had he been ane o' worth fu' scant,
Wha wadna work, an' wadna want,
Fu' o' hypocrisy an' cant—
      Yer pleasure, then.
But ane wha's praise we a' should chant,
      The wale o' men.

"I put it tae ye, fair an' square—
Na! haud ye yet, jist haud ye there;
Don't interrupt, I've something mair
      Tae say, my man,
That aiblins will make ye declare
      Ye'll watch yer haun'.

"He wasna ane tae cheat an' wrang,
Tae glunch an' gloom, tae bash an' bang,
Or side wi' a' the thochtless thrang
      Wad dae or say ;
Or cause his fellow mortal pang
      By nicht or day.

"His heid was clear, his heart was hale,
His mind aboon the sland'rer's tale—
Misfortune's sel' could ne'er avail
      Tae dump him lang.
He could the weary heart regale
      Wi' canty sang.

"What then, ye dreaded ne'er-dae-weel,
Made ye approach tae sic a chiel?
Can ye no' some compassion feel
      For noble worth,
An' spare sic men a while tae heal
      The ills o' earth?"

"Man, Davie, dinna ca' sae fast,"
Death ventured tae exclaim at last.
"Life's long allotted time was past,
  Ye will admit.
I ne'er wi' mair regret hae cast
  My shaft tae hit.

"I grant that a' you've said is true—
O' better men there's unco few.
The fact is this, 'twixt me an' you—
  If I maun tell—
I couldna langer life alloo,
  Or help mysel'.

"The job I hae is hampered roon'
Wi' strict conditions frae aboon;
An' gin I dinna mak' the stoon
  A vital prob,
Some ither chiel may fill my shoon,
  An' tak' my job!"

"Weel, after a', ye may be richt;
See, there's my haun', we winna fecht.
We a' maun gang, be't day or nicht;
  Say, is't agreed?
God grant I live wi' honour bricht,
  Like Ritchie, deid!"

———

EPISTLE TO A. CROCKET.

Dear Crocket, man, I got your note
 This morning, very early,
An' must confess, upon the spot,
 It flattered me fu' rarely

Tae learn a kindred chiel o' rhyme
  In sympathy was present,
Tae share my troubles at this time,
  An' wish me convalescent.
      But duly, an' truly,
        I here confession make :
      My fever was never
        Ocht but a mental ache.

Ye ken that whiles, for want o' ocht
  Real serious tae perplex us,
We do imagine evils wroucht,
  An' nurse them till they vex us,
Sae 'twas wi' me—I feared some ill
  Had overta'en oor papers,
An' couldna rest a minute still—
  Ye smile, an' say : " What capers!"
      But, mind ye, you'll find aye
        Imagined ills the warst ;
      At least they oor peace aye
        Hae much the oftener cursed.

But, noo that I hae thus explained
  What really was the matter,
I hope ye werna muckle pain'd
  By my unthochtfu' letter.
I didna mean tae wauken fears
  On my account whatever,
An' if I caused ye ony tears
  I'll blame mysel' for ever.
      For ever, an' ever,
        As lang as life is mine,
      I'll rue it, eschew it,
        By a' I hold divine.

Your kindly wishes, couched in rhyme,
  Hae set my heart aglowing,
Sae thus, withoot the loss o' time,
  My best regards I'm showing.
But, Andra, lad, my Muse, puir thing,
  Can scarce express my pleasure,
Or commonsense in couplets string,
  Tae pay ye back in measure.

      Sae hazy, an' lazy,
        The jaud has grown o' late
      That coaxing, or boxing,
        Wad scarce improve her state.

This morning, jist nae farther gane,
  When I got your epistle,
I thocht—alas! the thocht was vain—
  She'd blaw her penny whistle;
But deil ae blaw the bitch wad gie,
  Which put me in a fury.
I nearly swore; but no, not she
  Could see what was the hurry.

      But sulking, an' skulking
        'Mang reasons for delay,
      She teased me, displeased me,
        Ilk hour that passed away.

"Come here, ye jaud," quoth I at last,
  "Hae ye nae sense o' honour?
Come, pay in kind Kincardine's blast,
  You'll aiblins be the woner,"
She shook her heid in dolefu' mood,
  Entreating me tae spare her;
But a' her pleadings I withstood,
  Tho' seldom she looked fairer.

Sae sweetly, an' meekly—
  Her een dooncast the while;
An' blately, sedately,
  An' dootfu' did she smile.
What fears hae ye, you glaiket thing?
  What noo has taen your fancy?
Will you let Crocket pipe an' sing,
  Withoot the least response aye?
What will he think aboot us twa,
  But that we are fu' saucy?
Come, sit ye doon; cast care awa',
  My bonnie, bashfu' lassie.

  Thus, pleading and leading,
    My point I partly gain;
  But jimply, an' scrimply,
    An' no' her usual strain.

Wi' tearfu' e'e she bent her head,
  An' pled her want o' learning,
Her rugged notes, an' damaged reed,
  Her dress in need o' derning;
Her hamer-made attire, she pled,
  Was course an' oot o' fashion.
I owned the truth o' a' she said,
  An' quelled my former passion.

  For Truth, sir, like Youth, sir,
    Is ever fresh an' fair,
  An' wiles ye, beguiles ye,
    Frae anger an' frae care.

"Ne'er mind your garb," quoth I, "sweet lass,
  Nor yet your uncouth manner;
Many hamely folk you'll dootless pass
  When under Nature's banner.

The freaks o' Art may please the vain
  Wi' transient delusion,
But never can usurp the reign
  O' Nature in confusion.

      Nor alter what culture
        A' honest hearts confare—
      Enriching, bewitching,
        A' that its blessings share.

An' dootless, Crocket, cantie chiel,
  Indulgently will treat us,
An' can appreciate as weel
  As us the natural status.
If no', he's no' the man, I think,
  His writing clear discloses;
An' if he can, his health I'll drink
  Before the evening closes

      In whisky, fu' frisky.
        Here's tae ye, Andrew, lad;
      Your rhyme, man, was prime, man,
        An' tickled me no' bad.

But what a lang fraca' I've made
  In answer tae your letter,
An' left unwritten an' unsaid
  The most important matter!
I meant tae say: I wish ye weel,
  Wi' routh o' rhyme an' reason;
Wi' heid aye clear an' heart tae feel
  A' pleasures in their season.

      Fu' cantie; may want aye
        Gang by your door in haste,
      An' virtue support you
        In a' that's guid an' chaste.

.May ilka care an' dread o' ill
  That soors oor cup o' pleasure
Gang by your biel, an' never fill
  Your luggie wi' their measure.
May a' that sweetens life be yours,
  As lang as life ye claim it;
An' guard, O guard, wi' a' your powers
  Against ocht that can shame it.

 A guid name's the best fame
  We e'en may hope tae leave aye;
 Sae guard it, an' ward it,
  'S the wish o' Dainty Davie."

REPLY BY A. CROCKET.

Your rhyme has set a-jingling
  The music o' my heart;
My very nerves are tingling
  Wi' your poetic art;
And while I sit and ponder
  O'er measure, tread, an' style,
I notice, withoot wonder,
  You in the foremost file,

 Sae jaunty, sae cantie,
  Your thoughts, they jink alang;
 Sae breezy, sae easy,
  Ye mak' a lightsome sang.

Like sleigh-bells in the winter
  Your notes hae merry ring;
They e'en defy the printer,
  Your pen has sic a swing.

Their silvery chimes dae enter
  The portals o' my soul;
There they fin' nae dischanter
  Against their sweet control.

    An' moving, an' soothing,
      The lines a' seem tae be;
    Advising, surprising—
      A perfect melody.

I really think your labour
  Deserves a word or twa.
'Tis pleasant when a neighbour
  Upon a frien' does ca';
But when a brither poet,
  Wi' soul o' love divine,
Fraternally can show it,
  It floods this heart o' mine.

    Sae sweetly, completely,
      Your thrilling numbers flow;
    Sae grandly, sae blandly,
      Their kindness they bestow.

An' a' yer hamely phrases,
  Free o' deceit an' art;
Each sentiment surprises
  As coming frae the heart.
Though polished rhymes an' fancies
  May catch the cultured eye,
The Dorio still enhances
  Oor love in passing by.

    Its meetness, its sweetness,
      Fill a' oor hearts wi' joy.
    The Rhymer's the primer
      Wha can it richt employ.

An' you've the gift tae use it
  Wi' vigour an' wi' power;
God grant ye ne'er abuse it,
  Though tempted every hour;
For then a mither's prayers
  Wad be o' sma' effect,
If 'mang oor land's betrayers
  Her son stood shamed an' wreck'd.

    But, laddie, yer daddie
      Has learned ye better sense ;
    Yer singing, its ringing,
      Is ower true an' intense.

Noo, a' your kindly greeting
  I do reciprocate ;
An' I'll defer the meeting
  On which you do dilate,
For thochts that's suicidal,
  Or homicidal tend,
If no' checked wi' a bridle
  May bring things tae an end.

    'For wasting, an' hastin',
      Oor lives a' seem tae be ;
    But mendin', no' endin',
      Is best for you an' me.

Noo, be attent', an' listen :
  If prints the truth dae show,
Your very een dae glisten,
  Your heart wi' love does glow,
An' I am proud tae own ye
  A brither doobly tried,
An' in my heart enthral ye
  Wi' a' a brither's pride.

Then duly, an' truly,
    My heart comes wi' my hand,
Tae bless ye, an' wish ye
    The best in a' the land.

An' if we e'er foregather,
   In this or other clime,
In fair or stormy weather,
    We'll hae a pleasant time;
For brithers aye should strengthen
    The stakes that hold the tent,
The cords o' love aye lengthen,
    An' a' that's ill prevent.

For guidin', no' chidin',
    Should be oor daily end,
Ne'er grievin', deceivin',
    A brither an' a friend.

IN MEMORIAM.—JOHN LANG.

" In the service of the Corporation forty-one years.   .   .   .
    Those who knew him longest liked him best, and
    would most miss him."—Lord-Provost Richmond,
    at Council Meeting, 30th Nov., 1896.

Saint Mungo sat on the "Bridge of Sighs,"
    And a careworn look had he,
As the tears rolled down from his brimful eyes—
    'Twas a sorrowful sight to see.

He seemed like a sprite from the long gone past,
    And his frame was bent and worn,
And his long white locks o'er his shoulders cast,
    Spoke well of the cares he had borne.

He sighed—such a sigh as the heart sends forth
  When it otherwise needs must break,
At the loss of some object of priceless worth,
  Whose province none else may take.

He rock'd to and fro, and the gathering gloom
  Of a chill November day
Made sadder the path to the neighbouring tomb
  Of all who held that way.

His voice, like a voice from the tomb close by,
  On the evening air fell low,
I paused for a little, perchance that I
  His burthen of grief might know.

The tale of his woes was short but sad,
  As if born of black despair,
And told of a loss that but lately had
  Indented his heart with care.

"Wae's me," he sighed, "for this guid auld toon,
  Whaur the peaceful arts abound,
Ane mair o' her sons to the grave goes doon,
  And whaur will his like be found?

"So skilled in the lore o' her ancient guilds,
  So ready her rights to shield,
So full o' the love that oor greatness builds,
  And proud o' the power we wield.

"So ready to chide, aye almost severe
  When persuasion else might fail,
With a heart that could neither fawn nor fear,
  Nor in foemen's presence quail;

"So ready to shield what he deemed was right,
    And denounce what he thought was wrong.
Like Achilles of old, he was first in the fight,
    And in valour steadfast—strong.

"No bribe could corrupt, nor fear could divert
    His course from the treasured goal;
The Chambers of Justice were dear to his heart,
    And their honour the light of his soul.

"But never again shall her courts resound
    With his sage-like counsel clear,
Nor his exposition of laws profound
    Claim Mercy's pitying tear.

"Yet, though he has gone, his name shall live
    Through the ages yet to come;
And the homage his friends were proud to give
    Shall cluster around his tomb."

SKETCHES OF SCOTTISH CHARACTER.

I.

"Man, it's a strange worl' this, Tam," remarked ma frien' Sandy M'Neil ae nicht as we sat in Luckie Fulton's "wee snug" haeing a bit dram, a smoke, an' a crack the-gither. "It's a strange worl' this. There's that wee plumber body, Davie Gray, gaun tae get married again an' his first wife scarcely a year deid."

"An' what altho', Sandy? Losh, I think it's aboot the best thing the body can dae. Ye ken, men in his position are something like weans—they need somebody tae look efter them; an' Davie hasna been remarkable for being ower able tae look efter himsel'."

"Weel, there's maybe some truth in what you say, Tam; but I was thinking he micht hae waited a wee while langer, especially as he made sic an ongaun aboot his first ane. But Davie seems tae be ane o' thae kind o' bodies whose affection gangs frae the freezing to the burning point jist as easily as I can tak' aff ma dram."

"Ye'll no' be gaun tae the waddin', are ye? I hear it's tae be a grand affair, an' oor ane was jist wondering what way we hadna got an invitation alang wi' the lave, but Davie an' I haena been that lang acquainted, altho' we've met occasionally on the Booling-green, an' forgathered at an odd time doon the water."

"Weel, I hadna jist made up ma mind, but Meg's in a great state tae gang. She says that Davie an' I are that weel acquainted that it wad be 'daft like' were I no' tae be there; but I hae an idea that she (Meg) wants tae show aff her new harnish plaid that I bocht her the ither week.

She's an awfu' ane for grandeur, an' altho' she is ane o' the best wives in creation she jist jumps at every occasion for showing hersel' off: 'Keeping up the family dignity' she ca's it."

In the foregoing, four characters hae been introduced tae the reader, destined, mair or less, tae figure in this an' the following sketch:

Sandy M'Neil is oor local shoemaker—nane o' yer "done while you wait" sort o' tradesmen, but ane wha can either cloot or mak' a pair o' 'understandings,' frae the daintiest lady's kid tae the navvy's ironshod. In knowledge he's a perfect storehouse o' information, especially o' a local character, an' he can trace the geneology o' maist o' the families in oor toon through three or four generations. His present age is between fifty an' sixty, an' he can brag o' ne'er haeing had a day's sickness since he had the measles, an' even that is only hearsay tae him, as he was ower young at the time tae keep mind o't. In disposition he is kind-hearted tae a fau't, slow tae anger, ready tae forgive, an' at a' times an entertaining an' sociable companion. He is fond o' a dram nae doot, but never gangs far wrang in that direction; slightly philosophical in reflection, and, as a rule, sound in judgment.

David Gray, or "Wee Davie," as he is ca'd by his mair intimate acquaintances, is, or rather was, oor local plumber until a few years ago. Having acquired a sufficiency o' this worl's gear, he retired frae business tae leeve in the enjoyment o' his well-earned an' carefully-husbanded means, nae doot looking forward tae years o' happiness an' comfort, but alas! "Man proposes but God disposes." A year or twa after haeing retired, the partner o' his joys an' sorrows was suddenly seized with a fatal illness, an' she wha had been tae him a helpmeet in the truest sense o'

the word was laid beside her ancestors in the village church-
yard. The calamity was as unexpected as it was great, an'
threatened tae crush for ever that buoyancy o' spirit that
had always characterised "Wee Davie." His family were
young, an' required the care an' attention o' the maternal
mind. Davie, like most men similarly situated, felt himsel'
unfitted for the task o' guiding the youthful fancy, an'
shortly cast aboot tae secure the services o' a middle-aged
lady o' sedate an' unpretentious habits, who, having been
duly installed as housekeeper, soon installed hersel' as
mistress o' Davie's affections, an' shortly will be Mrs. Gray
No. 2. In justice tae Davie it must be said that if his grief
for the first Mrs. G. was short it was none the less sincere.
Those who think otherwise are ignorant o' facts, an' are
unacquainted wi' the genuine qualities o' the man, impulsive
in a high degree, warm in his affections, an' volatile in
spirits.

Margaret M'Phail, that's oor Meg, is a typical woman in
mony respects, possessing mony rare qualities, both as a
housewife an' the mither o' a family; an' altho' there are
mony slight peculiarities o' character in her composition,
there is wi' a' such a strong fund o' shrewd commonsense in
some o' her remarks an' in maist o' her dealings that ane
canna help admiring her tact an' discernment, even tho' it
pinches ye at times. I'm perfectly taen aback wi' her whiles
wi' the way she upsets some o' ma best-laid schemes an'
soundest logic jist wi' twa or three words. Of course, these
are the strong points o' her character, but she has some weak
anes tae, an' it's the latter I hae made a particular study
o', an' that for a very substantial reason, altho' it may no'
be quite apparent tae everybody, an' paradoxical as it may
appear it pays me best. I find that I can mak' maist o'
her by takin' her on the saft side—of course, in such a

way as she disna ken o't : ca'ing a calm soogh when a storm's brewing, an' hauding ma tongue a'thegither when the danger signal's up. Noo, some o' your readers'll be thinking that this is cowardly on ma pairt, but the fact is I don't like tae leeve at loggerheads wi' onybody, faur less wi' oor Meg; she has sic a knack o' letting things fa' oot o' her haun' in ma direction—such as bowls an' sic like, or whatever she may be handling at the time—that it wad be nae less than a tempting o' Providence tae cross her when she's put aboot. I wonder whiles if it can be nervousness, but it canna be that, for the articles a' fa' in a given direction, an' wonderfu' near ma heid, so that you'll see that it pays me best tae " jouk, an' let the jaw gie by." Of course, these are only occasional weaknesses on her pairt ; ordinarily speaking, she's as safe as a mail-coach, an' wonderfu' kind baith tae the weans an' me. An' were onybody tae say a word against either in her hearing guid help them !— I wadna gie saxpence for their hide. Another o' Meg's weak points is her love o' grandeur, maistly o' a showy kind, tho' as a rule her taste is regulated by the cost o' the article. She wad as soon think o' gieing five pounds for what's ca'd a fashionable dolman as I wad think o' fleeing in the air. Indeed, the fashions hae little or nae attraction for her; gie her something oot o' the common, an' cheap enough, an' you'll find Meg in the market. Then, as for news, she's a perfect almanack. Whaur she gethers it a' is past ma comprehension, especially as there's never a household duty neglected in the acquisition o't, so far as I can see. She kens a' the oots an' ins o' the neighbours for a mile roon' : hoo mony clubmen ca' on Luckie So-an'-so, hoo mony sewing machines hae been lifted for breach o' contract, an' whose things hae been poinded for non-payment o' rent. Her capacity for acquiring, an' her memory for retain-

ing, information o' this kind are only equalled by the volubi-
lity wi' which she can rattle't a' off the reel; indeed, her
tongue is ane o' the maist extraordinary anes I ever listened
tae. I don't ken hoo far *doon* in the gaumit o' contention
she can gang, but the *hicht* is something wonderfu'. I min'
ae day a neighbour woman cam' tae check her aboot some
trifling clash or anither, when Meg opened on her at the
tap o' the scale. Had an earthquake opened at that
woman's feet she couldna hae been mair dumbfoonered.
She's been wearing flannel up her chaffs ever since.

These are some o' the traits o' oor Meg's character; ithers
will come oot as we gang alang.

The ither character is ane that I wad much rather hae
left for ithers to describe; but the ane wha kens me best
is sae unfair in her estimate o' ma abilities that I canna
think o' leevin' it tae her. Ane wha tells ye tae yer face
that "there's naething in ye but what the spin puts in" is
hardly the ane tae choose for your biographer.

It may be sufficient tae say that I was born in the City
o' St. Mungo, an' am a burgess o' that ilk, an' am weel kent
in the east-end, whaur, though comin' o' guid auld Hieland stock, ma forefathers, for several generations, hae lived
an' died. I was bred tae the weaving trade, which is no'
tae be wondered at, for in ma young days it was aboot the
only trade that was worth learning, an' unless in periods o'
trade depression we, as a class, were fairly weel aff an'
comfortable.

Being the auldest o' a large family, I was, at an early
age, set tae learn the trade, an', consequently, had few
opportunities o' improving the mind. There was nae school
boards in those days, an' the palatial palaces that noo represent the centres o' education were things undreamt o'.
Not unfrequently the badly lit single apartment, or an empty

four-loom weaver's **shop,** had tae dae **the** duties, or rather **fulfil the** uses o' oor present commodious, well-aired, an' well-lighted colleges ; an' it was nae sma' accomplishment in **those** days when the diligent student managed tae get the **length** o' the "Juvenile Reader," wi' a smattering o' Bible knowledge, limited, it might be, tae the six days o' Creation, **an'** I micht, tae ma shame, confess that it **was** only when I began tae look efter the lassies **that the necessity o' self-**improvement dawned upon me wi' its full significance. **This,** dootless, has been the **case** wi' mony besides masel' ; **hoo**ever, having ance tapped the fountain o' knowledge, **I drank** wi' increasing thirst until this very hour when, I think, I'll ne'er **be** slockened. I stuck tae the weaving trade through **a'** its vicissitudes, an' having accumulated a few pounds, I'll **no' say** hoo mony, I started in business for **masel'** on a sma' **scale, hence I'm** a wabster in the true sense o' the word.

Twa or three years efter **haeing** commenced business on **ma ain** account I entered into a co-partnery concern o' quite **an** opposite character, **the** principals, an' only pairtners o' which were Miss Margaret M'Allister, spinster, **an' Mr.** Thomas M'Phail, bachelor. The concern has flourished **in oor haun's, an' altho'** we haena added much tae oor bank **account oor** stock has multiplied an' grown immensely, **so much** so that we **hae been under** the necessity o' removing tae larger an' **mair commodious** premises twa **or three times.**

Meg an' I hae **got on rale** weel, notwithstanding a certain lack **o' confidence on her** pairt o' **ma** ability tae watch **masel'.** Indeed, if she were half as ootspoken before ithers as she is before me, strangers micht think that "the grey mare was the better horse."

"**Man,** Tam, whan will ye learn tae hae a little smeddum?" is a favourite expression o' hers, an' at ance marks the degree o' respeot an' veneration in which she holds ma abilities as the predominant partner in the ooncern; an' if I venture tae remark that it's time enough, she closes me by saying that "you're jist a muckle sumph." Mony a bit tift we've had but that was in the early days o' oor co-partnery. On coming tae learn ane anither's disposition, an' learning ane anither's ways better, we seldom ever—in fact, never—hae a rale serious cast-oot. I'm a wee inclined tae leave the management o' maitters very much in Meg's haun's, an' sometimes, maybe on that very account, ower ready tae spend an hour or twa ower the toddy or whaur the crack's guid, either o' which wad be sufficient tae claim ma attention at ony time, but, baith combined, imperatively command me.

He must be a strange being wha hasna a failing o' some kind, an' ane o' mine is a partiality for guid company, whaur the flow o' soul is unrestrained; but I've maybe said as much aboot masel' as need be at present. The following sketches'll dae mair tae redd up ma character than ocht I could say here.

We will noo return tae the quiet "wee snug," whaur I first introduced the reader tae ma frien' Sandy M'Neil.

"Ye were sayin' it was a strange worl', Sandy. That's usually an assertion that's accepted withoot question; but, for argument's sake, what dae ye mean by the worl'? Is it this bit planet o' oors, that gangs swirlin' thro' space like a stane oot o' a sling? Or is it the folk wha inhabit it, eh?"

"Come noo, Tam, nane o' yer hairsplittin' wi' me. I'm ower auld in the horn tae be drawn that way; an' if ye will hae a bit argument, jist let us see what ye'll mak' o't. Suppose I say that it's neither the ane nor the ither that I mean but baith thegither, whaur's your argument?"

"Oh, weel, if you say that that's your meanin', that puts

an end tae the argument; but it micht be a difficult matter
for ye tae prove that your meanin' had the backin' o' facts,
a' the same."

"'That's jist whaur you're wrang, Tam, an' I'll show ye
at ance. It wad be ane o' the easiest things imaginable.
It doesna need a great deal o' gumsion tae see that the
planet, withoot the folk, wad jist as little be the worl' as the
folk withoot the planet wad be, if you can conceive o' sic
a thing. When I said the worl' I meant the worl', the hale
worl', an' naething but the worl'; an' it's a wonderfu' worl'
baith the animate an' the inanimate—so whaur's your argument?"

"Man, Sandy, you should hae been a meenister. Ye
could knock lumps oot o' some o' the chiels wi' white
chockers: but ring the bell. If I canna haud ma ain wi' ye
in an argument o' this kind, I'll warrant I'll no' be last wi'
the dram. But you were saying that you thocht it strange
that Wee Davie should get married again. Noo, Tam,
you're no' exactly correct; an' if I've tae hae ony chance
wi' ye in an argument o' this kind ye maun quote me
correctly. What I did say was: 'There's that wee body,
Davie Gray, gaun tae get married again, an' his first wife
no' that lang deid,' ma remarks applyin' no' tae the fact o'
his gettin' married sae much as tae his gettin' married sae
sune. Losh, help me! tae get married again is quite a
natural thing, an' I wad be mair than stupid were I tae
rin' fau't wi' that. It's the time, man; it's the time. Dae
ye no' see that caused ma remark?"

"But, Sandy, Time is simply a comparative factor in
matters o' that kind. A man maun be guided by his circumstances. For ma pairt, I think whaur there's a lot o'
sma' bairns tae look efter, an' the mither's taen awa', the
sooner her place is filled the better for a' concerned."

"Weel, I'll no' argue that point wi' ye, Tam. There's a deal o' truth in what you say; but surely an expression o' surprise is excusable, especially whaur there's nae harm meant. I don't wish tae insinuate that Davie's daein' wrang; indeed, I believe it's aboot the maist sensible thing he could dae under the circumstances, an' I only hope he may be as weel as I wish him."

"I see there's nae gettin' roon' ye, Sandy; your answers are aye ready as your logic's clear. But we'll let that flee stick tae the wa' in the meantime. Hoo are things goin' on wi' ye at hame?"

"Weel, Tam, I've naething tae brag o'. What between heelin' an' solein' I aye manage tae get ends tae meet, but wi' enough tae dae. As far as new wark is concerned, the last I saw o't was in a shop window. Things are comin' tae a fine pitch nooadays in oor trade: hardly ever a new pair come ma way. What between bankrupt sales an' machine-made goods there's little chance for a fellow working on his ain can, as I dae. I hae had thochts o' gaun intae the factory masel' this while back; but, man, the very thocht o't nearly gars me tak' ma bed. What a sacrifice o' liberty that wad be, Tam, tae ane wha for nearhaun' thirty years had been his ain maister, wi' ne'er a ane tae say: 'What doest thou?' except the guidwife, an' she's no' the warst in that line, especially if I'm no' in the way o' takin' a dram. Ye ken I've been in the way o' mendin' a' ma days, an' I'm aye thinking things'll tak' a turn an' mend tae; but they're unco lang aboot it. I've mony a time thocht if I had ma days tae begin ower again I wad join the sodgers, whaur ane's bread, butter, an' bed wad aye be sure, wi' ne'er a factor or laird tae fash ye aboot rent."

"Man, Sandy, I wonner tae hear ye. Ye're no' a meenit dune sayin' that were it no' for the sacrifice o' yer liberty ye wad gang intae the factory an' work, an' here, in your concluding sentence, you're eulogising the advantages o' a life the very antithesis o' what ye admire. You're paradoxical, Sandy; you're paradoxical in the extreme! I canna understaun' ye at a'."

"Weel, Tam, you're no' sae quick in the uptak' as I took ye tae be. Dae ye no' see that the twa theories are perfectly reconcilable? In the first place, if I had ma life tae begin again I wad be unacquainted wi' the measure o' liberty that may be enjoyed untrammelled by the supervision o' supervisers; an' in the next place, having enjoyed the aforesaid liberty for the length o' time that I hae, it wad be perfectly heartbreaking tae lose that liberty; but we're gaun ower deep intae thae things, an' it occurs tae me that as oor crack gets warm the water is getting caulder, an' we canna get guid toddy wi' cauld water, sae tak' aff yer dram, Tam, an' tell us hoo yer gettin' on yersel'."

"'Deed, Sandy, I've been daein' no' that ill ava this while back, altho' Meg says we're no' makin' muckle o't, an' seein' she's baith purser an' book-keeper, she should ken; an' I wad be inclined tae believe her were it no' that I ken she's a gatherin' body, an' thinks she's stirrin' me up tae greater exertion by pleading poverty. Of course, prices are no' what they used tae be, altho' for the rale hame-made article there's a fair figure gaun yet. Ye see, we've the same thing tae contend wi' in oor line that ye hae in yours: factories an' steam power hae played the mischief wi' us; but, man, the haun'-made article has aye a grip on some minds, an' I can get twopence an' threepence mair a yard for ma winceys than they can get in the shops, an' they're worth it a'. Tak' tweeds, for instance. I could gie ye the makin' o' a suit for little mair than ye wad pay in the shops, an' mine wad last twa o' them."

"I'm glad tae hear it, Tam; but hoo dae ye get on wi'
your accounts? There's masel'—mony a braw pair o' soles
I lose, an' mony a dainty foot is clad wi' ma gear that never
was paid for."

"Oh, wo get on no' that ill at a'. Nae doot we lose
a bit making here an' there, but, considerin' the quantity,
wo canna compleen. Whiles we hae a little bother wi' a
customer wha's ill tae draw, but Meg's a born collector o'
accounts, an' whenever I fa' in wi' ane that looks like hope-
less, I jist hand the case ower tae her, an' ten to one she
manages it a' richt. Hoo it's dune I canna tell, but some o'
the customers hae suggested that I micht ca' masel' for the
accounts. It's maybe jist a matter o' taste on their pairt,
but I never ask intae the particulars."

"You're blessed weel aff, Tam, wi' a wife like that. Ma
ane wadna gang the length o' hersel' tae crave a customer,
oven though they werena leaving me a pair o' uppers."

"Weel, as far as that goes, I canna compleen, an' I daursay I may hae the advantage o' ye; but nae doot you'll hae
the advantage o' me in ither respects. I don't suppose your
wife wad turn her tongue on ye though ye were gaun tae the
deil; but wi' ma ane it's a different story. Were I tae be
hauf-an-'oor late o' gaun hame, even were it only frae a
charity concert, I wadna hear the end o't for a hale week,
an' wadna daur tae mention concert tae her for a week efter
that, so that ye see 'there's aye a muckle slippy stane at
ilka body's door.'"

"It's maybe jist as weel that things are as they are,
Tam. The back's aye made for the burden. I don't know
that I could staun' tae be badgered like that by ony woman."

"Badgered! I wadna like Meg tae hear ye use that in
relation tae her conduct; an' as for staunin' it I hae nae
doot but efter the first twa or three trials ye wad be able

tae staun' it weel enough, an' wad learn that discretion
was the better pairt o' valour.   I tried tae haud ma ain wi'
her ance, but it was a failure, an' I hinna tried it since.
Someway things didna turn oot as I expected."

"Ah! but, Tam, that's maybe jist whaur you erred.   Had
you asserted your supremacy at the first ye wadna likely
hae needed tae try again."

"Supremacy, Sandy!   Losh! if I were tae mention ony
sic thing tae oor ane I wadna hae the hoose ower ma heid for
hauf-an-hour—I wad get it aboot ma ears in five minutes."

"Ye seem tae thrive wi't a', Tam.   I ne'er saw you lookin'
better in a' ma life."

"Oh, aye; ye see, it's jist like Paddy wi' the hangin'—ane
gets used tae't, an' wi't a' I hae come rather tae like it.
Wi' a little tact I've learned tae manœuvre her in sic a way
that while she thinks she's gettin' on finely, wi' a' things
her ain way, I'm jist ca'ing ma ain pirn."

"There's mair real philosophy aboot ye, Tam, than I
thocht."

"It's no' philosophy at a', Sandy; it's jist what oor
Meg wad ca' 'rumblegumption'—a knack o' puttin' this
an' that thegither, an' sine coontin' the cost."

"That may be sae, but it's for want o' that 'rumblegumption,' as ye ca't, that hauf the failures in marriage tak'
place, an' mony o' the warst ills o' life arise; but tempera-
ment, I think, maun hae a guid deal tae dae wi't.   Some,
maybe, could thole whaur ithers wad howl oot, an' it's there,
it appears tae me, whaur the grand secret lies.   There's
yoursel' noo, for instance; you're an easy-ozy lump o' guid
nature compared wi' the like o' me.   I wad burst a bluid-
vessel were I no' tae get vent tae ma feelin's.   Things that
wad sink intae ma very marrow wad jist rattle aff your
hide like peas aff a drum."

"That'll dae ye, Sandy; dinna be gieing me credit for virtues that dinna belang tae me. Meg's aboot the only ane that canna raise ma daun'er. The ae-hauf that comes frae her, comin' frae ony ither ane, wad hae me up in a bleeze in hauf-a-meenit."

"Ye're haverin', Tam. I don't believe ye could get angry if you were tae try."

"Maybe no': but I sometimes get angry withoot tryin'."

"Dod! I wad like tae see ye angry for ance, if it were only tae see hoo ye wad look. Are ye real frichtsome, na? Does yer anger manifest itsel' in an expostulatory manner, or does it jist burn itsel' oot in the inner regions o' your heart?"

"Nane o' your jokin', Sandy. Jist ask wee Pate Galloway, the tailor, what it's like, an' he'll maybe tell ye. He should hae as vivid an idea as onybody that I ken. It nearly cost the body his life, an' it was jist touch-an-go for a Coort case ower the matter."

"Oh, by-the-bye, I heard something o' that affair. What was it a' aboot? I thocht you an' he were real thick, an' I could hardly believe ma ears when I heard you had baen an oot-cast. Ye had shurely waukened aff your wrang side that mornin', Tam."

"Weel, I daursay I was maybe pairtly tae blame: but the body took it oot o' me, an' I'll haud ye he got mair than he bargained for."

"I've nae doot he did, Tam, considering the difference in your bulk."

"Weel, ye see, Pate an' I hae had dealings thegither, back an' forrit, for a considerable time. He gets a lot o' stuff frae me, an' his account comes tae something in the year. Weel, he's been fa'in' ahin' this while back in his payments, an' I was beginning tae get uneasy aboot them, sae I daunert roon' tae Pate that morning, jist tae remonstrate wi' him, an' tae see if I could squeeze onything oot o' him in the way o' payment.

"'It's a fine morning that, Peter,' I said, gieing him his Sunday name, as I stepped intae his bit workshop—I think that's the name he dignifies it wi, though it's only a mid-room on the same stair-heid wi' his hoose.

"'Oh, it's you,' he replied (without losing a steek). 'I'm glad you're pleased wi't.'

"Tae say that I was rather taen aback is putting it in the very mildest form I possibly can. In fact, I hardly kent whaur I was staunin', the retort was sae unlooked-for. I felt quite taen-doon like. I was fairly nettled, an' the hauf-smothered snigger o' his only journeyman an' a lump o' a halflin 'prentice that he keeps didna mend maitters, I can tell you. I felt, as it were, put upon ma mettle, an' no' wantin' tae get a showing-up, I replied : 'I didna say whether I was pleased wi't or no', Mr. Galloway ; I was merely biddin' ye the time o' day. I think ye should, at least, be civil when a body looks in on ye.' Ae word borrowed anither, until he ca'd me 'A muckle bubbly lump.' That was the straw that broke the camel's back. I fairly lost a' control o' masel', an' before you could say 'Jock Robinson' I had him by the cuff o' the neck. The body was gaun tae show fecht, but he was like a wean in ma haun's. Sae, telling him what I could dae, an' what I had a guid mind tae dae, I gied him a bit shake, an' threw him doon amang his pairings, mair frichtit than hurt, an', turning on ma heel, I left his place before I should further commit masel'. Pate's voice was ringing in ma ears wi' threats o' law an' prosecution, but there ne'er was ony mair aboot it. He kent better, tho' I daursay I was wrang tae assault him on his ain premises. Had he taen me tae the Coort, I wad hae taen him tae anither ane that micht hae been his ruin, an' he kent that tae."

"I don't know but I wad hae dune the same masel', Tam, had I been in your shin; but what could be the body's reason for being sae short wi' you, especially as he was behauding tae you mair than ye were tae him?"

"I canna tell, Sandy, unless he'd been roused before I gied in. We're no' aye in the same mood, ye ken, an' as ye hae said yoursel', temper has a guid deal tae dae wi't. But, bless ma soul! there's eleven o'clock. I'll hae tae rin. Oor ane'll hae been waitin' on me this 'oor. I'll see ye shortly again. Guid-nicht the noo."

———

II.

"Come awa', Tam; I've been waiting on you this half-'oor an' mair, but I kent ye wad turn up some time; an' I've been wearying tae hear hoo ye a' got on at the wadding. You're nane the waur o't onyway, I see. Was't a fine turn-oot? But, excuse me, jist weet your whistle before ye begin. What will ye hae?"

"Oh, jist a hair o' the dug that bit me last. Changes may be lichtsome for some folk; but it's whiles dangerous tae change the drink."

The reader'll easily guess wha the speakers were, an' whaur the above an' following conversation took place.

Having complied wi' the invitation, an' taen aff the first ane—I aye like tae tak' oot ma first dram—I settled masel' tae gie ma auld cronie an account o' Wee Davie's wadding; an' as it introduces a few new characters intae ma sketch, it may interest ithers as weel as Sandy.

"Man, Sandy, ye missed a treat, I can tell ye; it was ane o' the best nichts I hae spent for a lang time. The com-

pany were a' sae agreeable, especially efter the first kind
o' formal introduction was ower, that I felt masel' quite at
hame, e'en although I hadna seen the maist o' them before. There was nane o' that stuck-up nonsense that sours
an' sickens the sanguine-minded, an' operates like the pro-
verbial wet blanket. We were a' 'Jock Tamson's bairns,'
ilka ane vieing wi' anither in keeping up the harmony.
You'll no' expect me tae gie you a description o' the dresses
o' the ladies—that wad be far aboon ma poo'rs, an' wad
dootless be as tasteless tae ye, Sandy, as toddy withoot
sugar; suffice it tae say that they were awfully braw, an'
maistly a' in unco guid taste. I canna say that I fash masel'
much wi' what folk hae on—it's what they hae in them
that interests me maist. Gie me either the man or woman
wi' a warm he'rt, an' their cleading may be as thin an' bare
as a withered leaf."

"Jist the sentiment I wad expect frae ye, Tam; but
allowance maun be made for rank an' age. If a man or
woman's station in life is aboon the cobbler's bench or the
pirn-wheel, I see naething wrang wi' them putting on an
extra steek, cleanliness, of coorse, aye understood; an'
there's an excuse for the young keeping themsel's a bit
tipie, especially when they're on the "look-oot"—they're
no' like you an' me, wha hae oor markets made, they hae
their's tae mak'."

"That's a' richt enough. I side wi' ye there; an' as
there's nae matter o' dispute betwixt us, I'll jist proceed.
We met aboot eight o'clock in the Masonic Hall, a fine wee
hall—it is weel lichted, clean, an' weel adapted for a thing
o' the kind; an' among the very first tae shak' haun's wi'
me was oor auld frien' Hughie M'Sausage, as hale an'
he'rty as he was twenty years ago, wi' a big black swinger
on, an' a flower in the breast o't like a cabbage stock.

Hughie an' auld Faither Time seem tae be on the best o'
terms, an' agree rale weel. He is maybe no' jist as souple
as he used tae be, but he's as heart-hale an' hearty an' cheery
as in his best days. He's the life o' a company, fou o'
guid nature, an' a splendid singer. I whiles think he should
hae been a precentor—his voice wad hae din credit tae ony
choir. I'll back the kirk wadna be toom whaur Hughie
sang. The next tae salute was Jock Shavings, fair set, I
could see, for a nicht's fun, cheerfulness an' mirth beaming
in every feature, an' displaying an expansion o' starched
linen on his ample breast that micht hae dune credit tae
a meeting o' aldermen. Jock's ane o' the evergreens. Nae
sign o' withering aboot him. The very grip o' his haun' wad
maist bring the tears tae yer een : it's firm as a vice, as if his
heart was in what he was daeing, as it is in everything he
does. He seems tae be getting on rale weel, as he deserves.
His love o' pleasure ne'er interferes wi' his business. He
had it hard enough for a while when he started business
for himsel', but that never damped his spirits; an' noo
that things are gaun better he bids fair tae become a happy
auld man, a living example o' the saying that 'Persever-
ance overcomes difficulties.' Then there was Sandy Brae—
ye ken Sandy fine?—quiet an' retiring in his disposition,
but wi' a relish for guid fellowship that is only second tae
his overflowing guid nature. He is no' ane o' your garrulous
sort o' chiels, believing mair in deeds than words, an' these
maistly o' a beneficent character. Mony a puir soul has been
behaunden tae Sandy, an' a' dune in that kind o' style o'
'no' letting the left haun' ken what the richt ane's daeing.'
He is makin' lots o' siller, tae, and dootless putting't tae a
guid use. He doesna waste onything, an' he's far frae
mean. Then there was Jock Smudge, the plumber. I'm
no' sae weel acquainted wi' him as wi' some o' the ithers :

but he seems tae be a' there, an' contributed no' a little tae the nicht's enjoyment. He has some queer antics wi' him, an' the way he can crack his thooms wad mak' ye think he had a pair o' clappers in his haun's. I've heard waur in a band o' negro minstrels. Indeed, Sandy, tae gang ower a' wha were there wad tak' ower lang tae tell; ye ken maist o' them as weel as I dae. Efter the ceremony was ower we a' sat doon tae a substantial supper, purveyed by Jamie Dough, wha had the tables a' set oot wi' substances, the very name o' which are enough tae fill ye—wi' mystification. I did ma share, as far as the eatables were concerned."

"Aye, an' the drinkables, tae, Tam, or it wasna your ordinar'."

"Man, that's jist whaur you're wrang, for ance, Sandy. I had the pin in that nicht, at least during the supper!"

"Ye what?"

"I had the pin in."

"But it wad be greasy, Tam?"

"Weel, I'll no' say what happened later on; but at the supper I washed the solids ower with a mouthfu' o' water."

"Weel, weel, wonders'll never cease. Hoo did that come aboot?"

"Weel, ye see, the last time I was at a thing o' the kind Meg maintains that I was the waur o't, sae she wad hae me tae promise that I wad be T.T. on this occasion, iist tae let folk see that I kent hoo tae behave masel'. I promised that she wadna see me put a glass tae ma mouth that nicht, an' I kept ma word wi' her tae efter the supper was ower. When I got dry I jist gaed oot tae the stairheid an' had a *smoke*."

"Ha, ha! no' bad, Tam; I thocht there was a wheel within a wheel somewhere. Did she no' suspect onything?"

"Weel, maybe towards the end she did; but she was too 'cute tae let on that she had been oot-generealed, an only remarked that I was surely gaun through an' awfu' tobacco the nicht! The supper ower, the hall was cleared for the dancing. Wee Archie Pinleg had charge o' the band; an', man, he's a great worthy, Archie. Besides being a first-class fiddler himsel' he's a capital singer an' dancer, an' he's no' feart tae put tae his haun' at either. Tae hae seen that body gaun swinging roon' that hall wi' his pin ane wad mak' the teeth o' a dancing-master water, an' his singing o' 'Molly and I and the Baby' was sufficient tae secure him an engagement at a music hall. But I maun try tae gie ye an account o' the different events in their proper place, an' no' put the cart before the horse in that way. The dancing was begun wi' great spirit, the auld anes vieing wi' the young in the enjoyment o' the sport. As for masel', I don't know hoo I got on. I was shoved aboot here an' there in the first set tae sic an extent that I began tae think it was a game o' 'I'm on Toddie's Grun'.' An', of course, whaurever I gaed Meg followed, wi' the result that we were often in ither folk's road. Ane wad say, 'This side, Tam. this side; an' before I could get there anither ane wad say, 'Swing, man, swing,' ane wad tell me tae advance, while anither said, 'Retire, retire, man, an' cross over.' I got fairly bamboozled between ane an' anither, an' was michty gled when the dance was finished, an' I got time tae hae a *smoke*. Ae dance followed anither, jist like a regular ball; an' in an interval o' the fantastic we had songs an' recitations. We had 'Jeanie's Black E'e' frae M'Sausage. He was in fine form, an' when he cam' tae that pairt aboot 'kissing her frae lug tae lug,' I had mind o' the time when I was coorting masel', an' remarked, lood enough tae be heard a' roon', 'Meg, that puts us in mind o' auld langsyne.' I got a glour frae her that reminded me I was treading on delicate grun', accompanied wi' the remark that I should speak for masel'. We had a reading efter this frae Miss Shavings, wha bids fair tae be a guid reader yet, when she gets rid o' the bashfu'ness incidental tae a beginner. I think the piece she gied was the 'Spanish Champion,' an', considering her years an' experience, she did it rale weel. Then we had a comic sang frae young M'Sausage, entitled, 'Eight Hours a Day.' This sang took rale weel, an' was loudly encored; an' nae wonder, for he did it wi' the airt an' finish o' a professional. He's a chip aff the auld block, in mair ways than ane, an' I wadna wonder if he should wear some o' the same laurels that his father has won. Then we had as wonderfu' a performance as ony o' these, nae less than a sang frae auld Mr. Gray, the young guidman's faither, an auld man aboot 80 years o' age—ane o' the liveliest auld souls ye ever saw, an', even at his time o' life, as licht on his fit as a commercial traveller. He's a widower for the third time, an' I wadna put it past him if he should try the matrimonial lucky-bag for the fourth time. There wasna ane in the hall had mair chaff for the lassies, his years gieing him a licence that wad be refused tae his juniors. He sang the 'Battle o' Waterloo,' an', considering that he himsel' was born in the army, ye may be shure that the martial spirit wad be a' there, though his voice hadna the depth an' resonance o' youth. I got in tow wi' the auld fellow later on, an' we had a *smoke* thegither. He's fou o' auld worl' crack, an' minds o' the demonstrations o' joy throughoot the country when news o' the overthrow o' Napoleon reached these shores. The passing o' the Reform Bill, in 1832, is like a thing o' yesterday tae him, an' the Chartist agitation o' 1838, wi' its many stirring events, are maitters o' comparatively recent date. It's a pleasure tae hae a crack wi' him ; an' as showing his interest in present-day politics, he an' a few o' the auld stagers meet regularly tae discuss passing events.   If, as Ferguson says, 'The mind's aye credled when the grave is near,' then he has a lang while tae leeve yet.   There's nae sign o' repose in his mental faculties.   May he be lang spared tae gladden, wi' his cheerfu'ness, an' guide by his example, a' wha hae the benefit o' his acquaintance."

"By ma faith, Tam, there's been nae scarcity o' talent!"

"Talent, man, that's no' half o't!   There was nae scarcity o' onything; it was jist fill an' fetch mair the hale nicht."

"Did ye no' gie them a bit stave yersel', Tam ?"

"Oh aye, I did that tae, na ; but it was efter I had haen a *smoke* or twa."

"What did ye gie them, Tam ?"

"That auld favourite o' mine, 'Oor Tibbie.'"

"I don't mind o' hearing't, Tam.   Hoo does it go ?"

"I'll repeat it tae ye if ye hae time tae listen.   The words are—

"OOR TIBBIE.

"Oor Tibbie is a thrifty body,
    She's nae gowling dame;
We hae been married twenty years,
    An' still she is the same :
As kind an' thrifty aye as ever—
    Seldom seen tae pine;
Far India's wealth I winna niffer,
    Sic a wife as mine.

" We hae haen mony ups an' doons,
    An' poverty oor share;
We've tasted pleasure's choicest cup,
    An' drank o' bitter care.

But a' the ills that e'er befell,
　　Though sickening for a while,
Wad like the mountain mist dispel
　　Before my Tibbie's smile.

"When on a bed o' sickness stretch'd,
　　When fever's fired my frame,
Wi' fostering care she o'er me watched
　　Life's faintly flickering flame,
Through long and trying hours o' pain,
　　When frien's were unco few,
An' scarcely ane enquiring came,
　　My Tibbie aye was true.

"I fearna fortune's sullen frown,
　　Nae cares has she for me ;
An' were I honoured wi' a croon,
　　Nae happier could I be.
I ask nae mair than dae my turn ;
　　An' while I've strength tae toil,
I'll ne'er be heard tae fret or mourn,
　　While blessed wi' Tibbie's smile."

"Capital, Tam! Man, that was maist appropriate. Jist befitting an occasion o' the kind. Nae doot the sentiment wad be highly appreciated."

"As for that it seemed tae tak' no' bad ; but while ithers clapp'd their haun's, I could notice that Meg kept hers employed apparently counting the beads on the front o' her dress, wi' a modesty becoming the days o' oor courtship. Auld Mr. Gray asked me oot for anither *smoke* efter't, an' the dancing was resumed. Someane got me advised tae try a waltz, an' I was foolish enough tae tak' their advice.

It looked sae easy tae gang swirling roon' the hall, but o' a' the dances ever I tried yon's the tickler, especially if you've been *smoking* heavy. I hadna gaen half roon' the hall when I was fain tae sit doon. The floor began tae get unsteady, an' the emblems on the wa's were a' jumbled thegither, an' I'm certain I wad hae fa'en had I no' taen the precaution tae drap intae a seat. Country dances, there were plenty o' them; polkas an' schottisches, a' in turn, an' ane hardly kent the time gaun by tae the next interval was announced. By this time it was coming on tae twal o'clock an' we had a cup o' tea—jist a 'cup in your haun',' in the guid auld fashioned style; an' as Mrs. Shavings was announced for the next sang we a' crowded intae the big hall— some o' us had been oot on the stairheid, hae ing a *smoke*, of course. Jock's wife—that is Shaving Jock, as we whiles ca' him, by way o' variety—is a rare singer, dae ye ken? She did 'Dark Lochnagar' aboot as weel as ever I heard it, an' it's no' ane o' the easiest sangs tae sing, you'll admit. She's a rale free wee body, an' nae way sweart tae gie a bit verse, nae doot kenning that she's braw an' able for't. A chiel, in kilts, then gave us the Hieland Fling, an' skipped it ower twa sticks crossed, as if he had been dancing for a prize. Jock Smudge gied us the 'Bells,' wi' an original introduction o' his ain, an' Shavings gied us the 'Pra' Lad, ta Clerk in ta Office.' Jock can sing, mind you; but there's no' the same finish aboot it as there is aboot his better half's. Sandy Brae sang 'Afton Water,' a favourite o' his, as it seemed tae be wi' the maist o' us. He sings wi' great feeling an' pathos, an' acquitted himsel' wi' considerable credit. In fact, the maist o' us there could pass oor turn, an' were called upon twa or three times during the nicht. I gied them a reading that I learned lately, an' as I don't think you'll hae heard it I'll repeat it tae ye :—

"THE GENUINE RING.

"Do you know the man, if but by name,
  With a reputation crack'd;
A stranger to honesty and shame,
  And by self-assurance back'd.
A fawning chiel with a sickly smile,
  That chills like the Winter King,
And freezes the fount of peace the while:
  He hasn't the genuine ring?

"No doubt you do—he is not so rare
  That he may not be often seen;
You may meet him almost anywhere—
  Well, in certain spheres, I mean.
Though most at home with a certain class,
  Where doubtful dealings cling;
With the best, for a time, he whiles may pass,
  Though he hasn't the genuine ring.

"He may be skilled in the art of grab,
  And stick to whate'er he can;
His coat may be glossy black or drab,
  But with all he is not a man.
He may figure well at church or 'change,
  And may play, or dance, or sing;
But what of that, tho' wide his range,
  If he hasn't the genuine ring?

"He may excel in the gift of speech,
  Like a Writer to the Signet write,
May point by moral, and glibly teach
  That black isn't black but white.
He may, by a twist, make cause effect,
  And to that persistently cling;
He may be with Knox, yet D—— the elect,
  If he hasn't the genuine ring.

"He may, in appearance, be stout or slim,
    And he may be weak or strong;
His eyes may gleam, or they may be dim,
    But surely there's something wrong
When they shrink and shift from an honest gaze,
    And furtive glances fling
From side to side, as the pendulum plays,
    'Tis the lack of the genuine ring.

"He may be short or he may be tall,
    His skin of a yellowish hue,
And his beard may low on his bosom fall,
    Or be short, in the fashion new;
His hair may be either red or grey,
    Or black as the raven's wing;
But what of looks, I ask you, pray,
    If he hasn't the genuine ring?

"He may, by a subtle sleight-of-hand,
    Deceive the acutest glance;
And wealth of argument command,
    When his cause he would advance.
He may, in a circle of sophists, shine,
    And pride to their circle bring,
But he's hollow as any worked-out mine
    If he hasn't the genuine ring.

"He may, if it fits him, smirk and smile,
    And in rapture clasp your hand;
Disarming doubt of his dubious style,
    By the touch of his magic wand;
He may reprehend, in a fatherly way,
    But to please is the paying thing.
With him it is Mammon, night and day,
    But not the genuine ring.

"If such you have known, or know him still,
   Withdraw yourself in time;
Ere yet, by his craft and infernal skill,
   He besmirches your name with crime.
Seek not his court, though his rank be high,
   And jewels to his person cling;
Remember the spider and silly fly,
   And the lack of the genuine ring."

"Hear, hear, Tam! Whaur did ye get a haud o' that? Man, it's true tae the very life. Wha hisna fa'en in wi' customers o' that kind? They're as plentifu' as bad debts in thae dull times. You're fairly coming oot o' your shell."

"I drapped on it jist the other week, an' it describes a character I fell in wi', some time ago, sae accurately that I was struck wi' the likeness. The author maun hae hain some ane o' the same stamp in his mind's eye when he penned these lines. I ken ane masel'. The very colour o' his hair, the bulk o' his gut, the cast o' his e'e, an' the colour o' his skin staun oot as plain as the Tron Steeple, when you can read between the lines."

"Dae ye tell me that? Dod, ye were lucky in finding him oot in time. Hoo did you mak' the discovery? An' hoo did ye act when ye did mak' it?"

"Sandy, I've heard ye saying that wee words were best. We'll no' be ower particular aboot the first pairt o' your question; indeed, it wad tak' ower lang tae tell. Wi' regard tae hoo I acted, I telt him tae his face, in the presence o' ithers, that he was a ——— fraud, an' that I dichted ma haun's o' him."

"Gie's your haun' for that, Tam. Maybe your language wasna what it micht hae been, but your action was a' that could be desired. It's a wonder he didna try tae mak' a case o't, seeing he had witnesses."

"Witnesses! The same witnesses were witness tae his duplicity. But we're getting awa' frae the wedding. If it werena tae tak' me ower lang, I could keep ye an 'oor or so wi' the various incidents that took place. There was ane that I maunna overlook. In fact, I think, next tae the knot-tying, it was the event o' the nicht—a sang by the guidman himsel'. Ye ken, Davie's nae singer, in the real meaning o' the word, but he's made a particular—I micht say a life-lang—study o' ane that's maist aye shure tae bring doon the hoose. He only sings it on particular occasions, an', of course, this was ane o' them. There's no' much in the sang itsel', but when sung by Davie, accompanied wi' the gestures requisite in its delineation, an' the break-doon dance at the end o' each verse, its influence is irresistible, an' you feel yoursel' half-inclined tae accept the invitation o' the singer, an' 'shake your trotters at Finnigan's wake.' But, Sandy, I maun draw tae a close, an' it wad be a pity tae dae sae withoot rehearsing a piece that Miss Shavings gaed us. There was sic a touch o' genuine feeling in the lines, an' it was sae pathetically rendered, that I ask'd her tae gie me a copy o't. Here it is :—

"THE WEE DEID CAT.

(Found dead on a cold morning in December.)

"Puir wee gangrel, hameless thing,
  Nae mair thou'lt loup, wi' lichtsome spring ;
  Some fell mischance has nipped the string
      That did thee lead,
  And tae my bosom sent a sting—
      Since thou are deid.

"Aft i' the morning's early dawn,
  Thou haild'st me wi' thy purr an' fawn,

An' greet me sae till I wad staun'
  An' straik thy head,
Or gie thee crumbs oot o' my haun',
  O meat or bread.

" Aft, aft I've watch'd thee frisk fou fain,
Withoot a care, withoot a pain,
Whiles jinking roon' a muckle stane,
  You'd dart wi' speed,
Then, like a flash, quick back again—
  But noo thou'rt deid.

" Ye made fraeca' wi' young an' auld;
A' bodies' pet, sae fearless—bauld;
E'en o' a dog, I hae been tauld,
  Ye hae nae dread;
But aye wad set thysel' tae scald,
  But thou are deid!

"Ilk rustling leaf, before the win',
That fell or fluttered on the grun',
Was aye tae thee a source o' fun,
  An' test o' speed,
As darting efter't ye wad run—
  But noo you're deid!

"Nae cosy creel, nor woollen rug,
Had ye whauron tae lay your lug;
But curled up, content an' snug,
  On some stair-heid,
Ye'd snoose as soun' as some fell drug
  Had laid ye deid.

"Nae fash o' fairleys made ye sad,
  Nor greed o' gear your passions bad;
  Your spunk was a' the wealth ye had
      Tae fash your heid;
  Wi' mair ye micht, like some, gane mad—
      Far better deid.

"Thy sma' desire o' meat was a'
  The fash ye seemed tae hae ava';
  Thy sleeket coat o' grey, sae braw—
      Like cosy tweed—
  Kept aff the keenest blasts that blaw,
      Yet thou art deid!

"Wae's me, wee baudrins, for thy fate,
  Ae heart at least bemoans thy state,
  An' tho' nae tablet may relate,
      In measured screed.
  Some *fancied* action that was great,
      I mourn thee deid.

"May it be mine, when death draws near,
  Tae hae ae mourner as sincere,
  Tae ease my pain or drop a tear
      Aboon my heid,
  When a' is ower an' finished here,
      An' I am deid."

"Tam, I wadna hae missed that for a' that has gane before.
It has raised a lump i' ma throat, an' made ma een water.
Ye maun gie's a copy o't. There's something in't that ap-
peals tae oor better nature. I see you're affected wi't
yoursel'. Ring the bell, an' we'll hae a 'douchandorus'
before we go. I'm glad that you enjoyed yoursel' sae weel;
indeed, you couldna dae otherwise in sic company."

III.

"Come awa', Tam; I'm no' long in before you. Here's Jock Tile, Jamie Bane, Jock Downie, an' Jamie Slag a' as dry as a lime-basket, an' jist wishing ye wad drap in."

"Dod, Sandy, there's no' mony o' ye; but you're no' badly picked. Hoo's a' wi' ye the night, freen's? What hae ye ca'd? Oh, jist the auld thing ower again! Weel, jist book me as a pairtner. Oor ane's awa' tae tak' the seats, an' I thocht I wad jist look in an' see if there were onybody here, tae beguile an hour or sae. She's never in a hurry back when she gangs there. Her an the Beadle hae aye tae set the affairs o' the congregation a' richt before they pairt; an' while they're making it hot for ithers, there canna be much wrang wi' me making it comfortable for masel'."

"Spoken like a sensible man, Tam. It's a pity but ye had been a cobbler. Ye wad hae been a credit tae oor profession."

"Sandy, had that been the case, there micht hae been rivalry between you an' me, an' that wad hae been a social calamity I shudder tae think o'."

"Hear tae him, chaps! He's getting as sharp i' the wit as an Irish cadger."

"An' as dry i' the pipe, Sandy, as an auctioneer. Send roon' the dram, man, an' let the crack follow't. Hoo are ye the nicht, Tile? Are things busy wi' ye the noo?"

"Weel, efter the last storm we had a bit burst for a day or twa, but there's a lull again, an' I canna say that we're owre thrang."

But before introducing the company tae the reader in this unceremonious manner, I should first tell wha an' what the different members were. It mak's ane feel mair at hame when ye ken wha you're talking tae, an' you're better able tae understaun' the peculiarities o' sentiment an' speech that occasionally crop up. Hence, in the interest o' the reader, it will be as weel jist tae gie a bit ootline o' the characters wha hae been thus hurriedly introduced.

The first twa need nae introduction ava', that ceremony having been gone through with on a former occasion under circumstances somewhat similar tae the present, an' wi' the same surroundings. The others, being introduced intae these sketches for the first time, deserve a mair detailed description so that nae misunderstanding may arise.

Jock Tile is a man bordering on sixty, thin but wiry, an' aboot the average heicht. He's been in business for himsel' for a considerable number o' years, an' tho' no' apparently revelling in the luxuries o' wealth, he has evidently secured a comfortable living—that is, he has a bit guid-gaun business, wi' twa or three men working tae him, an' an apprentice or twa. I had maist forgot tae say that he's a plasterer, but nae doot the intelligent reader has gathered that already frae his remark aboot the storm. It says a great deal for him that, beginning life in the very humblest possible sphere, he has managed tae climb, step by step, the social ladder, until now, if not in a position o' glorious independence, he is at least in one of comfort. In politics he's a strong Conservative, but no' o' the unreasoning class. He can aye gie a reason for the faith that is in him, an' altho' that reason may no' at a' times be acceptable tae his political opponents, no' ane for a moment doots the sincerity o' his convictions. He likes his bit taste, like the lave o' us, but ne'er forgets what's due tae self-respect. He's cautious almost tae a faut, but has sufficient spirit tae resent an affront. He's a wise monitor, a safe guide, an' a sociable companion.

Jamie Bane is a much younger man, unmarried, but auld enough fashioned tae haud his ain wi' the auldest. He's exact an' methodical in manner; **an' hoo he** has managed tae **escape** the matrimonial snare **is** mair **than I** can tell. He's **no' ill-looking,** an' sports a wonderfu' **big** moustache. He's **steady an'** intelligent, an' **in a twa-handed crack** can haud **his ain.** He's a butcher **tae trade, an' nae** doot in **course** o' time hopes tae set up for himsel'. **I wadna** be surprised if he started twa things on his ain account at the same time, namely, housekeeping **an' shopkeeping. He'll** mak' a **guid** man, get him wha may, **or he's no' the chiel I** tak' him for.

Jock Downie's a widower, a boilermaker **tae** trade, an' by **skill an'** industry has wrocht himsel' **intae a** position o' trust **in a large establishment,** whaur his services are highly appreoiated. He has travelled a guid deal, an' has seen a **bit o' the world** beyond the limits o' St. Mungo. Being a boiler-**maker, he's a** wee dull o' **hearing, but** his sense o' fun an' his appreciation o' a guid dram are in nae **way** blunted. When **in the** way o' fun he's as tricky as a circus clown, an' ne'er haggles aboot what's tae pay. I've haen some rare nichts wi' Jock, an' hope tae **hae** mony mair. He's haen a lot o' trouble in his day, puir fellow, especially during the long an' protracted illness o' his wife, wi' an ailment that **was** beyond the reach **o' medical skill.** He was **braw an' guid** tae her, altho' she wasna **in** a condition tae appreciate his **kindness;** yet, wi' a', it hasna left **a scaur** on his big an' generous heart, an' **if** ony warm-hearted woman was tae **throw in** her **lot wi' his she wad fin'** him little the waur o' **the wear.**

Jamie Slag, **or** Slagie, as we sometimes ca' him, is ane **o' thae** pleasant-faced, even-tempered souls wha mak' us **think that** mankind is no' sae bad efter a', notwithstanding the Scriptural declarations that **"the** heart is deceitful above **all** things and desperately wicked." He's as frank an' free

as a successfu' horse couper, an' as warmhearted as a lassie
in love. He lost the partner o' his joys an' sorrows a few
years ago, an' hasna yet seen anither worthy o' her place.
The care o' his bairns claims the bulk o' his spare time, but
he can spare a bit hauf-oor noo an' then tae join in the
feast o' reason an' the flow o' soul. He's manager in a
pretty steady-gaun concern, whaur he has been for years, an'
it's nae sma' testimony tae his worth an' ability that he has
been able tae work himsel' frae the humble position o' a
clerk tae ane o' sic importance. In politics he's a staunch
Liberal, but no' ane o' the offensive kind—he's fair in discussion, open tae conviction, an' applauds the guid actions
o' either party. He an' Tile are auld opponents in argument, but the best o' freen's as soon as it's ower. Jist hint
that the Liberals are losing grun' wi' the electorate, an' that
the Conservatives'll sweep the polls at the next election, an'
you'll hae him an' Tile intae ane anither's necks before ye
ken whaur ye are. He's ane o' Nature's noblemen is Jamie,
an' wad spurn a mean action as the Deil wad spurn Holy
Water. His name may be a little significant o' the baser
metal, but his heart is o' pure gold. Is it tae be wondered
at that wi' a company o' this kind ane's happy tae meet,
sorry tae part, an' happy tae meet again?"

"I say, Sandy, will ye pass the gargle, an' no' sit there
wi't before ye like an object for microscopic inspection.
Whisky loses by exposure, an' is aye best under cover."

"Tam, if ye keep on as you're daein', there's nae saying
hoo high ye may rise in philosophy; but, when a's said an'
dune, maybe the safest place for't is in the barrel. What
say ye, Tile?"

"Dod, I'm no' an authority on maitters o' that kind;
but it appears tae me that if it was aye tae be kept in the

barrel we wad miss a lot o' fun. Ye ken what ane said,
wha wasna a bad judge o' a dram—

> "It waukens wit an' kindles lear,
> An' bangs us fu' o' knowledge."

"Thank ye for that, Tile. Sandy's on the wrong tack
this time."

"Say rather that my witnesses are too bias'd tae gie im-
partial evidence," retorted Sandy.   "When I start tae gie a
dessertation on total abstinence, I'll no' look for ony o' the
present company tae support ma views."

"Maybe there's as much chance o' us supporting your
views, Sandy, as there is o' ye gieing the threatened dessertation," interposed Slagie, at which the ithers interjected wi'
a 'Hear, hear!'"

"Weel, I'll no' say but you may be richt, an' as this
is likely tae be a too labsided argument, we'll be as weel
tae change the subject."

> Here's tae the land o' the heather,
>   The land o' the mountain and flood ;
> May her sons, when they kindly foregather,
>   Aye taste o' a croggie as guid.
> May her daughters be braw, strapping hizzies,
>   An' virtuous aye as they're braw ;
> Nae waur be amang us than this is,
>   The best the distiller can draw.

> May the loon wha is gien tae contention,
>   An' sours a' aroon' wi' his fash—
> Gang aff tae that place I'll no' mention,
>   Whaur the drouthy their teeth ever gnash.

May he ne'er hae a bicker tae cheer him
    Nor slocken his thirst wi' ava';
Nor a frien' when he's needed be near him,
    An' a' that is ill be his fa'.

May the cobblers wha sit in St. Stephen's
    Repair a' the wrangs o' the State,
An' aye hae a drappie an' leavings
    Tae oil the machine o' debate.
An' may they jist noo hae the gumption
    Tae ask oor auld frien' Uncle Sam
Tae meet withoot grudge or compunction,
    An' settle their score ower a dram.

"Your sentiment's grand, Sandy. If some o' the big haun's wad jist tak' your advice there wad be less cause for uneasiness. What dae ye think's likely tae come oot o' that Yankee business, Sandy? Dae ye think they'll gang tae war?" This enquiry was ventured by Jamie Bane.

"War! Dae ye think we could mak' the Clyde rin backward?" retorted Sandy, wi' a look o' compassionate indulgence on the butcher. "Man, the ane wad jist be as unnatural as the ither. I canna say what a' may come oot o' it yet; but there's ae thing certain—that ance oor cousins across the water get time tae cool doon, an' realise the consequences that may spring frae an act o' belligerence, they'll gar their President dance tae a different tune. It's a michty pity that ae man should hae the power—we'll no' speak o' the inclination—tae set twa nations at luggerheads. What say you, Slagie?" Slagie, whose Liberalism had jist the faintest suspicion o' Republicanism, and who can hardly allow the head o' a Republican State tae be condemned in this summary manner, is called upon to reply, which he does in a very guarded manner,—by suggesting that Cleveland has doubtless simply been acting as the mouthpiece of the governing classes, an' probably had been forced into his present action, much against his will, by the impetus from within.   Tile, wha cocks his birses at the very suspicion o' onything being said favourable tae Republicanism, seizes on this opportunity tae remark that "Ony man wha doesna like his job should gie it up."   This was the spark that was required tae get the twa o' them in a lowe.

"Dae ye propound that as a general principle, Mr. Tile, or are ye simply making it as a casual remark ?"

"I propound that as a general principle, as applicable tae nearly a' the dealings o' life."

"Then I beg tae differ frae ye, an' can show ye that your principle wad lead tae mischievous results in a great many concerns."

"Oh, but I am quite prepared for you tae differ frae me on almost ony matter ; but gie's ane o' your cases in point."

"Weel, I'll jist tak' the case we're discussing. Suppose Cleveland, finding that he couldna endorse the sentiments o' the Senate or o' Congress, or even o' the great class o' paid officials that keep the machinery o' Government working, had tendered his resignation, dae ye think the result wad hae been less embarrassing an' critical than it is?   Supposing he had exerted his influence in guiding an' directing the current o' American opinion, instead o' fanning the flame o' national jealousy, Slagie, don't you think he wad hae risen tae a higher standard o' statesmanship than he occupies at the present time?"

"That's no' an answer tae ma question," replied Slagie, "an' jist gangs tae prove what I'm contending for—that there are cases whaur the application o' your general principle wadna work,—or if work at a', wad work mischief—if universally applied."

"Dod, Tile, I think he has the best o' ye this time. It's a dangerous thing tae han'le wi' general principles, especially in relation tae politics," interposed M'Neil.

"Weel, I maybe was hardly guarded enough in ma assertion; but I wad as soon be in the wrang in staun'ing up for a principle o' this kind as be in the richt defending the contrary, an' I'll maintain yet that were there mair o' this principle in evidence among politicians an' place-seekers there wad be less noise."

"Ye shurely don't mean tae insinuate, Mr. Tile, that America's the only place whaur an absence o' this principle, as ye ca't, is in evidence. There's oor ain Government, for instance; if we kent a' the oots an' ins that tak' place ye wad maybe hae a less exalted idea o' their integrity an' ability."

This was an unfortunate remark, an' fairly roused Mr. Tile tae a sense o' his responsibility in defending the integrity an' entirety o' the British Empire. He rose to the occasion like a true son o' the Conservative party, and, assuming a look o' the utmost severity, he enquired:

"Dae ye want tae add disloyalty tae yer ither shortcomings, Mr. Slagie? When had ye a better Government than the present? When had ye a series o' delicate matters treated wi' the same masterly diplomacy? When had ye a Government enjoying the confidence o' the nation tae the same extent?"

"Whan the Grand Old Man was in power," interjected the irrepressible Slagie; "whan the Grand Old Man was in power——"

"Whan the Grand Auld Man, as ye ca' him, was in power, whaurin consisted his grandeur? Keeping aff his unblemished character, which I'm willing tae concede, was it in raising the expectations o' a nation tae the verge o' revolution an' then quietly skedaddling, leaving tae ithers the task o' carrying on the fecht? Did his grandeur consist in the ability an' effectiveness wi' which he wrecked his ain pairty? If so, then you're welcome tae a' the glory an' grandeur that attach tae his name."

"Dod! bless ma soul, Tile, ye've very nearly taen the wind frae me wi' that ootburst o' eloquence. Efter that ye'll be ready tae say he was naebody ava'. Maybe he had naething tae dae wi' the disestablishment o' the Irish Church, an'——"

"Haud ye there na. Granting that he had something tae dae wi' that measure, is it ane tae pin his reputation tae? Did it bring in its train the blessings o' peace an' guid-will that was prophesied o't, eh? Losh, the less you say aboot the Irish Church the better!"

"Oh, aye! but there are mony ither measures that I could name that he was instrumental in carrying through."

"Aye, an' a gey lot o' them he wad hae been better tae hae left alane. Wha was it wha left puir Gordon tae his fate, until an indignant nation almost led him by the ear tae see his duty? The Grand Auld Man, indeed!"

"Ma certie, Tile, you're on a high horse the nicht, an' if it wasna that I ken your bark's waur than your bite I wad be inclined tae retaliate. Strong language micht be used against baith parties, but I'm content tae leave tae future generations the task o' saying whether he deserved the title or no'. The contemporaries o' a man are no' aye the best judges o' his actions, and dootless the heat o' your argument can be traced tae that cause an' tae the disappintment ye hae felt at the passing o' some o' the great measures o' reform wi' which his name'll aye be associated. Were I tae carry the war intae yer ain camp, an' prove tae ye that ony bit scrap o' usefu' legislation the Conservatives hae managed tae pass was, in reality, forced upon them by the Liberals, ye wad dootless begin tae think ye had taen up wi' the wrang pairty."

"Naething wad gie me mair pleasure than tae hear ye mak' the attempt."

"Oh, we'll no' bother! Ye ken, Tile, it's no' the first bit tussle you an' I hae had; an' if the present instance can be taen as an indication o' the progress o' your conversion, politically, I doot the task's gaun tae be ower much for me. What dae you say, Tam? You're keeping unco quate the nicht."

"Oh, I daurna interfere whaur twa sic gladiators as you an' Tile are engaged; but it appears tae me that a guid deal o' valuable time is wasted, if ane has tae judge by the results. Ye mind o' that game we used tae play, when we were laddies, aboot the rule o' contrary—When I say 'Hold fast,' you let go: when I say 'Let go,' you hold fast. Weel it appears tae me there's a guid deal o' that in political arguments."

"No' bad, Tam; an' if thae twa wad jist lay by their political tomyhawks for a time, we micht enjoy the pipe o' peace."

The above remark was hazarded by oor frien' Sandy, an' as it seemed tae meet wi' the approval o' a' present, no' even exceptin' the twa combatants themsel's, the glasses were replenished, oor pipes trimmed, an' we settled doon tae a mair enjoyable entertainment. Efter we had had a bit crack o' a desultory character for a few minutes, in which a' took pairt, Sandy, wha was aye looked upon as chairman, suggested that we micht hae a bit verse o' a sang, an' as oor frien' Downie had been keeping wonderfu' quate, it was suggested that he micht open the concert. Tae this Downie demurred, on the ground that he had naething new, an' those that he had were a' threadbare; but as we wad tak' nae denial he was obliged tae gie us that auld favourite o' his, "Pour Out the Rhine Wine," which he did in excellent style—I don't mean the wine, but the sang; an' tae mark oor appreciation o' the command, we a' emptied oor glasses at the end o' the last verse.

Slagie was next ca'd on, but he only sings on set occasions, an' this no' being ane o' them, we were obliged tae let it pass his door. It was nae use me trying tae prompt him on, putting him in mind that I had heard him singing "What is the Use of Repining?" He replied that he had only learned the chorus o' that sang, an' he was a wee oot o' practice. I reminded him that the practice he had had on one occasion micht hae been sufficient tae hae dune for a lifetime—he sang it a' the road hame frae Paisley on one occasion; an' when we gaed in tae hae a hauf when we arrived in Glasgow he commenced tae sing it again, an' as the waiter failed tae appreciate the beautiful sentiment, either because he hadna an ear or had too much o' an ear, an' ordered us oot o' the shop, he (Slagie) sang it a' the way hame on the tap o' a car.

As it wad be a pity tae let this beautiful scrap become obsolete I here reproduce it, for the benefit o' the desponding—as near as I can recollect—

> "What is the use of repining?
>   Where there's a will there's a way.
>   To-morrow the sun may be shining,
>   Although it is cloudy to-day."

The above was all that oor frien' Slagie had learned o' the sang, an' I can assure the readers o' this sketch that the lines lose nothing o' their attractiveness even when repeated for the thousandth time, as they were on the occasion referred to; but he was proof against a' encouragement on the present occasion. Sae we were obliged tae ca' on his political adversary, Mr. Tile, wha gied us a fine rendering o' "The Pedlar ca'd in by the Hoose o' Glennuik."

> "Thus the time drove on wi' sang an' clatter,
> An' aye the yill was getting better,"

till that inexorable fiend an' enemy tae a' guid fellowship, Forbes M'Kenzie, reminded us o' oor duties as husbands an' faithers, an' a' signs o' controversy haein' laug syne been laid tae rest,

> "We each took aff oor several way,
> Resolved tae meet some ither day."

IV.

TAM McPHAIL LEARNS THE BICYCLE.

"Come awa', Tam; I'm jist waiting on ye. Here's a machine that'll fit ye up tae dick; it's no' ma ain ane, but it'll staun' mair knocking aboot than mine."

"Dod, don't speak aboot 'knocking aboot.' If ye'll promise that it'll no' knock me aboot, I'll gie ye ma word that I'll be as canna wi' it as ever I can."

"I ken that, Tam; but let us see hoo ye get on. See, I'll tak' a turn roon', jist tae let ye see hoo it's dune," and wi' that Measles vaulted intae the saddle, an' was a' roon' the recreation ground in a jiffy. It was awfu' easy like, an' I felt as if ma courage was reviving.

"Noo, I'll haud the machine till ye mount, Tam; an' dinna forget tae work the han'le bar. Whatever side ye feel the machine gaun tae, jist turn the han'le baur in that direction, an' there's nae fear o' ye."

"That's a' richt noo. Steady yoursel'. Are ye a' richt?

Weel, off ye go." Aye, an' off I did go, as fast as if somebody had felled me wi' a brick.

"Dod, Measles, that's rather a bad beginning, I doot," I muttered, gathering masel' thegither, wi' a vague idea that something had gane wrang, an' trying tae mak' as licht o' the matter as if I had been expecting something o' the kind, while a sharp sting at ma elbo' reminded me that I had a funny bane thereaboot.

"Is there onything wrang wi' the machine, Measles!" I thocht it best tae appear concerned aboot that, for, mind you, it wasna me that Measles flew tae lift, it was the machine.

"Oh, there's naething wrang wi' it."

"That's naething at a', man; you'll get ower a' that by-an'-bye."

I said I had nae doot but I wid, if it wadna last long, or if I lived long enough!

"Here you are. Have another go. Noo, I'll steady ye a wee bit. Don't be feared; ye canna hurt yersel'."

Ma elbo' gied him the lee direct, an' I hypocritically murmured, "I see that."

"If you fin' yoursel' gaun tae the side jist put your fit doon on the ground an' come aff. See, it's as easy as cast peas in your mouth."

"So it is," I murmured. "There's no' much in it, efter a'. Here goes again! I'll dae better this time. There noo; gie's a bit push, an' steady us a bit. Dash the thing! It's gaun a' tae the ae side. Haud on a bit tae I get ma fit on the pedal."

"Ah! ye maun keep pedalling. Dinna tak' your feet aff at a' unless when you're stopping a'thegither."

"That's jist whaur the secret o' the thing lies, Measles. I forget a' aboot the pedal in wondering what side I'm gaun tae fa' on."

"Och, man, don't talk aboot fa'ing; ye canna fa' if ye keep the thing gaun. There noo, you're daein' fine. You'll be scorching directly." And wi' words o' encouragement like these, Measles kept trotting by ma side ance or twice roon' the ground, till he was fairly oot o' puff an' the perspiration was streaming doon his face, as if he had newly emerged frae a Turkish bath. Up tae this point I had reason tae be fairly well satisfied—for, be it understood that the chiel wha rins by the side o' a learner, an' guides the machine, has the heavy end o' the stick; therefore, I wasna surprised when Measles suddenly remembered that he had some important duty tae perform at hame that wad detain him—maybe—aboot half-an-hour; but I was iist tae keep at it masel' until he came back. I promised tae persevere, and, profiting by the lesson he had gien me, I stuck tae ma guns—as the saying is—like a man. It was then that ma real difficulties began tae dawn upon ma mind; and then only that I began tae realise what hard work it was tae learn. How often I mounted and dismounted has never been recorded. Whiles hopping for a dozen yards or so on ma ae fit, with ma ither resting on the step o' the machine, until the necessary impetus had been gained. I wad seize an opportunity o' slipping intae the saddle, only tae find that the pedals eluded ma most earnest endeavours to secure them wi' ma feet, with the result that a revolution or two o' the wheel was sufficient to exhaust the little speed at first acquired, an' doon went —no, not M'Ginty, but—Tam M'Phail mair nor aince, with the machine sometimes below an' sometimes on the top o' him!

It is said that "There's a Divinity that shapes our ways, rough hew them as we will." There maun be a special Divinity, I think, for cycles an' cyclists, an' especially for

learners. Hoo every bane in ma body wasna broken I
canna tell ; that remains ane o' the unsolved mysteries that
may puzzle future ages, at least it has aye been, an' will
likely aye remain, a mystery tae me. Tae say that I got
an awfu' shaking is simply stating a bauld truth, an' as for
the machine, I'll gie ma word that it deserved a' the praise
that Measles gied it at the commencement o' the lesson, wi'
the exception o' a bit twist tae the han'le-bar, an' the chain
knocked oot o' gear at an odd time, an' a bit odd spoke or
twa oot o' the wheels tae mak' room for ma fit tae get on the
pedal, there wasna much wrang ; indeed, when Measles returned he seemed baith pleased an' surprised tae see us
baith sae weel.

"Hoo hae ye been getting on, Tam ?" was his first enquiry, on his return.

"Oh, like a hoose on fire. I've been roon' the place twa or
three times, an' I'm beginning tae like it ; but it's awfu'
tiresome at first. I'm nearly done up."

"Ah, but you'll get ower a' that. Jist hae anither turn,
an' let us see the shape ye mak'."

Feeling a wee vain o' the progress I had made, I mounted
again, an', determined tae excel a' previous performances,
I rattled roon' the enclosure once more, of course, taking
the whole width o' the road in doing so. Had I rested content with one round, I should dootless have established ma
reputation ; but—O vanity, vanity !—elated with success, I
determined tae astonish Measles by an exhibition o' ma pro-
ficiency, and went on for another turn ; but Nature's long
suffering has its limits o' endurance. Tired with ma
previous exertions, an' somewhat dazed with emotion, I lost
control o' the machine on a slight incline, and part o' ma
unmentionables on a hedge. Hoo I came tae get there I
canna tell yet, it a' happened sae sudden an' unexpected.

I mind o' getting oot at a terrible sacrifice o' claith, an' a few scratches, but itherwise no' muckle the waur. I felt rather taen doon a bit by the mishap, an' felt as if called upon tae show that I could dae better; but Measles expressed himsel' as perfectly satisfied, an' if I micht judge by his looks there was nae doot he was telling the truth—his features were beaming wi' pleasure, but I had a strong suspicion that a guid deal o' it was derived frae the awkward predicament that I got intae in the hedge.

"Man, Tam, I never saw onybody making a better shape; but ye've had plenty o't for a first lesson. Ye've got ower the warst o't noo; a' that ye need is a little practice tae mak' you perfect."

"An' a new suit o' claes tae mak' me appear decent; hoo in a' the worl' am I tae get hame wi' these? The folk'll think it's a tattie bogle deserting his post if they see me in this state! Have you a preen or twa, tae I see if I can fix up the seat o' ma trousers a bit?"

"A preen or twa! Tam, if it was a clean rent it wad be naething; but you've left pairt o' your trousers sticking in the hedge. There, come awa' roon' tae oor hoose, an' I'll lend you an auld pair tae gang hame wi'. Here, put ma topcoat ower a', an' naebody will be dafter or wiser. That's the thing."

"I hope your machine is nane the waur o' that spill. It's a guid ane for that kind o' work, at onyrate."

"It's jist the very thing, Tam. Man, you could hardly hairm it wi' a forehammer."

I was satisfied that it was worthy o' a' the praise he bestowed upon it; but I had an inward hankering that I wad jist hae liked aboot five minutes at it wi' the instrument mentioned. I back it wadna hae run awa' wi' anither.

But what am I blethering at? It was dootless a' ma ain faut.

Hoo I got hame, an' the reception I met wi' frae Meg, I'll maybe tell some ither time; suffice it tae say that the foregoing wasna ma last adventure on the bicycle, by ony means; an' as the cycling season opens shortly, an' I'm likely tae be oot occasionally, I'll maybe hae something tae say by-an'-bye that may interest an' amuse your readers. We hae started a club in Parkhead, an' there's aboot 50 members in it already, an' Tam M'Phail's ane o' them.

CYCLING SONG.

Let the huntsman attend to the horn,
  When Phebus enlivens the east,
An' the hounds rush through thicket an' thorn
  To share in the spoil an' the feast.
More gladly I spring to the saddle,
  More joy I certainly feel,
While guiding with bar and with pedal,
  I speed with the wind on my wheel.

The huntsman, no doubt, has his rapture,
  And the hound may enjoy the chase,
And glut their desire in the capture,
  When long and successful the race.
But sweeter to me is the pleasure
  And joy that over me steal,
As mile after mile I measure,
  Astride on my wondrous wheel.

The landscape, continually changing,
  Variety gives to the scene,
Like an artist some picture arranging,
  With shadow and light between.

While the song of the blackbird and mavis,
　　Through the grove and the woodlands peal,
.As they flit through the sylvan mazes,
　　Away from the silent wheel.

I mark, with delight, how in wonder
　　The rustics incredulous stare,
As I rush past the cottage out yonder,
　　Away in the distance, where
The din of the city is silent,
　　And the fragrance of flowers you feel,
Make you strong, aye, fearless and valiant,
　　While speeding along on your wheel.

ARCHIE.

A PAGE FROM THE PAST.

It is many years now since the worthy whose name heads
this paper passed to that bourne whence no traveller e'er
returns. Yet methinks I see him now, as vividly as he appeared
in his best days. Eccentric in many ways, but kindly disposed and beloved by all. Archie M'Lean was his real name—
sometimes called Daddy M'Lean, but oftener Noble Archie.
How he came to be so designated is immaterial. That he
was so designated by his most intimate acquaintances is
sufficient proof that it was in no derisive spirit that he was
so named. He was a M'Lean of the original stock, and I
remember that on more than one occasion he claimed that
at the time of the Flood his ancestors had a boat of their
own, thus putting the matter of antiquity beyond dispute.
I remember, too, the first occasion on which I heard this
extraordinary claim put forward. If it did not convince all

who heard it, it at least effectually silenced them, and especially the individual against whom the thunderbolt was launched. The circumstances were, as near as I can bring to mind, as follows:—Some half-dozen of us had met to "hang the New-Year," in other words, to have a small jollification, as a wind-up to our New-Year's festivities; and crack, joke, and song enlivened the minutes as they winged their way unheeded. There were Noble Archie, Peter M'Kay, Sandy M'Neil, Big Willie Hill (the sinker), Willie Little (nicknamed " The Doctor "), your humble servant, and one or two others—as sociable a lot as ever couped a glass or paid a reckoning. We had been at it mair or less the whole day, and when the evening shadows fell and the gas was lit there we were, as brisk as ever; nay, our spirits seemed to rise as time went on, and although none o' us were what you call " fou' " we had had sufficient to sharpen our keenest perceptions, though, perhaps, hardly enough to slocken our drouth. Now, although we were all the best of friends, and would have stood by one another against outside interference that did not prevent a considerable amount of banter taking place; and as Peter M'Kay and Archie were old opponents in argument, it was no difficult matter to draw the two to an encounter. Though Peter invariably had the advantage in point of education, this was more than counter-balanced by Archie's mother wit, which generally exploded all Peter's long-drawn arguments and rounded periods—very often to the blank astonishment of Peter himself and to the no-small amusement of those present. Occasionally Archie came off with flying colours and the palm of victory. If there is one thing which a Highlander prides himself upon above all others it is the antiquity of his ancestors. Peter and Archie, though long resident in the neighbourhood of St. Mungo, had lost none of their

Highland pride, the love of their Highland ancestry, and that determination which upholds both at any sacrifice.

Now, it may not be generally known that there exists a strong and deep-rooted rivalry between the M'Kays and the M'Leans; but such there is. At least there did between the two representatives under notice. We all knew this; hence the facility with which they could be, figuratively, brought to draw the claymore in defence of their claims. How to manage this none knew better than M'Neil; and this is how he did it.

"I say, Archie, is there nae word o' you getting that estate in the North yet?"—(This had reference to a prospective inheritance that for years had been one of Archie's pet expectations).

"No, man, Sandy; I'm looking for word every day. The lawyers have had it in haun' this mony a day; but it's bound tae come."

"I doot, Archie, there'll no' be much o't left when they're done wi't."

"Left! I tell ye they couldna gang through it, tho' they were tae employ a' the big wigs aboot the Court o' Session."

"There maun be a dainty lump o't then, for yon's the chiels tae run up an account."

"Oh, they're no' hindmost at that; but the interest on the siller wad mair than pay the expense."

"An' has it been lang in the family, that there's sae much bother in getting't?"

"Ower lang in the family wha hae it the noo, M'Neil. They've nae claim tae't at a'. It should hae fa'n tae my grandfather, wha was an only son an' gaed awa' tae sea, an' wha everybody thocht was deid, until he cam' back, only tae fin' his kinsman in possession, an' wi' nae chance o' proving his right."

"Then your family maun be the auldest branch o' the name?"

"Oor family's no' a branch at a'. Oors is the trunk; the ither is the branch."

"Ye micht hae some trouble tae prove that."

"Prove! I can prove that the M'Leans hae an unbroken line o' descent frae before the time o' Malcolm Canmore, an' that's what no' mony can prove."

"I hope you're no' referring tae me, my noble boy, for the M'Leans'll hae tae tak' a back seat tae the M'Kays," interrupted Peter, who felt as if his own family reputation was at issue. "A'body kens that the M'Kays hae a history reaching back tae Noah's flood. Ye canna gang beyond that, my man."

"Aye; an' whaur were the M'Kays at the time o' the Flood, Peter, if it be a fair question?"

"Man, they were in the Ark, Archie. That'll astonish ye, nae doot. Ye didna ken that before," and Peter laughed as if he had scored a point. This certainly would have been a poser to most people, but to Archie it seemed only to serve as a starting point; and with one of the slightest twinkles in his eye imaginable, he replied:

"Oh, no' sae fast, Peter. We've a' read o' there being *Kye* in the Ark, an' dootless they were ancestors o' yours; but the M'Leans were aboon taking a free passage, even wi' Noah: they had a *boat o' their ain,* showing that even in thae antedeluvian days we were o' some standing."

How shall I describe the scene that followed this sally? It must have been the first time it had been hurled at the head of poor Peter, for he utterly collapsed, while the rest of us felt as if electrified. The tone in which it was said and the circumstances defy the most vivid imagination to pourtray its effect upon the company. M'Neil, who had been instrumental in bringing the exchange of civilities about, relished the result like unto a wean taking saps, while the "Doctor" and the sinker exchanged a series of nods and winks, brimful of appreciation. As for me, I could not repress my feelings—never an easy task for me at ony time—but broke out in the hamely Doric, as I invariably do when strongly moved, in something like the following :

"Dod, lads, isn't he an awfu' body ? Nae getting ower him, either in drinking or joking. What dae ye say tae that, M'Neill ?"

"I say that if ane were tae judge by the expression o' Pate's face, it wad be hard tae tell whaur the joke cam' in."

"Aye, an' if they were tae judge by the lear in your ain e'e they could tell at aince."

"Tam, you're getting too smart for me. If you keep on as you're daeing there'll be nae hauding o' ye in in a short time ; but I'm thinking the sound o' your ain voice betrays your ain feelings in the matter."

"Losh, I canna help mysel'. I think that as smart a thing as ever I heard—an' as harmless tae. Pate himsel'll relish it by-and-bye, when he has haen tae digest it. It's no' gien tae every ane tae be a born wit."

"A born wit !" retorted Pate. "Say rather 'a born leer.' Wha ever read o' the M'Leans haeing a boat o' their ain at the Flood ? It's a' a thing o' the imagination, like the estate in the North."

Archie, who felt called upon to maintain his veracity, did so by suggesting that the record of the antedeluvian M'Leans would be found in the same book that chronicled the presence o' the M'Kays in the Ark. The fact is that Peter was no match for Archie in a banter of this kind ; and although a real serious out-cast had never really taken place, there was no saying what might happen if this banter were allowed to go much further; therefore, with a view to laying whatever differences may have been raised, M'Neil, with his usual adroitness, gave a turn to events that, for a time at least, quelled the spirit of banter and raised the spirit of song.

"What dae ye say, lads, if we hae a verse a' roon'—jist tae show that there's nae ill-feeling?"

"I hae nae objection tae that," interposed the "Doctor," "if you wad first attend tae the mair immediate requirements o' my patients."

"Weel, jist gie your prescription, 'Doctor,' an' if it's guid for's dinna stint it."

"Weel, I don't approve o' changing the medicine when it's working weel. Ye'll better renew the bottle, an' repeat the dose."

"Ye hear what the 'Doctor' says, lads? It's bound tae be guid for ye, seeing he's sae fond o't himsel'."

"Watch yoursel', Sandy; and nae insinuations, or I'll pronounce you convalescent."

"Guid forbid, 'Doctor!' I hae nae wish tae get better; an' my trouble 'grees wi' me. Here, Baillie, anither o' the same; and dinna forget the bannock"—(a piece of oat cake usually brought in with the dram in those days).

The Baillie thus addressed was the landlord, who not unfrequently made one of the party—not one of your sordid, greedy, grasping landlords who disgrace their calling, and who, while sweeping every available sixpence into his till from the pockets of his customers, never thinks it is his own turn tae "stand." No, the Baillie was a gentleman, in the truest sense of the word—notwithstanding what has been and is still said against his calling. Large-hearted and sympathetic, I have frequently seen him refuse to supply where he thought sufficient had been imbibed. I have even seen him take the money from some of his most foolish customers, carefully wrap it up, and send it along to the wife who had been waiting in vain for her erring lord with his pay. Did he not get into trouble over matters of this kind? Never. The man's character was as much above suspicion as his nature was above all that is mean. Quarrel with the Baillie? Why, the very idea is preposterous! Quarrel with the man whose bounty was shared by all, irrespective of claim, so long as it was deserving? Many a hungry child and shivering mother have reason to bless his name. He, too, has long since passed away; but the very remembrance of him tends to lift the mind—even as I pen these lines—above the sordid surroundings of everyday life, and strengthens me in the belief that there is something truly noble in the human heart after all. My readers, I feel certain, will bear with me in these digressions. They, to me at least, are the little flashes of light that illumine what might otherwise be the dull monotony of simple rehearsal. Could they but convey to the reader half the pleasure they give to the narrator, then my task would be lightsome indeed; but let us return to the scene where we left off so abruptly.

The measure, a "tapit hen," having been replenished—none of your gentle, modern "ha'fs"—the management of the carousal developed, as it usually did, upon Sandy, who always acquitted himsel' with entire satisfaction. He inaugurated the exercise of his authority on this occasion with a short address, in something like the following terms:

"I think, lads, we couldna dae better than ca' upon oor auld frien' Tam M'Phail for ane o' thae hamely sangs that wauken oor better feelings an' sends a' spleen an'

animosity tae the wa'. Of course, I need hardly add that
he's no' what ye micht ca' ane o' the sweet singers
o' Israel, but he has the knack o' letting himsel' be understood, which is mair than can·be said o' a' wha try it.
Come on, Tam, gie's ane o' your auld anes."

"Man, Sandy, I've naething new; but if ye care tae
listen tae a Masonic ane I don't mind trying."

WI' HIGHEST HONOURS GREET HIS NAME.

A' ye wha work wi' Plumb an' Rule,
   Fu' conscious that ye dae richt,
Lay by wi' care ilk working tool,
   An' let's be blyth this ae nicht.
This ae nicht, this ae nicht,
   We're brithers a' this ae nicht;
An' fickle Care may, in despair,
   Gae droon hersel' this ae nicht.

Oor brither bard, whas memory dear
   We seek tae pledge this ae nicht,
Implored, wi' melting heart an' tear,
   We wad dae sae this ae nicht.
This ae nicht, this ae nicht;
   His memory pledge this ae nicht.
May garland Fame aye guard his name,
   Is oor prayer here this ae nicht.

The winter win' withoot may roar,
   Wi' angry growl till daylicht,
An' farmers wail their ruined store,
   But we'll be blyth this ae nicht.

This ae nicht, this ae nicht;
   We'll banish Care this ae nicht,
Wi' deep regard, "Oor ploughman bard"
   Shall be the theme this ae nicht.

Wi' highest honours greet his name—
   In daeing sae ye dae richt—
He's worthy o' the highest fame
   Ye can bestow this ae nicht.
This ae nicht, this ae nicht;
   Oor hearts, aglow, this ae nicht
Shall sing his praise, an' chant his lays,
   An' happy be this ae nicht.

The applause which followed the singing of the foregoing needs no description, suffice it to say that it was loud and sincere; and no one was more demonstrative in their appreciation than my auld frien' Sandy, though it was not by any means the first occasion on which he had listened to it. Yet, strange to say, he did not belong to the Craft, and consequently could not appreciate its hidden meaning. Perhaps his partiality for me blunted the critical faculty so predominant in his character. Be that as it may, there was no dubiety about the warmth of his applause.

"I telt ye what he could dae. Here's tae ye, Tam!

"May ye ne'er want a groat when its needed,
   A heart aye tae gar it gae roon';
A bumper fa' fu' an' weel beeded,
   Whaurin a' your troubles tae droon."

"Noo, lads, we've made no' a bad start wi' the harmony. What dae ye say if we ca' on the 'Doctor' noo for ane o' his love lyrics? Tae be a bachelor, he gies wonderfu' expression tae the softer sentiments o' the heart, an' nae doot has his ain reason for shirking the matrimonial snare."

"M'Neil, I'll reduce your prescription if you carry on as you're daeing."

"Don't dae that, 'Doctor,' or you'll lose a patient. I don't grudge your fee, an' you micht get waur than me; but it's your sang we want, no' your advice, in the meantime. Come on wi' it."

The "Doctor," thus urged, commenced with

THE BONNIE LASS O' LICHTBURN.

The sun's gane doon, the gloaming fa's,
  The gathering gloom looks ocht but cheery;
But what care I? I'll tak' my wa's,
  An' blythly meet my bonnie deary.
I ken she's waiting at the stile;
  But waiting sae as nocht could move her,
Although her bosom heaves the while,
  Impatient tae embrace her lover.

Her bonnie een o' azure blue,
  Her cheeks that shame the cherry blossom
I'll tell a tale o' love as true
  As ever fired the human bosom.
I'll strain her tae my heaving breast,
  An' pledge anew the love I bear her;
Tell hoo frae her I am distress'd,
  Hoo bless'd an' happy when I'm near her.

Her looks o' love'll licht the gloom,
　The music o' her voice enthral me,
Her breath the silent shade perfume,
　An' dread o' danger ne'er appal me,
While clasp'd within my fond embrace,
　My brightest, purest, dearest treasure,
Nae wanton fear shall haunt the place
　Tae dash my brimfu', blessfu' measure.

"Did I no' tell ye what he could dae, lads? Losh! 'Doctor,' ye deserve a taste o' your ain gargle. That puts a body in mind o' langsyne, when the step was licht an' the heart was warm. What say ye, Tam?"

"Weel, no' being o' a poetic turn o' mind, I can hardly say. Wi' regard tae the sang itsel' it's no' bad; but I think it owes much tae the feeling wi' which the 'Doctor' rendered't, an' if we may tak' that as an indication o' his true state o' feelings under the circumstances related in the verse it's a won'er tae me that he didna marry the lass."

"Tam, your medicine's no' 'greeing wi' ye. I'll hae tae prescribe sma' Pale, an' put you on a diet o' red herrin'," retorted the "Doctor." "Your sense o' penetration becomes too acute."

"Blister his heid, 'Doctor,' an' send him tae bed," added M'Neil, while the ithers laughed an' rattled their glasses. I joined in the laugh mysel' at the tables being sae cleverly turned upon me, but I wasna satisfied that I said onything oot o' place.

"Noo, lads, gin ye hae dune cangratulating the 'Doctor,' I'll ca' on Willie there tae favour wi' the next verse; an' if he does onything like as weel as the last time I heard him I promise ye a treat. Dae your best, Wull, an' knock the cobbler doon," I whispered loud enough for them a' tae hear.

"Tam, you're jist aboot as sharp i' the wit as the tip o'
ane o' your ain shuttles; but it'll no' dae this time. Ye
ken brawly what I mean. Come on, Wull, an' let them
ken I'm richt."

Willie, whose knowledge o' musical notation—well, we'll
no' say ony mair—being thus urged, responded with

TAM STRACHAN.

Tam Strachan was big an' was strong;
   His wife was a wee wiry body.
Tam whiles gaed a wee kenning wrang,
   An' then he was thrawn as a cuddy.
Jist then he wad fecht wi' the win',
   An' few cared his powers tae tackle;
But Meg took the job aye in haun',
   An', faith, she could han'le the heckle.

Chorus.

Sing hey for the wife wha can rule,
   The ane ilka wrang that can richt it;
The wife wha can keep hersel' cool,
   An' ne'er o' a tyrant be frichtit.

Ae nicht Tam cam' hame on the spree—
   Three sheets in the win', I am certain—
Wi' a dangerous licht in his e'e,
   That had dootless been lit at the pairting.
The neighbours, wi' fear, kept aloof,
   An' gied a wide berth, I am thinking,
But Meg cried, "You great muckle coof,
   Whaur the Deil were ye daffing an' drinking?"
     Sing, hey for the wife that can rule, etc., etc.

He tried tae look bold; but, alas!
  Meg peppered him weel wi' her flyting.
She ca'd him a big silly ass,
  An' vowed that her peace he was blighting.
He stammered oot some lame excuse.
  She caredna for that—no' a spittle:
And unless he wad stay in the hoose
  She wad scald baith his feet wi' the kettle.
    Sing, hey for the wife that can rule, etc., etc.

Lod, Tam couldna venture a word;
  Like a sumph, he was sulky an' silent,
While still, like a torrent was heard
  Meg raging. wi' passion fu' violent.
He kent she was aye in the richt,
  An' she a' his fau'ts an' his failings.
She kent when tae screw him up ticht,
  An' when tae relax in her dealings.
    Sing, hey for the wife that can rule, etc., etc.

Thus Tam, wha could twist a horse-shoe
  Wi' a wrench o' the haun', like a docken,
Was held-by his wife under coo,
  Like a coute that has newly been broken:
An' yet the twa 'greed unco weel.
  For the flyting was unco ae sided.
Tam simply wad say, "Weel-a-weel,
  I'll jist by your counsel be guided."
    Sing, hey for the wife that can rule, etc., etc.

"Bravo, Willie; ane o' the best I ever heard ye sing.
Did I no' promise ye a treat? Hoo dae ye relish that, lads?
I am thinking there's nae scarcity o' talent. here the nicht.
Dod, 'Doctor,' your medicine's working brawly. I hope

that has nae effect in keeping ye awa' frae your bonnie lass."

"Ne'er fash your thoom aboot the lassies, Sandy; your market's made langsyne."

"Aye, an' I micht hae made a waur bargain o't."

"Noo, Pate, it's your turn; an' I ken ye can dae't. Gie's either a sang or a sentiment, Pate. Ye can dae baith if it's needed. I don't know when I saw ye keeping as quate as you're daeing the nicht. Never mind Archie; his turn's coming."

"Oh, I'm no' thinking o' the body. He's welcome tae a' the honour an' glory his imagination can bring him."

"Noo, noo, Pate; let sleeping dugs lie. Archie'll pay for't a' when he gangs hame the nicht."

"An' as for you, M'Neil," retorted Archie, "if you hae tae pay for't the nicht it'll neither be the first nor the last."

"Capital, Archie," I chimed in. "Serves the cobbler richt. I like tae see him getting paid back wi' his ain siller."

"Lod, Tam, you needna craw; it's no' sae lang since you were served sae yoursel'. But if I alloo the ragging tae gang on like this I'll lose control o' the meeting, an' maybe my situation as chairman. Noo, Pate, if you're ready, we'll hae your pleasure."

"Weel, I suppose there's nae getting oot o't; an' as I wadna like tae be a mar tae the harmony"—casting his eye in Archie's direction—"I'll jist try a bit verse or twa o' a rhyme:

"LAND O' MY FOREFATHERS.

"Land o' my forefathers, land o' my birth!
The dear land of Freedom, the dearest on earth!
Thy cloud-kissing mountains, uprearing high,
The step of the slave and the tyrant defy.

"Thy far-stretching valleys I view with delight,
  Where the husbandman earns repose of the night;
  Thy green-mantled hills, where the herdsman reclines,
  To me are more precious than Indian mines.

"The castle, the keep, once so famous in war,
  I view with a rapture, more hallow'd far
  Than that which inspires and sustains in the flame,
  The victims of Buddha, the children of shame.

"The cot in the valley, thatch-covered and poor,
  The children at play on the green by the door,
  The kirk in the clachan, the mill and the wheel
  All fill me with pleasure no being can steal.

"Thy glens, where the hazel, the birch, and the fir
  Wave gentle salutes to the breezes that stir,
  And the blackbird and mavis rejoice in song,
  Are the sports and the pleasures I revel among."

Pate's effort was hailed with rapturous applause, and none more warmly than his erstwhile opponent, Noble Archie, who, striking the table wih his clenched fist, declared there wasna anither man in the clachan could equal Pate, either in sang or sentiment; and grasping his hand in the intensity of his admiration, he exclaimed:

"Man, Pate, you're a born patriot! Nane but a patriotic Hielandman could gie expression tae sic sentiments. There's my haun'. May ye never lose the smell o' the peat reek, nor forget the bloom o' oor native heather."

This sentiment was shared by all, tho' but imperfectly understood by some. Indeed, we were a' fairly in oor element, as the saying is; but M'Neil was not the man to let us forget ourselves, under any circumstances, and, having still another artiste in view, he broke the spell of oor admiration by ca'ing Order at ance. We were too sensible of the severity o' his censure to disregard his mandate. Having cleared his throat wi' a something, he said there was ane o' the company yet wha hadna dune onything in the vocal line, and he felt sure when he mentioned the name of his noble friend that everyane wad listen wi' attention tae either sang or sentiment frae him.

"Hear, hear! Come on, Bauldy; gie's your favourite: 'A Wee Drappie O't,' or 'The Brewing o' Yill.'"

Archie could not with grace refuse to comply, and although not what is called a finished singer, he rendered the following characteristc song with a clearness of voice and an assumed earnestness that must have been the result of deep conviction, from long experience, no doubt :—

WHISKY TODDY.

Ye chiels wha dree in dauldrums dull,
An' fain wad flee frae ilka ill,
Nae langer fret, but drink your fill
    O' steaming whisky toddy.

For it can droon ilk carking care,
Hope inspiring, life desiring,
Happier aye ye drink the mair
    O' steaming whisky toddy.

O' foreign wines, wi' sickening smell,
I canna frae experience tell
Hoo they may act; I drink mysel'
    The best o' whisky toddy.
    For it can droon ilk carking care, etc., etc.

The brewster may exhaust his skill
In perfecting his slushy yill.
I carena for't : gie me my fill
     O' steaming whisky toddy.
    For it can droon ilk carking care, etc., etc.

When tired at nicht, wi' labour sair,
An' ilka moment's weighed wi' care,
If I hae but a groat tae spare,
     I'll spen't on whisky toddy.
    For it can droon ilk carking care, etc., etc.

When summer heat mak's hot the bluid,
An' thirst oppressive drives ye wy'd,
Nae better cooling draught nor guid
     As steaming whisky toddy.
    For it can droon ilk carking care, etc., etc.

When winter freezes keen an' snell.
An' shivering souls their hardships tell,
They wad dae weel—I dae't mysel'—
     Tae drink o' steaming toddy.
    For it can droon ilk carking care, etc., etc.

When jilted lovers, fu' o' gloom,
Resolve tae seek an early tomb,
Tak' my advice, ne'er fash your thoom.
     Forget your grief in toddy.
    For it can droon ilk carking care, etc., etc.

When gout or toothache drives ye mad,
Or influenza—quite as bad—
Mak's baith yoursel' an' ithers sad,
     There's nocht like whisky toddy.
    For it can droon ilk carking care, etc., etc.

> For ilka ill that hampers life—
> The want o' work, a scolding wife,
> Domestic jars, an' family strife—
>   There's nocht like whisky toddy.
> For it can droon ilk carking care, etc., etc.

The foregoing song, like the ithers, was hailed with rapturous applause, and Archie was greeted on all sides as the hero of the evening. Not one present doubted the sincerity o' Archie's sentiment, and not one of them was better able to expatiate on the virtues, real or imaginary, of the stimulating cup. Wife, weans, and home were too often left to take care of themselves, while Archie drank deep and long at his favourite draught; indeed, it was Archie's besetting sin, and while he could and did earn good wages at the loom, when sober, he was often fain to make of himself a menial of the humblest class when on the fuddle. No office was too humble for him at those times—from running messages to carrying coals. The present occasion was one suited to Archie's mind—sociable company and a guid dram. No wonder, then, that he did ample justice to the foregoing characteristic song; and no wonder that it met with the reception it did. The glasses rattled and the jest went round until it was time to think of home and the "pickled tongue." Under a less experienced chairman than M'Neil, the company might have oversat itsel', but Sandy, while he could enjoy himsel', wi' the daftest o' us, had firmness enough tae draw the reins at the proper moment; and although it was suggested that he micht gie us a verse or twa himsel' for a wind-up he put us off wi' "Some ither nicht, lads; some ither nicht. It's time we were a' hame."

LINES SUGGESTED BY THE DEATH OF MY FRIEND AND BROTHER, C. GALLETLY, DIED 21st NOVEMBER, 1897.

He was one in a thousand.　Our hearts said so,
　As we stood by his lowly grave,
Recalling the graces his life could show—
　So unselfish, generous, brave.

He was one in a thousand.　In act and thought
　As pure as the prattling child;
In practice as pure as the precepts he taught,
　When the Lodge was closely tyled.

He was one in a thousand.　Where shall we find
　His equal in goodness of heart—
So wide in its range, and so unconfined,
　So free from deceit and art?

He was one in a thousand.　So good and rare,
　So far from guile removed.
Go, tell of his virtues everywhere,
　And how he was beloved.

EDITORIAL MUSINGS.

A' ye wha think it unco nice
　Tae edit a bit paper,
Had better ponder o'er it twice
　Before you try the caper,
Else ye may rue, when rather late,
　An' bann the hour ye tried it,
An' wish for ony ither fate,
　Although ye try tae hide it,
　　Wi' smile serene.

Here hae I sat for five lang hours,
　'Mang reams an' reams o' matter,
Straining, taxing a' my powers,
　Wi' scarce ae drink o' water,
Tae pick an' wail frae 'mong the lot
　Some gems o' composition
That may be read an' then forgot
　Wi' careless indecision,
　　　　By 'tentless cuifs.

Still, there's a pleasure in the task,
　Tho' cares around do warp it,
What sphere o' life's a' bliss, I ask,
　Let's ken, that I may start it.
Kings, counsellors, and princes fair,
　As weel's the common ploughman,
Hae maist their pleasures mix'd wi' care,
　An' dread some muckle boo-man,·
　　　　Wha mocks their fun. ·

My boo-man is my readers' frown,
　My readers' condemnation;
My rich reward, my laurel crown,
　Their smiles o' commendation;
Hence, hour by hour, I ponder o'er
　What dainties tae provide them,
An' tax my editorial power,
　A' blemishes tae hide them,
　　　　Frae prying een.

Some write tae say they're gey weel pleased,
　Some ominously grumble,
Some flatter, whiles wi' some I'm teased,
　An' some are unco humble;

Some want a letter's lang's my arm
  Inserted holus-bolus,
Regardless o' the scath an' harm
  Their writing wad embroil us,
        Wi' ither chiels.

Some chant in rhyme, while decent prose
  Wad serve their purpose better,
An' dootless turn up their nose
  When we return their letter;
Some quiz an' question 'bout the law
  O' precedence Masonic,
An' ithers write without a flaw,
  Wi' reasoning quite platonic—
        ' But they are rare.

Wi' these we've little fash tae thole,
  Their periods are so measured,
So rythmical, an', on the whole,
  Their thoughts should aye be treasured,
But, oh! it is the budding scribe
  Wha puzzles an' perplexes,
Wha's rigmarole we canna bide,
  Wha's manuscript aye vexes
        Our anxious minds.

A NEW- YEAR'S GREETING TO OUR READERS.

A Guid New-Year we wish ye a',
  Ye sonsie chiels o' square an' level;
Lang may Fortune's sunshine fa'
  Across your path, without an evil;
Lang may Love fraternal bind
  And knit ye closer athegither,
Leaving ilka care behind,
  Like autumn leaves, tae fa' an' wither.

Cantie, couthie, be your wives,
  Obedient be your thriving bairns,
Happy, cheerfu' a' your lives—
  'Tis but the bliss your virtue earns.
May Poverty, that scowling loon
  That haunts the poor man, never fear ye,
An' a' that's guid, below, aboon,
  Be yours, tae strengthen an' tae cheer ye.

May comfort cleed your happy hames
  Wi' a' that's needfu', an' wi' plenty
Aye tae fill your hungry wames,
  An' health in store tae mak' it dainty.
May Envy never cross your door,
  Tae taunt ye wi' anither's measure.
Remember that, though e'er sae poor,
  Contentment is the greatest treasure.

I'M UNCO CONTENTED AN' WEEL.

I'm unco contented an' weel,
  · Though at times, like a' ithers, I grumble,
An' think that a's gaun tae the deil,
  If I noo an' then get a bit tumble.

But wha disna fa', let me ken,
  An' wha disna frown when they're fa'ing?
The best I hae seen among men
  Are cross when wi' Fortune they're thrawing.

I hae health, that's aye something, I trow,
  That canna be bocht like a bonnet.
    An' grey faces, tae, no' a few,
Though I canna be said tae be moneyet.

But riches mair precious than they—
  I've a wife, in hersel' a rare jewel,
An' my heart is kept het ilka day
  Wi' abundance o' love's lowing fuel.

Besides, I've a bonnie wee bairn—
  Guid spare her! she's really a treasure—
An' I dote on her.   What am I carin'
  Though some think that weak beyond measure?

Ca't weakness, or love, if you like.
  Wha likesna their ain likes but little.
The parent's a passionless tyke
  Wha cares for his ain no' a spittle.

FREEDOM.

Free as the air we are breathing,
  Our thoughts, all unfettered, should be;
Unbeguiled, and ourselves undeceiving,
  We then shall be happy and free.
The parsons may preach of the blessings
  The death-bed repenters enjoy;
Let Time share Eternity's wishings,
  And guidè us our lives to employ.

To-day is the time for life's battle,
  To-morrow we ne'er may behold;
Then live so that pleasure or sorrow
  May still find us valiant and bold.
The soul that's continually sighing,
  A heavenly bliss to obtain,
Should rather on strength be relying,
  Still fearless, come pleasure or pain.

Life is not a sham; it is earnest.
  Its laurels are still for the strong.
The happiest heart is the firmest
  And foremost to rectify wrong.
The holiest life's the most active,
  When Truth is the cause to defend;
The freest from all that's deceptive,
  Where Virtue and Truth ever blend.

Then let us be earnest, my brothers,
  And active while life is our own,
In sympathy sharing with others
  The comforts we've fought for and won.
Thus Heaven, the home of the blessed,
  Shall then be established on earth;
And Man, then no longer oppressed,
  Shall grow both in goodness and worth.

BY NETHAN'S BOWERY BANKS.

By Nethan's bowery banks I stray,
  As gloaming shadows, lengthening, fa',
To muse upon my own sweet May.
  Her charms o' grace, sae airtless a',
She kens the trysting place, whaur love
  We've plighted o'er an' o'er again.
I'll hie me there, an' constant prove
  I'm still her faithfu', loving swain.

The river, murmuring, laps the bank,
  The trout, in wid'ing circle, springs.
A' Nature, joyous, seems tae thank
  The Power aboon, wha e'ening brings.

The cushet cooing in the grove,
  The blackbird on yon thorny tree,
A', lingering, tell their tale o' love,
  But nane are half sae fond o' me.

I mark, wi' pain, the slow-gaun hour
  That brings my charmer tae my arms.
The flowery bank and shady bower
  Withoot her hinna half their charms.
Ae smile o' hers mak's licht the shade,
  Her voice the tunefu' sangsters shame;
And, pressed within my sheltering plaid,
  Her heaving breast my own inflames.

With love as pure, as warm, an' true
  As ever fired angelic breast,
I kiss her cheek an' cherry moo',
  Tho' fain her shyness wad resist.
I pledge ance mair my constant love
  Shall shield her frae a' thocht o' harm,
And vow by yonder stars above
  To guard her love and every charm.

WINTER.

Nae langer summer's balmy breath
  Sweet blooming flowerets fan,
And leafless are the forest trees,
  Where sweet the warblers sang,

While ilka plant that bloomed sae bright
  In summer noo lies dead—
Cauld winter seemed tae hate the sight,
  And spoilt ilk flowery bed.

He came upon his annual raid,
  An' little flowers grew wan;
Ilk plant an' tree his victim made;
  Nor has he yet withdrawn—
See hoo the wee bit warblers shake
  An' shiver in the blast.
They seem as if their **hearts** wad break,
  An' wish for winter **past**.

They, cowering, seek the shelter **still**
  O' yon cauld, leafless wood;
An' often brave the blast **sae chill**
  In searching for their food.
An' still cauld winter lingers yet,
  With fierce tyrannic sway,
Wi' icy mantle lying yet
  O'er woodland, glen, an' brae.

NEW-YEAR'S SONG.

Again auld Faither Time brings roon'
  The New-Year's social meetings,
And friendship, blyth o'er sic a boon,
  Is spendrift wi' her greetings.
"A guid New-Year tae auld **an'** young,"
  She sings, wi' muckle **cheer**;
And echo, quite as loose **o'** tongue,
  Cries, "Hail the infant year!"

Chorus.
  Then welcome ye the infant year,
    Wi' hearts as blyth as mine;
  An' let us be as blyth as were
    Oor forebears o' langsyne.

'Tis noo that couthy cronies meet,
  Forgetfu' o' ilk care,
Tae crack o' auld langsyne sae sweet,
  Tae age aye doubly dear.
'Tis noo that youth, rejoicing, tae,
  Forgets ilk suffered wrang,
And dedicates the year's first day
  Tae merriment an' sang.
    Then welcome ye the infant year, etc., etc.

Fu' happy may the year gae roon',
  Unscaured by haggard care,
May Plenty shower her treasures doon,
  Till hunger cries nae mair;
May Friendship, tae, aye haud her ain
  'Gainst a' the ills that mar,
An' mak' them reel wi' cries o' pain
  Throughoot the dawning year.
    Then welcome ye the infant year, etc., etc.

EPISTLE TO J. KERR, TOLLCROSS.

Man, Jock, I don't know what you're thinking—
Perhaps that I've been deid or drinking;
At ony rate, I'm further sinking
    In your esteem.
For no' replying tae yon clinking
    Little rhyme.

The fact is, I've been unco thrang,
An' hadna time, for things gaun wrang,
Tae write ye either prose or sang,
    Though I'd been stickit
Wi' either sword or serpent's stang,
    Or soundly lickit.

But noo, since I've a blink tae spare—
'Tho' jist a blink, an' naething mair—
I'll rin ye aff, wi' Deil-ma'-care,
      A line or twa,
Although the Muse should start an' stare,
      An' me misca'.

Deil tak' the Muse, the fickle jade,
Noo, that I think o't, since she's fled
Frae me, wha wad hae gladly bled
      Tae keep her favour,
An' Tollcross noo her hame has made,
      Wi' great palaver.

Nae doot you're proud she's eastward gane,
An' think tae ca' her a' your ain,
An' laugh within yoursel' fu' fain,
      Ye pawky devil.
I maist could swear, but maun refrain
      Frae sic an evil.

You're no' tae blame; 'twas her, the slut,
Wha whispered in your lug tae put
Your thochts in rhyme, an' nicely cut
      The flowing measure—
Mixed weel wi' sense an' mither wit—
      Nae common treasure.

My certie, ance it's better kent
That ye can rhyme, you'll hae tae prent—
E'en though it be against your bent—
      A sang or twa;
An' dootless, man, you'll ne'er repent
      The deed ava'.

But, though you shouldna soar sae high
As measured sang or elegy,
Keep rhyming on, an' you'll descry
          The pleasure o't,
Though no' refined wi' learning high,
          The measure o't.

It's weel kent nane o' us hae lear
Tae mak' oor meaning unco clear;
But that's nae reason we should fear
          Tae state in rhyme
Oor notions o' the true an' queer
          At ony time.

Oor mind's oor ain you'll no' deny ;
Though no' refined wi' learning high,
'Twould be a sin tae let it lie
          In dormant state ;
Unexercised, 'twould get as dry
          As copperplate.

But, Jock, I maunna keep ye langer,
Lest at me ye should tak' a scunner.
Whilk, if ye should, wad be nae won'er—
          But let it pass.
You'll say I'm neither saint nor sinner,
          But jist an ass.

Weel, weel, I maybe jist deserve it ;
Sae, when you've read this, don't preserve it,
But tae the fire fu' speedy serve it—
          There let it burn ;
Or intae sma', sma' pieces carve it—
          I winna mourn.

TO A COUSIN.

God guide and guard ye safely through
  This life o' trials here;
May wisdom ever cling tae you,
  Thy pilgrimage to cheer;
May she be thy companion still
  Through a' life's varied scene,
To cheer and comfort thee; then will
  Thy years have happy been.

Remember, tae, as lang's ye leeve,
  Your mother true and kind,
For, though I rhyme, this rhyme believe:
  You ne'er sic love will find.
Watch o'er her age wi' tender care,
  Where'er thy lot be cast;
An' if a groat ye hae tae spare,
  Share't wi' her tae the last.

SUMMER.

Welcome simmer—
Winsome kimmer—
Wi' your bonnie frock o' flowers
Lying lightly—
Daily, nightly—
O'er the lea an' woody bowers.

Welcome ever;
Lea' us never;
See what happiness ye bring!
Hear how sweetly
Warblers greet ye—
E'en the meanest loves to sing.

All are singing;
Vendure springing
Now proclaims dull winter gane.
Ilka creature,
Viewing Nature,
Hail the simmer here again.

Zephyrs blawing;
Nightly fa'ing
Dews bespangle budding boughs;
All extending
And expanding—
Brighter as the season goes.

Ilka floweret
That can spare it
Lends a fragrance tae the air;
Ilka gowan,
Meekly bowing,
Claims the simmer sunshine there.

Laverocks, soaring,
Sing inspiring
Songs o' welcome in thy praise;
And the linnet,
Sharing in it,
Does his best in humble lays.

Come, then, simmer—
Beautous kimmer—
Tarry wi' us for a while,
Cheering Nature,
And ilk creature,
With thy life-restoring smile.

TO SCOTLAND.

Farewell, Scotia, I maun leave thee,
  Land of Wallace, Bruce, and Burns,
But I love thee—oh! believe me!—
  Though my fancy from thee turns.

Still I love thy towering mountains,
  Crested by the heather-bell;
Still I love thy silver fountains,
  Sparkling in the rocky dells;

Still I love thy flowery meadows,
  Where the lambkins sportive play;
Still I love thy sylvan shadows,
  Echoing the warblers' lays.

Still to me thy name gives pleasure
  Dearer than I can express;
Still I fondly prize and treasure
  All the glories you possess.

Glories, brighter by that freedom
  Which our fathers guarded still;
Glories that shall never perish
  While the sun shines on ilk hill.

Or while yet the thistle, proudly
  Waving, rears his downy head
O'er the dust of great and lordly—
  Scotia's dear, illustrious dead.

Why, then, should I not revere thee,
  Land that gave my fathers birth,
Land of liberty? Oh, hear me!
  Still I prize thy priceless worth.

Though I seek a land where riches
  Lure the humble toiling swain;
Though far from thee as ocean stretches
  I shall seek thy shores again.

WISDOM, STRENGTH, AND BEAUTY.

Long may this Lodge in prosperity shine,
  And its members still vie with each other
In spreading the light of our Order divine,
  And relieving the wants of a brother.

May envy and malice ne'er enter the door
  That is aye closely tyled tae the cowan;
And peace, love, and harmony aye be in store,
  More abundant the older you're growing.

May he who presides, like the Master of old,
  In Wisdom excel, and astonish,
And never be heard erring brothers to scold,
  But with brotherly love aye admonish.

May he in the West, like the sun's setting ray,
  Illumine the golden horizon;
May his Strength never fail with the burden of days,
  But increase every moment that flies on.

And he in the South, like the Beauty of day,
  May he gladden the worn and weary;
And cheer with his smiles, when they rest by the way,
  The toilers, and make them fu' cheery.

And ye whom the Master is honoured to rule
  And instruct, be ye sober and steady;
Expert in the use o' each working tool,
  And aye hae them handy and ready.

Thus will the Temple we seek to upraise
  Be completed, when all do their duty ;
And your voices unite in a chorus of praise
  To Wisdom, to Strength, and to Beauty.

HAIL TO OUR CHIEF !

(Respectfully dedicated to Major F. W. Allan).

Hail to our chief ! in virtue growing grey ;
  Mature in wisdom, vigorous in mind.
May we, for years to come, his worth survey
  In active exercise among our kind.
Possessing virtues rare in man to find.
  Envy herself cannot asperse his name,
And old and young their praises have combined
    To swell the chorus of his deathless fame,
    In paths where virtue ever feeds the flame.

Wide as the earth, and ceaseless as its roll,
  His sympathies extend to every class.
No narrow crotchies can enslave his soul,
  To bid the hungry poor, unheeded, pass.
All are his kindred, though their lot, alas !
  Precludes their entrance 'mong the favour'd few,
Where want nor care the fleeting hours harass,
    And every moment brings them pleasures new.
    Too oft, alas ! obscuring what is good and true.

Swift to correct the erring, ever strong,
  Where rectitude her limits would define,
Ready to redress oppression's wrong,
  And with discretion charity combine.

Straight as the Plumet leads the hanging line.
  His every action marks the soul within—
Pure and unselfish—aye, almost divine,
    Yet to humanity's best force akin
    In deprecating each besetting sin.

Vast as the store of knowledge he has drawn
  From Nature's storehouse and from mystic art,
And all the honours he has nobly won
    Have not with empty pride enthralled his heart;
He thirsts for knowledge that he may impart
  To others all the blessings it can give,
And bid the soul with emulation start
    With resolution strong henceforth to live
    More self-reliant, more determined, brave.

By precept drawn from musty ages past
  He eloquently points the onward way
That leads to happiness secure and fast,
    A monitor of bliss from day to day.
Nor is it of his rhetoric a vain display,
  The enraptured crowds his life's example know
Else how could he their various passions sway,
    And fire their breasts with virtue's purest glow,
    And bid desire in smoother channels flow?

Long may he guide our thoughts, command our hearts,
  And cheer us with his kindly, beaming smile,
Nor ever grudge the comforts he imparts
    To all who love and venerate his style.
May every blessing be his own the while,
  And years weigh lightly on a heart so kind.
May pleasant recollections oft beguile
    The hour of rest, and soothe the troubled mind
    With thought to leave an honoured name behind.

AULD CANNY TAM.

A kindly auld body ance lived in oor toon,
An' respected was he by the neighbours a' roon'.
The worst o' his fau'ts was he liked a bit dram,
But a couthy auld body was Auld Canny Tam.

He could crack o' the wars an' the battles o' yore,
O' the time o' the Flood, an' a lang time before;
Ilka thing that had happened lang syne he could tell,
As if he had actually seen them himsel'.

He leeved in a wee cot that stauns a' alane,
An' dearly he loved it, baith rafters an' stane—
Lov'd it a' did he, an' weel micht he, tae,
For a cozy wee beil was't by nicht or by day.

Contented was Tammy—contented, I throw—
An' tho' he had battles he warstled them through—
Warstled them through, tho' at times clouted sair.
When the tussle was ower he wad think o't nae mair.

But time wore alang, an' his hair turned grey,
His step grew unsteady, an' oft wad he sway;
Auld age was upon him, wi' shortness o' breath,
Which kindly gied warning o' what we ca' Death.

Ah! Death came at last, wi' his cauld icy haun',
An' touched the auld body as by he was gaun;
An' those wha had loved him in storm an' calm
Closed the cauld eyelids o' Auld Canny Tam.

LET US NEVER LOSE HEART.

Let us never lose heart tho' our lot may be poor,
An the pock in the cupboard be empty;
Though want noo an' then should keek in at the door,
Ne'er faint wi' his figure fornent ye.

The warst o' oor ills, like the cloud in the lift,
  May daurken the sun, though it's shining.
But never lose heart.   There is dootless a rift
  Through which we may glint on the lining.

The house may be sma', an' the wa's may be bare,
  An' the store o' a' comforts be scanty ;
But tent ye tae this : Ye hae something tae spare
  If you're routh o' guid health, an' content aye.
The laird may look big wi' his acres o' lan',
  An' glunch wi' disdain when ye meet him.
Jist say tae yoursel', wi' a wave o' the han',
  "In a' that's worth while I can beat him."

DESPONDENCY.

(Written in a fit of despondency),

Thou soul-corrupting evil.
Go, seek the shades.   For ever there
  Attend thy parent Devil.

Why torture me with doubt and fears,
  Perpetually distressing,
And cares too numerous for my years,
  Eternally oppressing?

Why rob me of life's golden hours
  In manhood's early dawning?
Why, oh! why, ye torturing powers,
  Delight to hear me groaning?

Avaunt! withdraw thy mantling cloud,
  And leave me as of yore,
Or wrap me in Death's solemn shroud,
  And rest for ever more.

DEATH OF STRAFFORD.

(Late Manager at Parkhead Rolling Mills).

Trials, such as seldom mar domestic bless,
  Were thine, nor murmured thou at what befell.
The rod that chastened thou didst humbly kiss,
  Nor in despondency thy troubles tell.

Could emulation kindle at thy tomb,
  And fire the breast of all who mourn for thee,
Less would be felt the all-pervading gloom
  That gathers round the lifeless form we see.

But, ah! how slow we are to emulate the wise
  In aught that Virtue hallows with her name!
Appreciation may, at times, arise,
  But oft, alas! the heart withstands the same.

Not so with thee. Thy heart, like to thy mind,
  Continual enlargement ever knew.
Free from all pride, by avarice unconfined,
  You generously gave to not a few.

For other motives, purer far the glow
  Too frequently beheld in this our day.
For other motives, purer far the glow
  Than some designing hypocrite's display.

But now, alas! the yawning tomb awaits
  All that remains of thee—our common end.
The voice of friendship now in vain relates,
  Nor half can tell the worth of such a friend.

To deck thy tomb the sculptured stone may rise—
  The last sad gift surviving love bestows;
But not the highest, tears from sorrowing eyes
  A higher tribute is to life's calm close.

That tribute's thine—the rich reward of worth,
  More precious than the trumpeting of fame.
Long be it paid.   May other sons of earth
  Reap half the praise that hallows Strafford's name.

FROM A LOCAL PAPER.

JANET HAMILTON.—We have been favoured this week
with a letter and poem from Mr. David Willox, Parkhead,
which will explain themselves. Mr. Willox is a horny-
handed son of toil, almost wholly self-taught. Young,
temperate, unassuming, with a prospect of much future
culture, and withal gifted in no ordinary degree with the
poetic faculty, he bids fair to obtain a niche in the temple
of the Doric muse, to judge from various productions of his
which have appeared elsewhere, as well as from the con-
tents of his note-book, which we have partially perused, and
from which we trust to be allowed to take frequent selec-
tions. On a recent occasion he paid a lengthened visit to
dear old Janet, whose converse, presence, and enthusiasm
he found altogether congenial. To this visit we are indebted for the letter and poem above alluded to, which we
feel sure all our readers will be pleased to read:—"Parkhead, March 29, 1869. Dear Sir,—I take the liberty of
forwarding you the enclosed lines, trusting, if you deem
them worthy, you will find a place for them in your very
valuable paper. I need hardly tell you that the subject
of my rhyme is Scotland's aged poetess, Janet Hamilton—

a poetess dear to the hearts of all true lovers of poetry, and especially so to the sons and daughters of auld Scotland.—Yours respectfully, D. WILLOX.

OUR MINSTREL MOTHER.

Janet Hamilton, **Poetess,** Langloan.

Tell me not our Scottish muse
    Wi' Robin sang her latest song,
Nor that the Nine since then refuse
    Their sacred dictates to prolong.

Tell me not they have forsaken
    Scotia's sons and daughters all,
For now sweet notes reverberating
    Chain the heart in Music's thrall.

Hark! how sweet our minstrel mother
    Tunes our ancient native lyre.
Soul and genius sing together,
    Forming an immortal choir.

Hark, how sweet her notes are falling
    On our pleasure-spellbound ear,
Former days and scenes recalling,
    Welling from the heart a tear.

Now they thrill the pensive lover,
    Now they stir the hero's heart,
Now they nameless grief discover,
    Now they solace sweet impart.

Now they lift the soul sublimely,
    With the skylark, in the air;
Now they touch the heart divinely
    With a mother's earnest prayer.

Praise, then, Scotia, this your daughter;
  Trace her name in pages grand,
And extol the Muse that wrought her
  Greatest of our minstrel band.

Fame hath wrapped her robes around her,
  And proclaimed her list complete;
Genius, proud to own she found her,
  Strews her laurels at her feet.

NEW-YEAR GREETINGS TO THE NURSES OF BELVIDERE HOSPITAL.

(Suggested by a visit to that Institution, on 1st January, 1897, by the Visiting Councillors).

Ance mair upon the dial of Time
  A New-Year's smiles appear,
And happy hearts in every clime,
  Rejoicing, greet the year.
Hope's ruddy glow, reflecting, springs
  To light our toilsome way,
And guide, as if on angel's wings.
  Our path from day to day.

We seek not to forget the past,
  Where love and friendship strong
Around our hearts their pleasures cast,
  Like chords of heavenly song.
Such memories can but swell the store
  Of comfort and of cheer
We hope for, as we have before,
  When dawned a new-born year.

But upward, ever upward, still
  Hope points the path beyond,

That crowns with bliss life's toilsome hill,
  Where our reward is found.
Reward: a peaceful, honoured age,
  With conscience calm and clear,
We've merited at every stage,
  An' endless, blissful year.

May such reward, thou noble band,
  Be thine. Thy labours claim
Our highest praise, almost command
  The laurel wreath of fame.
To help the helpless day by day,
  And stem the rising tear,
Is surely what makes light the way
  Towards the endless year.

Remote from social pleasures far,
  Self-sacrificing few,
Where dangerous diseases war,
  Ye constant are and true,
To cool the fever-heated brow,
  Like angel presence near,
And teach the sinking heart to know
  That ever endless year.

Long may you live, your labour blessed
  To cheer and comfort you
For all the pleasures ye have missed
  Of home and friendship true.
May grateful hearts your praises sing,
  Where'er in life you steer,
And circling seasons ever bring
  You all a Guid New-Year.

NOW AND THEN.

(On learning of the great loss of my esteemed friend, Mr.
Gavin Ingles, whose wife and only son died within
fourteen days of each other).

As dowie by the ingle side
  I wistfu' watch the dancing lowe,
My memory travels far and wide
  O'er what I was and what I'm now.

I ance was blithe as blithe could be,
  Wi' scarce a care my heart to move;
Three happy hearts, yes, only three,
  Made glad my home wi' constant love.

Full thirty years o' married bliss
  I can recall without a jar,
O! that it e'er should come to this
  I should my loneliness declare.

She who had hallowed with her love
  My humble hearth, when first she came
A blushing bride her worth to prove,
  And be the sunshine o' my hame,

Has passed beyond that darksome vale
  Whose further side no eye hath seen,
Nor strongest love can e'er avail
  To guard against its anguish keen.

And he, the darling of our home,
  Whose infant years such promise gave,
Cut off in manhood's early bloom,
  Now shares his mother's lowly tomb.

Nae wonder that I dowie bend,
  And wistfu' watch the dancing lowe,
While groans and sighs my bosom rend
  As memory pictures then and now.

THE GIFT.

(The following verses were written for the Rev. A. D. Tait
on the occasion of his being presented with a very
handsome staff by the members of the Parkhead Parish
Bible Class, of which he was the talented and respected teacher).

'Tis good at times to feel we are
  By others much esteemed,
It gives an impulse to the heart
  Which stoics ne'er redeemed.

It cheers us in our solitude,
  And makes our bosoms swell;
It speaks of mutual gratitude
  That language cannot tell.

For words are tiny little things,
  And often can't reveal
The language to the heart that clings,
  Nor half the love we feel.

The heart is still the casket where
  The purest gems lay hid,
And words may tell they're treasured there,
  But cannot lift the lid.

Therefore I trust, though half expressed,
  My thanks will be accepted,
And find with you an honoured rest
  In your esteem respected.

For thanks are all I can bestow
  To mark my admiration
Of this a true symbolic shew
  Of your high estimation.

And while I tread the busy path
  Of life to age declining,
'Twill comfort me to find I have
  On friendship been reclining.

For thus I name this handsome staff,
  The name it's most deserving ;
Though you incredulous should laugh,
  It all of us is serving.

'Twill lend me first its strong support,
  When journeying from home.
Nor fret nor grumble nor get short,
  No matter where I roam.

And then again 'twill bring to mind
  The friends I'm proud to own.
And speak, though silently still kind.
  Of each and every one.

'Twill speak of friendship which I feel
  Is mutual to us all,
And which I trust will ever seal
  Our hearts 'gainst evil's thrall.

'Twill stand in friendship's social stead
  When distant from this hall.
And as I grasp its glossy head
  I grasp the hand of all.

LINES COMPOSED BY COUNCILLOR D. WILLOX
ON THE
OPENING OF TOLLCROSS PUBLIC PARK
BY
LORD PROVOST RICHMOND, ON SATURDAY, 19TH JUNE, 1897.

We hail with joy another breathing space,
  Where labour may relax her grip of toil
And Nature court, with sweetly smiling face,
  The weary labourer upon her soil.
Here no o'er-mastering task may spoil
  The golden hours of leisure, rest, and ease;
And peace and harmony may wile
  The troubled mind from care to themes that please,
  And bid the heart all-hopeful cherish these.

Here, when the gloaming shadows softly fall,
  The amorous lover may in peace repair
To breathe the troubles of his longing soul,
  In tuneful numbers to the ambient air;
Or, crowned with bliss, he wanders with his fair
  Through shady bower and fragrant woody grove,
Recounting oft her charms, to him so rare,
  And telling of his strong undying love
  In strains that win the heart he seeks to move.

Here, weary from the dinsome forge and mill,
  Young Vulcan may his steel-like sinews rest;
The scented air inhaling, he may fill
  With deep-drawn draughts the chambers of his breast,
And strengthened thus, of weariness divest,
  His aching limbs to meet to-morrow's toil.

With buoyant heart, and hope to do his best,
  He homeward hies, refreshed all o'er the while,
  Seeking his couch, no dreams his slumber spoil.

Here, careless childhood may disport and play,
  And gather flowerets from the grassy mead,
Or chase the bee throughout the summer day
  To steal the treasured amber-honeyed bead.
Unmindful of the pangs their thoughtless greed
  Inflicts upon the tireless, toiling bee.
With cap in hand they bound with deer-like speed
  To lead him captive, and his treasure pree,
  Then mangled leave him on the flowery lea.

Here settled sires may stroll with matron dames,
  And mark with pride their off-springs' growing powers,
Encourage or correct their childish games,
  Or help them busk themselves with garland flowers,
While speeds the all-unheeded summer hours.
  Parental pride and hope their bosoms fire;
They mark the virtue that outstanding towers,
  And say, "How like the lad is to his sire!"
  Affection strengthening the fond desire.

Here all may roam at leisure and in peace,
  And taste the pleasure which possession brings.
No tyrant lord can bid their wandering cease
  Nor damp the ardour which within them springs.
As free to roam as in the woodland sings
  The tuneful mavis, or at dawn the lark
When soaring high he upward heavenward wings
  His joyous flight, his rapture all to mark—
  This is our own, the People's Public Park!

IN MEMORIAM—JANET POLLOCK BLUER.

THE WITHERED ROSE-BUD.

[Suggested on being shown a flower culled from the grave of
Janet Pollock Bluer, a young lady of rare personal
beauty and natural endowments of heart and mind,
who died 10th Feby., 1895.]

It was only a flow'ret its fragrance shed,
 And the bloom from its bosom gone;
A pale little flow'ret all withered and dead,
 Ere the bud had maturely blown.

But it came from the grave of a favourite child
 Who died in her early years—
An emblem of innocent womanhood mild,
 And was wet with the parents' tears.

Its beauty was gone, to the casual eye
 It long since had shed its bloom;
But the wealth of the Indies could not buy
 That prize from the humble home.

'Twas an emblem of her who mouldering lay
 Where its infant fragrance spread
A hallowed incense over the clay
 That covered the peerless dead.

It shone like a gem to the parents' eyes,
 In its casket of earthenware;
And to them it was touched with a thousand dyes,
 In form and beauty rare.

'Twas so like the child they had lost, so sweet,
 And it came from her lowly tomb,
That its faded leaves ne'er failed to greet
 Their eyes with perennial bloom.

It spoke to their hearts in its voiceless way,
  Of the daughter they loved so well ;
And its fading leaves had been watered each day,
  With the tears from their eyes that fell.

It touched with a visionless hand the chords
  That swelled with undying love
For her who *was* theirs, but is now the Lord's
  In the Golden City above.

And in fancy they could hear her voice
  Amongst the angelic throng,
Whose voices, tuned in joyful noise,
  Raise high the Celestial Song.

They could hear her sing as they oft had heard,
  With her whole soul in the strain,
Vieing in tune with the soaring bird
  As he springs from the grassy plain.

They could see her still as she was, so fair,
  So gifted and full of grace,
That she vied with the loveliest angel there
  And shone in that peerless place.

And their hearts were touched by a holier fire,
  From the picture their fancy drew,
And strengthening Hope gave stronger desire
  To join the Celestial Crew.

They longed to be clad as their daughter was,
  In spotless robes of white,
And join in the praise of the Great First Cause
  Of Eternal Love and Light.

FIRST CORPORATION V. OFFICIALS BOWLING MATCH.

17th AUGUST, 1897.

Oor City Fathers hang their heid,
  An' oh! but they're protesting
Against the match whaur Lindsay led
  An' gied them sic a besting.
They say it was nae match ava,
  An' shouldna be recorded;
But lood the bold Officials craw,
  And as a win regard it.
            Fu' blithe this day.

Tae try their skill, three rinks were drawn
  O' Councillors, fu' cantie,
Against Officials, ilk man
  Of whom were unco vantie.
The match was set for Titwood Green,
  An' after twice postponing,
At last they played; but, oh, hoo mean!
  Five Councillors responding
            Tae challenge sent.

But, undismayed, they socht recruits,
  Tae mak' the needfu' number,
An' tackled tae, wi' mony doots
  Hoo far they would be under.
Twa rinks o' them did no' sae bad—
  Yin peel'd, the ither winnin'—
But, oh! the score the ither had
  Set them their loss bemoaning,
            Wi' grief that day.

A wily Lawyer skipped the foe,
  P.G. the Corporation.
Whit was the score ye needna know—
  We'll say it was vexation.
P.G. had never skipped before,
  Yet oot the match he lasted;
An' from the field fu' manly bore
  A reputation blasted,
        As skip that day.

He's aye the first in ilka fray,
  The soul o' wit an' humour;
But, oh, dear, no! he canna play,
  At least as skip, in honour.
Time after time, when telt tae draw
  A close yin tae the kitty,
His bool wad rumble yards awa'
  Intae the ditch, as pretty
        As ocht that day.

But what altho'? He's no' the chiel
  Tae be dooncast or daunted;
His heart's ower big sic fash tae feel—
  He's jist the man that's wanted
Tae gie a relish tae the game
  An' set the fun a-steerin',
Regardless o' defeat or fame,
  The price o' neither speiring
        His constant aim.

So, when we try oor luck again,
  He'll surely be invited;
An' should he win I'm shure ilk yin
  Will fairly feel delighted.

An' wha can tell but win he may,
  An' verify the sayin':
"The game's a kittle yin tae play"
  Tae e'en the best at playin',
    Hooe'er sae guid.

TO
COUNCILLOR ALEXANDER OSBORNE,
CONVENER OF THE WATER COMMITTEE,
ON
THE PRESENTATION OF HIS PORTRAIT
BY
THE CORPORATION OF GLASGOW,
31st AUGUST, 1897.

Hail, Osborne! father o' oor Board,
Oor greetings here, in blithe accord
But faintly mark hoo ye hae scored
    Wi' mony a dart,
An' pierced the very inmost chord
    In ilka heart.

Ye've served St. Mungo lang an' weel,
Watching, wi' jealousy and zeal,
Oor growing wants, an' aye could feel
    Oor needs were yours,
An' claimed your efforts a' tae heal,
    Wi' a' your powers.

Ye ne'er were loth, where work was gaun,
Tae lend a ready, helping haun';
Whaur ithers micht in swithers staun'
    Ye aye were ready,
Ne'er slothfu', critical or thrawn,
    But firm—steady.

For thirty years an' something mair
In Council work ye've taen a share,
An', even noo, we ill can spare
      Your voice an' guiding
When knotty problems fill the air,
      An' need deciding.

'Tis then, when ithers seek tae shine
Wi' points lang-drawn, some eight or nine,
Ye calmly interpose benign
      Wi' some past ruling
That bangs their rhetoric divine,
      An' leaves them cooling.

When great Demosthenes was young,
An' could weel control his tongue,
He to the waves, for practice, sung
      His perorations,
Until, wi' pith o' brain an' lung,
      He ruled the nations.

Ye need nae sic lang strokes o' art
Tae fire the mind or move the heart,
Ye've jist tae speak, when upward start
      Oor best emotions,
Ready tae tak art an' part
      In maist your notions.

We ken you're richt, your wecht o' years
Dispel oor doots an' quell oor fears;
The cuif wha hankers jist appears
      In need o' schooling,
Until the Provost's voice declares
      Ye richt in ruling.

Thus hae you won oor faith sincere,
Till ane an' a' your worth revere.
We fain wad hae ye aye appear,
    Tae guide an' lecture,
Ilka time we're gathered here,
    Sae hence your picture.

Lang may it fill its gauzy frame,
An' aye oor highest reverence claim
For ane whose work, whose very name,
    Has aye been dear
Tae a' wha love oor city's fame,
    An' labour here.

Lang may it guide aspiring youth
In paths o' temperance, peace an' truth,
Encouraging the early growth
    O' a' that's best—
A' that can cheer, will last, an' soothe,
    Within the breast.

An' tho' nae trumpet voice may blare
Your triumphs tae the echoing air,
O'er foes wha, shrinking in despair,
    You've fiercely battered;
Yet thousands still unborn will share
    The bliss you've scattered.

E'en while Loch Katrine's crystal tide,
In myriad streams, far-stretching, wide,
Shall bounteous bless, on ilka side,
    The poorest hame.
Oor sons an' daughters will with pride
    Recall thy name.

As lang's Saint Mungo's motto dear—
"Let Glasgow Flourish" year by year—
Shall on oor Civic crest appear,
    Tae keep us brithers,
Your work shall last, outstanding, clear,
    A guide tae ithers.

"CODNOR PARK."
For W. C. Pegg.

There may be scenes of sylvan shade,
  Where lovers roam at eventide,
There may be wilds of fairest glade,
  Where timid deer are fain to hide;
There may be meadows green and fair,
  Where rising hills the landscape mark,
But none to me are half so dear
  As thou, my home, dear Codnor Park.

Here childhood's happy days were spent
  'Midst friends whose hearts were true and warm;
Here both my parents' voices blent
  To guide my mind from thoughts of harm;
Here gathered round the glowing fire,
  When winter nights were long and dark,
I've met my friends, and so admire
  Thy homely comforts, Codnor Park.

Our cities may with wealth abound,
  And teeming thousands shelter there—
Give me the home where peace is found,
  And kindred spirits for me care;

There, though I own no mansion great,
　I anchor would life's fragile barque,
And bless the star that rules my fate,
　And love thee more, dear Codnor Park.

AULD GRANNY IS DEID.

Auld granny is deid, a' the neighbours bewail,
　For a couthy auld body was she;
Death claimed her as his when wan an' frail—
　Her age was a hundred an' three.

Fu' mony a change had the auld body seen
　In her wearyfu' journey through life,
But kind and affectionate aye she had been
　In the warst o' her warldly strife.

Nae sour, sullen frown as in age oft appear
　Cast a gloom o'er the auld body's face,
As careless an' happy we wee things drew near
　Tae her ingle—oor happiest place.

The wee bairns a' were her pride and delight,
　There was nocht that could please her sae weel;
Her heart would aye warm, her sorrows grow light
　As we played roon' her auld pirn wheel.

When ocht wad befa' us that caused us tae fret,
　Tae auld granny we greetin' wad rin,
And aye frae her something were sure for to get
　That wad cure ilka sorrow an' pain.

But thae days are gane, an' I think o' them whiles
  Wi' a tear growing big in my e'e;
In fancy I see her as sweetly she smiles
  At oor childish an' innocent glee.

Farewell then, auld body, tho' you are awa',
  I ne'er shall forget tae my last
The body wha aye was sae kind to us a',
  And often I'll think o' the past.

SAINT MUNGO'S WELCOME TO THE DUKE AND DUCHESS OF YORK,

10TH SEPTEMBER, 1897.

Saint Mungo bares his reverend pow,
And welcomes ye wi' mony a bow,
Fu' blithe tae think you've managed now
    'Tae come this airt,
And share the feelings that aye glow
    Within his heart.

Nae scrimped share o' loyal love
He offers ye, but bids ye prove
How deep an' strong the currents move
    Within his breast;
Imploring a' the powers above
    That ye be blest.

He bids ye welcome o'er an' o'er,
An' would that it were in your power
To tarry wi' us three or four
    Hale days or mair,
That ye micht hae a leisure hour
    Or twa to spare.

Then ye micht see, an' no be seen
As noo by countless glowerin een,
Oor stores o' wealth—a dainty wheen
    O' treasures rare,
An' works o' art that rival clean
    Sic like elsewhere.

Ye then micht saunter by the Clyde,
An' mark oor harbours far an' wide,
Whar ships o' ilka nation ride
    Safe an' secure,
Or bring wi' ilka flowing tide
    New wealth an' power.

Ye then could see, as 'twere by stealth,
The sources o' oor city's wealth,
An' marvel aiblins at the health
    An' vigour shown
In raising palaces o' wealth
    Whar grass had grown.

The river's rolling, turbid wave
Micht justly your attention crave,
A streamlet ance whar bairns micht brave
    The further shore,
An' crossing scarce their ankles lave
    In passing o'er.

Now rolling wide an' deep an' strong,
A stemless tide it sweeps along,
Where once the ancient native swung
    His ponderous oar ;
Braw steamers ply—a countless throng—
    Frae shore to shore.

The magic wand Alladdin swayed
Ne'er such a transformation made
As here, on ilka side portrayed,
        Can noo be seen—
Whar silence reigned, the roar o' trade
        Is morn an' e'en.

Oor boat-yards tae on ilka side,
Frae Linthouse a' the way doon Clyde,
Micht weel entice ye jist tae bide
        A kenning here—
Their fame, I'm shure's been warld-wide
        For mony a year.

There, 'midst the rattle, roar, an' din
O' countless hammers rivettin',
Ye aiblins micht some knowledge fin'
        Worth while to store,
An' learn hoo such fame they win
        The warld o'er.

Or should ye seek in thochtfu' mood
A cannie 'oor in solitude,
Then leave the din, the steer, an' crowd
        Wi' few remarks,
An' view oor truest "Common Good"—-
        Oor public parks.

There, musing, moralise at will
On a' you've seen o' art an' skill,
An' if ye other wonders still
        Wad like tae see,
Jist slip ye roon' by yonder hill —
        Oor water pree.

There frae the fountain's sculptured side
Unstinted draw the crystal tide
That flows beneficently wide
    O'er a' the toon—
Oor boast, oor joy, oor bliss, oor pride
    By night an' noon.

A' that is oors is yours to share,
E'en though its worth were double mair,
You're welcome tae't; jist you declare
    Your will an' pleasure;
Nae scrimpit coggie passes where
    Love heaps the measure.

May constant loyalty an' love
Your close companions ever prove,
An' ilka blessing frae above
    Your bosoms cheer
Through life; an' mind whare'er ye move,
    You're welcome here.

MASONIC ORATION.

Delivered at Funeral Lodge held October, 1895.

R. W. M., Wardens and Brethren:—The circumstances under which we are met are well calculated to awaken our most serious thought, indicating, as they do, the mutability of human life and the transitory nature of our existence. To-day, in the full flush of strength and vigour, we are breasting the waves in the ocean of life; to-morrow, we sink into the overwhelming surge. We mark with kindling eyes and emotions of pleasure the progress of our friends and loved ones, and we mourn with saddened heart, and in tears, at the close of their career.

This, brethren, is as it should be, and proves at once our kinship in thought and feeling—descendants from the same stock, partakers of the same nature, and sharers of the same hope. What a flood of sympathy there is in a single tear dropped by the grave of some beloved friend! What a world of emotion there is in a deep drawn sigh over the sufferings of some dearly loved one!

The present occasion is a particularly sad one for the members of this Lodge, 128, commemorating, as it does, the decease of several of our brethren who were wont to be with us in the working of our mystic rites, who have passed from labour to rest until the angel of the Lord shall call the last high twelve, when the assembling craftsmen from all countries, and of all creeds, shall take their instruction from the Grand Master of all.

It would be impossible, brethren, to do justice to the memory of all who deserve our remembrance in the time at our disposal. Their names, like their work, will long live in the remembrance of those who knew them; and their Mother Lodge will record, for the benefit of future generations of craftsmen, the excellence of their work.

Among the many good men and true who, within recent years, have passed away, three I remember whose memory I revere and who have left their mark in the annals of our Lodge. First, Bro. John Murray. Merchant, Parkhead; second, John Reid, Merchant, Parkhead; and George M'Leod, Springburn, all Past Masters, and worthy men.

Bro. John Murray, who predeceased both Bros. Reid and M'Leod by several years, was a man of sterling integrity and large sympathies. His heart was ever open to the cry of distress, and his hand was ever ready to relieve want. Many a poor family in the locality has reason to bless the bounty of the Bailie, as he was familiarly known, his benevolence extending far beyond the masonic circle.

Bro. John Reid, whose death took place a few months ago, was well known to many of you. For many years he occupied an important social position, influencing for good all who came within range of his friendship, or sought his advice in matters of perplexity or doubt. He filled several positions of trust in this Lodge, and discharged his duties in an exemplary manner; and after having filled the chair of King Solomon for a period of three years, he for many years discharged the duties of treasurer. In his latter years the sun of his prosperity seemed to be on the wane, but his spirit of integrity and honest dealing was as strong as ever. He enjoyed the sympathy and kindly feeling of all who had known him in his brighter days ; and when it became known that he was about to leave the home and land of his birth for a home on the other side of the Atlantic, we felt that we were losing a brother whose place it would be difficult to fill in the chambers of our affection. As an illustration of his strong sense of honour, and spirit of sturdy independence that had characterised him through life, let me cite one incident—time will not permit of more.

Knowing his straitened circumstances, and actuated by a feeling of genuine sympathy, a brother who had known him long, and had profited much by his kindness, sought to relieve his necessity in a small way by handing him a small sum of money. It was with difficulty that he could be induced to accept it, and then only that it should be considered as a loan, which was agreed upon for the purpose of getting over the difficulty. Judge the surprise of the brother when, on the morning of Bro. Reid's departure for America, he called upon the obliging brother and asked him to accept repayment, and his heartiest thanks. It was no use to suggest that he might retain as a parting pledge of friendship that which had been accepted as a temporary loan. He could not, by any amount of persuasion, be induced to keep it as a gift. His last few years were spent in the bosom of his family, some of whom had preceded him across the western ocean, and, although his latter days were spent in ease and comfort, he had occasional longings for the old home, the old friends, and the fraternal greetings of the brethren of his Mother Lodge.

Bro. George M'Leod, whose death took place so recently as the 1st September, must still be fresh in the remembrance of even some of our youngest members. It seems but yesterday since he occupied that seat beside you, sir, and it will be long before we can realise that he shall never again occupy it. Of his personal qualities it is perhaps needless to speak, as most of you must have enjoyed the pleasure of his acquaintance. Sociable in disposition, he was, notwithstanding, liable to resent what may be deemed the approach of premature acquaintanceship; and if somewhat restrained in the presence of strangers, he was altogether unconventional with those he knew. A strong stickler at times for the forms and ceremonies of conventional etiquette, he sometimes offended where he intended only to correct. Most of us, perhaps, have winced under the chastisement of his criticism, but have been compelled to admit if not the correctness of his judgment at least the purity of his motives.

Contentious at times, where a less robust individuality would have acquiesced, he found himself occasionally opposed to the popular will, but having himself wielded the mallet of authority with a firm hand, few yielded more readily or more cheerfully to the wish of the majority and the ruling of the chair. Strong and enduring in his attachments, he was slow to anger and ready to forgive; and if the range of his perception was obscured at times, and the soundness of his judgment faulty, the general impulses of his heart more than made amends for the imperfections of his actions. His failings were like the setting of the precious stone, but caused his virtue to shine with all the greater lustre. So much for his personal qualities as a man. Let us briefly consider his character as a Mason.

As a Freemason, few men can boast of a more distinguished career than that of our deceased brother, having been seven times elected to the office of R.W.M. Brethren, were this fact alone to stand as the record of his masonic work, it should endear his memory to every well-wisher of the craft, and especially to every member of his Mother Lodge. But when we consider that for nearly thirty years he took an active, a lively, and leading interest in all the concerns of this lodge, in addition to his services as a member of the Provincial Lodge of Glasgow, in which he held important offices, our wonder is aroused and our admiration is unlimited. Emulation shrinks from the ordeal of competition, and we can only hope, as Freemasons, to follow on. Who can measure the amount of labour comprised in this period of usefulness, or gauge approximately the cares, the worries, and anxieties, inseparable from responsibility? Who can estimate the amount of self-sacrifice required in the discharge of duties extending over such a period? Perhaps only those who have worn the badge of office, and realised their responsibility, can venture to reply.

When we further consider, brethren, that during the earlier years of his masonic life, and while he was invested with supreme authority over the lodge, the organisation of the craft had not reached that high standard of excellence which characterises it now, and that cases of insubordination were not infrequent, we can recognise the difficulty of piloting through the shoals of dissension this grand old barque, and we can readily understand that the brother who had skill and ability sufficient for the task was well worthy of the esteem and affection and confidence of those who acknowledged his authority. That he was considered worthy of their confidence, his frequent election to supreme power is sufficient guarantee. That he was worthy of this tribute to his memory, let our present grief testify; and while we deplore the loss of one whose work claims our highest admiration, let us hope that his labour has not been in vain. Let us hope that under the omniscient eye of the great Architect Divine, his work has been duly squared, marked, and numbered, and that the excrescences of the rough ashler have sunk into the quarry of oblivion never more to be remembered. Let the record of his work be told to succeeding generations of craftsmen, that it may stimulate them in the prosecution of their daily task until like he, whose memory we revere, they are called from labour to refreshment and rest under the watchful eye of the Grand Master of all.

OUR SOVEREIGN'S DIAMOND JUBILEE.

Ring forth, ye bells, with a joyous peal,
    Let your silvery echoes ring,
Proclaiming the love that the nations feel
    For our aged Empress Queen.

Ring forth, ye bells in your sweetest tones,
 Give your tribute of harmony
To the greatest of all on the world's thrones,,
 And her Diamond Jubilee.

Tell not of the length of her reign alone,
 Nor her power on land and sea,
But the goodness of heart she has ever shown,
 And her love for the pure and free.

Tell of her motherly, anxious care
 For her loyal subjects all,
And the joy that follows her everywhere
 Where her welcome footsteps fall.

Tell yo of her drawn to the humble cot,
 Where the suffering peasant lies,
And the sunshine that gladdens the sufferer's lot
 As soothing his cares sho tries.

Tell of her just as our mother was
 In our childhood's happy days;
A vision of light, and of love the cause
 In the lands where her sceptre sways.

Tell of her just and righteous reign,
 And how well her crown she bore,
Toll it again, again, and again,
 And repeat it for evermore.

LIST OF SUBSCRIBERS.

Adam, J. R., Parkhead, Glasgow.

Anderson, J., Falkirk.

Anderson, James, Parkhead, Glasgow.

Anderson J., Craigielea, Carluke.

Anderson, George, Tollcross.

Angely, Wm., 27 Millroad Street, Glasgow.

Aitman, R. B., Hamilton Street, Carluke.

Alexander, Wm., 4 Gray Street, Glasgow.

Anthony, George, Broxburn.

Armstrong, Rev. Hugh, 3 Bridgeton Cross, Glasgow.

Austen, Wm., 50 Wesleyan Street, Glasgow.

Bain, Dr., Carluke.

Baird, A., Stationmaster, Tollcross.

Balfour, James, 441 Kenmure Street, Pollokshields.

Ballantyne, Lanark Road, Carluke.

Barclay, John, Janefield Dairy, Broxburn.

Barkley, J., 276 Paisley Road, Glasgow.

Barrowman, Andrew, Parkhead, Glasgow.

Barton, W., Glenorchy Terrace, Edinburgh.

Bauer, F. W., Birmingham.

Baxter, George, 295 Dalmarnock Road, Glasgow.

Bennet, James, 32 Tower Street, Paisley Road, Glasgow.

Bennie, Robert, 339 Napier Street, Linwood.

U

Binnie, James, 14 Regent Street, Greenock.

Bird, Mathew, 109 Greendykes Road, Broxburn.

Bixby, C. S., Osawatomie, Kansas, U.S.A.

Black, D., Parkhead, Glasgow.

Black, A., Invergowrie, Dundee.

Black, J., Parkhead, Glasgow.

Black, Wm., Parkhead, Glasgow.

Bloomfield, John, Glasgow.

Bluer, R., Parkhead, Glasgow.

Blyth, D. W., 2 May Place, Shettleston.

Blyth, John, Edinburgh.

Boal, James, 20 Armadale Street, Glasgow.

Borthwick, Alex., 10 Holmscroft Street, Greenock.

Bowie, R., City Chambers, Glasgow.

Bowie, Robert, City Chambers., Glasgow.

Bradshaw Robert, 17 Garden Street, Glasgow.

Brocket, J., Parkhead, Glasgow.

Brodie, Wm., 32 Steven Parade, Glasgow.

Brough, J., Parkhead, Glasgow.

Brown, R., Parkhead, Glasgow.

Brown, Alex., 10 Argyle Arcade, Glasgow.

Brown, George, 2015 Market Street, Philadelphia.

Brown, Thomas, Parkhead, Glasgow.

Brown, W., 379 Gt. Eastern Road, Parkhead, Glasgow.

Brown, S., 96 Findlay Drive, Glasgow.

Brownlie, Wm., 22 Greendykes Road, Broxburn.

Brownlie, Alex., Parkhead, Glasgow.

Buchan, Joseph, Clyde Terrace, Tollcross.

Buchanan, Alex., Glasgow.

Buchanan, Tollcross.

Bukerton, D., 158 Buchanan Street, Glasgow.

Burk, Alex., Parkhead, Glasgow.

Caird, D., Parkhead, Glasgow.

Cairney, W. A., 32 Hamilton Street, Greenock.

Calderwood, Councillor, Glasgow.

Campbell, J. M'Naught, Kelvingrove, Glasgow.

Campbell, J., 21 Bernard Street, Glasgow.

Campbell, James, 396 Main Street, Bonhill.

Campbell, J., yr., Glasgow.

Cane, A., 97 Union Street, Glasgow.

Carswell, Councillor J., Glasgow.

Chyne, Alex. D., Spens Crescent, Perth.

Cook, Duncan, Scotland Street, Glasgow.

Cook, Wh., 10 Abbotsford Place, Glasgow.

Cooper, Thomas, Merchant, Rutherglen.

Cooper, Horace H., clerk, Berehaven, Cork.

Cooper, James, Edinburgh.

Cooper, Jas., Glasgow.

Cowan, Wm., 807 Gallowgate, Glasgow.

Crawford, Wm., High Blantyre.

Crocket, Andrew, 12 Regent Street, Kincardine.

Cross, Alex., M.P., Glasgow.

Cummings, Colin, Glasgow.

Cunningham, Councillor T. M., Glasgow.

Currie, John, 109 Cubie Street, Glasgow.

Dalglish, Wm., London Road, Glasgow.

Daniels, L F., La Parte, 1104 Main St., Ind., U.S.A.

Davie, Archd., Silvergrove Street, Glasgow.

Davis, Ed., Dollar.

Deans, James, Shettleston.

Deverty, Jas., City Chambers, Glasgow.

Dick, William, 144 Main Street, Tollcross.

Dickie, J., Aberdeen.

Dickson, Wm., Edinburgh.

Dieperink, Dr. W. H., Somerset, West, Cape Colony.

Dobbie, D. S., 3 West Campbell Street, Glasgow.

Donaldson, Peter, Glasgow.

Donnachie, Peter, 51 Springfield Road, Glasgow.

Dougan, Councillor, Glasgow.

Downie, Stationmaster, Lanark.

Drysdale, H., Glasgow.

Dunn, J. W., Craigmudie Terrace, Glasgow.

Duthie, Alex., Lilybank, Lenzie.

Fenton, Jas. B., City Chambers, Glasgow.

Ferguson, John, 15 Walton Street, Shawlands, Glasgow.

Ferguson, D. D., Poplar Place, Larbert.

Fife, G., 203 Dalmarnock Road, Glasgow.

Findlay, Wm., Councillor, Glasgow.

Finnie, John, 43 London Street, Glasgow.

Finny, Maurice E., Harrisburg, U.S.A.

Flockhart, R. L., 27 Patrick Street, Greenock.

Ford, David, 54 West Nile Street, Glasgow.

Foreman, W. J. G., Glasgow.

Frame, R. M., Dollar.

Fraser, Alex., Glasgow.

Frost, Donald, Inspector, Rutherglen.

Galbraith, H., Glasgow.

Gebbie, D. G., Shettleston.

Gibson, Alex., Blantyre.

Gilchrist, Robert, Parkhead, Glasgow.

Gillies, James, 14 Hamilton Street, Greenock.

Gourlay, Wm., Cambuslang.

Graham, Walter, Merchant, Strathbungo.

Graham, Wm., 22 Smith Street, Hillhead, Glasgow,

Gray, Wm., 3 Holmes Rows, Uphall.

Green, Wm., 1 Columbia Place, Clydebank.

Green, J., Stationmaster, Dollar.

Grubb, David, Police Barracks, Rutherglen.

Haddow, Alex., Parkhead, Glasgow.

Halket, Thomas, 3 Walworth Terrace, Glasgow.

Hamilton, Thomas, Glasgow.

Hamilton, J., Belvidere, Glasgow.

Hamilton, T., 107 Duke Street, Glasgow.

Hamilton, G., Merchant, Tollcross.

Hamilton, James, 224 Baltic Street, Glasgow.

Hamilton, J., Councillor, Glasgow.

Harper, John, Police Barracks, Rutherglen.

Harris, David, Glasgow.

Harris, Robert, Rosemont, Maryhill.

Harvey, J., Parkhead, Glasgow.

Hederwick, J. D., 79 George Place, Glasgow.

Hegieson, James, Blantyre.

Henderson, Wm., Dollar.

Henderson, Alex., Barnhill, High Blantyre.

Henderson, James, Parkhead, Glasgow.

Henderson, Wm., Queen Mary Street, Glasgow.

Hendrie, John, Edinburgh.

Hendry, W. R., Tillicoultry.

Henry, John, Police Station, Tollcross.

Higgins, Alex., Parkhead, Glasgow.

Hill, Alex., Parkhead, Glasgow.

Hislop, John, 20 Scott Street, Glasgow.

Hogg, R., Gallowgate, Glasgow.

Hood, George, 135 Parson Street, Glasgow.

Houston, R., Cathcart.

Houston, J., Parkhead, Glasgow.

Houston, James, Glasgow.

Houston, Thomas, 50 Orchard Street, Partick.

Houston, Thomas, 4 Craignethan Gardens, Partick.

Howard, J. W., Glasgow.

Howieson, John, 59 Bridge Street, Glasgow.

Hughen, W. J., Dunscare, Torquay.

Hulbert, Edward, Downfield, Stroud, Glo.

Hume, Alex., Glasgow.

Hunter, W. G., Dollar.

Hunter, J. D., Falkirk.

Inglis, W., 80 St. Andrew Street, Leith.

Inglis, David, 265 Great Eastern Road, Glasgow.

Inglis, John, 3 Columbia Place, Clydebank.

Inglis, Gavin, Glasgow.

Ireland, D., 85 Garnethill, Glasgow.

Jackson, Robert, 141 Allison Street, Glasgow.

Johnston, Dr. Alex., Belvidere, Glasgow.

Johnstone, Alex., 5 Flemington Street, Springburn.

Johnstone, Alex., Tillicoultry.

Keith, John, Tollcross.

Keith, John, High Street, Lanark.

Kennedy, John, Glasgow.

Kerr, J., Tollcross.

Kilpatrick, J., Kirkcaldy.

King, James, 6 Rutland Crescent, Glasgow.

Kiniburgh, J., 24 Antague Street, Greenock.

Laird, W. H., 419 E. 3rd St., St. Winona, Minn., U.S.A.

Lake, H., Alloa.

Lamb, Thomas, Port Buchan, Broxburn.

Lamb, Robert, 12 Kirkhill Road, Broxburn.

Leitch, James, Kerr's Buildings, Tollcross.

Liddell, Wm., 115 Claythorn Street, Glasgow.

Lindsay, J., City Chambers, Glasgow.

Lindsay, John, City Chambers, Glasgow.

Livingstone, A., 28 Preston Street, Glasgow.

Livingstone, Alex., Blantyre.

Lockhart, Wm., Stonefield, Blantyre.

Lothian, D. H., Tillicoultry.

Lyon, D. Murray, Grand Secretary, Edinburgh.

Macdonald, R., 37 Marquis Street, Glasgow.

Mackay, John, 27 New Stock Street, Paisley.

Maclay, D., Blantyre.

Macrae, A., 30 Neilson Street, Greenock.

M'Aullay, Robt., 380 Main Street, Glasgow.

M'Bean, Ed., Fullerton House, Tollcross.

M'Bride, J., Parkhead, Glasgow.

M'Cartney, Joshua, 21 Savoy Street, Glasgow.

M'Coll, H., Parkhead. Glasgow.

M'Coll, D., 12 May Terrace, Glasgow.

M'Cracken, Alex., 65 Red Vale Street, Glasgow.

M'Crone, R. 128 South Portland Street, Glasgow.

M'Donald, Robert, 53 Oswald Street, Glasgow.

M'Donald, A., Parkhead, Glasgow.

M'Farlane, D., 227 Saracen Street, Possilpark.

M'Gilvery, R., Glasgow.

M'Gregor, John, 37 Avon Street, Glasgow.

M'Guther, Wm., Dollar.

M'Innes, Archd., Bridgend, Bonhill.

M'Intosh, Chas., Eastfield, near Cambuslang.

M'Innes, John, Dollar.

M'Kee, A. J., 95 Gairbraid Avenue, Maryhill.

M'Laren, Rev. John, Kincardine.

M'Leod, M., 707 Duke Street, Glasgow.

M'Leod, Angus, Dollar.

M'Leod, Geo., Dollar.

M'Leod, Wm., 123 North John Street, Glasgow.

M'Leod, Hector, City Chambers, Glasgow.

M'Leod, John, Shettleston, near Glasgow.

M'Millan, Alex., Buckingham Terrace, Partick.

M'Millan, William, 10 Abbotsford Place, Glasgow.

M'Millan, Andrew, 20 Brisbane Street, Greenock.

M'Nair, P., Parkhead, Glasgow.

M'Naught, R. 21 Abbotsford Place, Glasgow.

M'Naughton, D., Commercial Bank, St. Enoch Square.

M'Nee, Jas., Parkhead, Glasgow.

M'Nee, H., Parkhead, Glasgow.

M'Neil, J. N., Parkhead, Glasgow.

M'Phearson, Alex., Mathieson Street, Glasgow.

M'Taggart, J., "s.s. Fingal," Oban.

M'Williams, Wm., Glasgow.

M'Williams, Archd., Parkhead, Glasgow.

M'Andrew, Wm. C., 900 London Road, Glasgow.

Maltman, Geo., Tillicoultry.

Maltman, Wm., Biggar.

Marshall, Archd., 142 Main Street, Tollcross.

Marshall, Thomas, Tillicoultry.

Marshall, Wm., Mill Street, Tillicoultry.

Marshall, A., Parkhead, Glasgow.

Martin, W., Parkhead, Glasgow.

Mason, J., Junr., 5 East Neilson Street, Glasgow.

Maxwell, Councillor J. Shaw, Glasgow.

Mellish, John, Glasgow.

Michie, John, Tillicoultry.

Middlemass, 11 Niddry Rows, Winchburgh.

Millar, A., 257 Saracen Street, Possilpark.

Miller, J., Parkhead, Glasgow.

Miller, Hugh, Glasgow.

Miller, C., Glasgow.

Milne, Alex., Auchvavie, Monymusk.

Mitchell, G., Councillor, Glasgow.

Mitchie, Thos., Dalmuir.

Moffat, G. S., 419 Langside.

Morgan, Andrew, Winchburgh.

Morrison, J. G., Tollcross.

Morrison, R., 96 Napiershall Street, Glasgow.

Morrison, John, Merchant, Parkhead, Glasgow.

Morrison, H., 14 Collins Street, Edinburgh.

Morton, James, 1 Dunlop Street, Tollcross.

Morton, James, Upper Dunlop Street, Tollcross.

Morton, R., Uddingston.

Morton, A., Paisley.

Muichie, Charles, Merchant, Ardrossan.

Muir, George, 213 Buchanan Street, Glasgow.

Muir, J., Cumbernauld Road, Glasgow.

Muir, John, 133 Parliamentary Road, Glasgow.

Munn, Dr. R. J., Gergia, U.S.A.

Munro, G., 14 Whitevale Street, Glasgow.

Murray, Andrew, 15 Columbia Place, Clydebank.

Murdoch, James, 253 Argyle Street, Glasgow.

Murphy, James, 26 Edmond Street, Glasgow.

Murray, James, P.M. 437, Glasgow

Murray, J., 52 St. Enoch Square, Glasgow.

Murray, Andrew, 15 Columbia Place, Clydebank.

Murray, H., Glasgow.

Neil, Alex., Mill Road, Kilmarnock.

Neilson, Walter, Blantyre.

Newton, R. W., Cameron Street, Glasgow.
Newton, W. W., 52 St. Enoch Square, Glasgow.
Nicol, Alex., Waverley Road, Nairn.
Nimmo, Zec., Blantyre.
Nisbet, Jas., Parkhead, Glasgow.
Ockburn, Wm., Edinburgh.
Oliphant, Peter, Dollar.
Oliver, J., Wellpark, Glasgow.
O'May, Wm., Duke Street, Glasgow.
Orr, Alex., Parkhead, Glasgow.
Paterson, Dr. Law, Carluke.
Paterson, Wm., Stare, Broxburn.
Paterson, Bailie, Kilmarnock.
Paull, Thos., Glasgow.
Peebles, Thos., South Street, St. Andrews.
Pegg, Wm. Carter, Codnor Park, Derbyshire.
Pettigrew, Wm., Waddel Street, Glasgow.
Plenderleith, Parkhead, Glasgow.
Pollock, Gavin, West Haughhead, Uddingston.
Pollock, Wm., Cripua Terrace, Uddingston.
Rae, Geo., Parkhead, Glasgow.
Rail, Wm., 5 Broomhill Terrace, Glasgow.
Rankin, Robt., Thistle Street, Glasgow.
Rankin, H., Glasgow.
Rankin, Jas., Glasgow.
Rankin, Jas. W., 4 Bell Street, Glasgow.
Rankin, W., Glasgow.
Ramsay, J., Glasgow.

Ramsay, Thos., Axminster, England.

Reid, D., Grand Treas, Edinburgh.

Rice, John, 134 Main Street, Tollcross.

Richardson, Thos., Edinburgh.

Richardson, George, 243 Mid Street, Broxburn.

Richardson, D., Church Street, Broxburn.

Riddell., D., Parkhead, Glasgow.

Robb, Wm., Redvale Street, Glasgow.

Roberts, D., 8 Whitevale Street, Glasgow.

Robertson, Samuel, 3 Regent Street, Greenock.

Robertson, R. R., Tollcross.

Robertson, R., Saracen Foundry, Glasgow.

Robertson, R., Parkhead, Glasgow.

Rodger, And., Dollar.

Ross, A., 223 Baltic Street, Glasgow.

Russell, J., Langside Road, Glasgow.

Scott, Adam, jun., 14 Roman Camp, Uphall.

Scott, Walter, Winchburgh.

Simpson, Jas., London Road, Glasgow.

Simpson, H., 44 Bardowie St., Possilpark.

Sinclair, Wm., 19 Armadale Street. Glasgow.

Sinclair, John, 29 Sword Street, Glasgow.

Smillie, J., 65 Bath Street, Glasgow.

Smirl, J., Gallowgate, Glasgow.

Smith, John, Edinburgh.

Smith, Jas., Glasgow.

Smith, L. W., 27 Ingleston Street, Greenock.

Smith, Jas., 3 Gardner Street, Glasgow.

Smith, D. Crawford, Perth.
Snedden, Wm., Parkhead, Glasgow.
Snowdoune, P., Dollar.
Sorley, R., 1 Buchanan Street, Glasgow.
Southy, E. L., Glasgow.
Sproat, Robt., Blantyre.
Stalker, A. B., J.W. No. 782.
Stalker, H. B., Tillicoultry.
Stark, Alex, Broxburn
Steel, M., Glasgow.
Stevenson, Alex., Buckingham Terrace, Partick.
Stewart, Jas., Bedford Street, Glasgow.
Stewart, Councillor P. G., Glasgow.
Stewart, Jas., Greendykes Road, Broxburn.
Stewart, Alex., Hanover Street, Glasgow.
Stewart, John, Tillicoultry.
Stewart, G., 41 Tobago Street, Glasgow.
Stirling, J. H., Crown Street, Glasgow.
Stirling, Jas., Glasgow.
Strang, Jas., 462 Gallowgate, Glasgow.
Strath, Jas., Parkhead, Glasgow.
Struthers, Allan, Tollcross.
Sutherland, J. R., 35 Kelvinhaugh Street, Glasgow.
Tatham, Walter, Ilkeston, England.
Taylor, Jas., jr., 61 Mitchell Street, Glasgow.
Taylor, D., 175 Thomson Street, Glasgow.
Taylor, Alex., Cambuslang.
Taylor, D., Police Station, Broxburn.

Templeton, David, 703 Gallowgate, Glasgow.

Templeton, Wm., 75 Brunswick Street, Glasgow.

Thom, J., Belvidere Cottages, Glasgow.

Thomson, D., Gartnavel Cottages, Glasgow.

Thomson, John, 14 Gloucester Street, Glasgow.

Thomson, W. J., Sandford, Montrose.

Thorley, R., merchant, Tollcross.

Torrance, Wm., Dollar.

Upton, Wm. H., Walla Walla, Washington, U.S.A.

Walker, Councillor J., Glasgow.

Walker, John, Parkhead, Glasgow.

Walker, Chas., Blantyre.

Walker, J., Parkhead, Glasgow.

Wallace, D., 1 Hamilton Street, Yoker.

Wallace, Jas., Dollar.

Warnock, J., City Chambers, Glasgow.

Warnock, Wm., 451 Gallowgate, Glasgow.

Warnock, J., City Chambers, Glasgow.

Warton, J., Parkhead, Glasgow.

Warton, S., Parkhead, Glasgow.

Watson, A. C., Largs.

Watson, Jas., 34 Dunn Street, Glasgow.

Watson, C. G., Parkhead, Glasgow.

Watson, J., 37 Marquis Street, Glasgow.

Webster, John, Uphall.

Whitton, Andrew, Constable, Limerigg.

Willock, Councillor J., Glasgow.

Willox, David, jr., Glasgow.

Willox, Jas., Glasgow.

Willox, C. M., Glasgow.

Willox, Alex., Parkhead, Glasgow.

Willox, J., Parkhead, Glasgow.

Willox, R., Parkhead, Glasgow.

Wills, Thos. Henry, 2 Market Street, Torquay.

Wilson, Thos., 45 John Street, Glasgow.

Wilson, H., 254 Saracen Street, Possilpark.

Wingate, Archd., Parkhead, Glasgow.

Wotherspoon, D., Old Stewartfield, Broxburn.

Yorston, Chas., 39 Hollygate, Broxburn.

Young, Thos., jr., Old Town, Broxburn.

Young, Archd., 49 Wilson Street, Partick.

Young, Wm., Rosebank, Cambuslang.

Young Wm., New Milns.

Yuill, Archd., 61 King Street, Rutherglen.

Yuill, David, Kilmarnock.

Printed by ALEX. MALCOLM & Co., 34 Ann Street, City, Glasgow.